GENESIS

Book #1 of Glory

Dale Mayer

Book in this series:

Genesis

Tori

Celeste

Glory Trilogy

About This Book

As an energy worker, Genesis Chandler's job is to protect the healing pools all over planet Glory. Yet, ever since her grandmother died and her sisters left their town of Little Glory, Genesis can't seem to find a purpose in her life anymore. She goes through her days with blinders on, reeling from having lost everyone and everything she knows and loves. Never does a person like Genesis, who is by nature gentle and unassuming, expect someone to take advantage of her grief and her disorientation …

As a recent contractor for the Glory Energy Council, Connor Bateman is called in to investigate the odd energy fluctuations affecting all the townsfolk of Little Glory. Connor discovers it is directly connected to the healing pools in the forest preserve. Only Genesis can help him deal with the inevitable crisis.

Unfortunately, Genesis is more than a little resistant to help Connor with anything, even this. Once upon a time she'd been in love with him, but then, after a disturbing fight, the next morning he had walked out on her abruptly, without another word.

Connor realized his mistake too late, but, not knowing how to take it back, he's avoided her all this time. Seeing her again assures him of two things that he does not want to consider: that he's still in love with her and that she doesn't want anything more to do with him.

Regardless of their personal feelings, Genesis and Connor must find a way to work together to discover who's destroying the energy reserve that's the key to all life forms on the planet. Their very survival depends on it …

Sign up to be notified of all Dale's releases here!
https://geni.us/DaleNews

CHAPTER 1

"MAY I HELP you?" Genesis Chandler kept her polite smile plastered on her face and her voice cool yet friendly, despite the fact that broken glass crunched underfoot and that her shop lay in shambles. A good shopkeeper would never show that anything was amiss. The two large black-suited males stared at her, not even the hint of a smile cracking their stern faces. They didn't acknowledge the mess around them either.

A large Paranormal Council meeting was scheduled this week, and, from the subdued air of power rippling from the men, Genesis had a good guess as to why they were here. She thought she recognized them. In fact, they might head the similar council in a different city. For all her attempts to stay removed from the dealings in the paranormal world, it was hard to not get glimpses of the goings-on. As anything in that line brought powerful memories to the forefront, she did her best to block it out immediately.

"Are you looking for something specific?" she asked, brightening the wattage of her smile.

The men never moved a muscle.

Her invisible familiar, Remi, being wise as well as cheeky, squeaked once and left. But then, what else did she expect? Rare plumers weren't known to be friendly in the first place. And Remi's instincts were finely honed, like any other wild animal.

As Genesis stared at the big square men, she realized she'd like to disappear too.

They stood just inside the doorway of her shop and finally surveyed the mess. Without a word, the older man turned and walked out. The younger man brought his gaze around to land on her. She kept a bright smile on her face. A customer was a customer, although she was pretty sure these men weren't here for a sleeping tisane.

With the faintest sneer marring his face, the second man exited as silently as he'd arrived.

"Goodbye. Have a nice day," Genesis called out, as a proper storekeeper should, then breathed a sigh of relief when the bells chimed, signaling the strangers' exit from her shop. They'd entered, damn-near filling the tiny interior of her shop, had never said a word, but had studied her for longer than was strictly necessary.

She'd been friendly. Polite. But she'd also instinctively pulled a protective layer of energy around her. She didn't know who they were or what they wanted, but the one thing she did know was that they weren't in the right place.

No one with their energy belonged here. And given their intimidating size and presence, she'd had a hard time holding that smile on her face and her nervousness at bay. She'd kept her own energy system well buttoned down. Another of Granny's lessons she'd learned well. Granny's words had rolled through her head, as she'd stared at the men. *Don't let anyone know who you are. What you can do. Everyone has an agenda. It won't be yours.*

That advice seemed appropriate right now.

With the men gone, the atmosphere inside lightened. Remi reappeared.

"There you are." She reached out and stroked a hand down his long back. "Fine bodyguard you are, leaving me with those two scary dudes."

She swore his grin, already wide and mischievous, widened yet again. He chattered once, then raced over to lie on the window shelf, where he could look at the people walking past.

It was hard to not be suspicious of everyone right now, after her shop's break-in by paranormal means. At least her intruder had only broken the energy lock on the back door instead of smashing the front windows. That was another reason to avoid law enforcement. They didn't work with those who had supernatural powers. The Paranormal Center in town would be policing that. Another group of people she avoided.

And the community? … Well, they mostly avoided her.

Just enough fear had been involved to spawn prejudice against energy workers in the community. Respect for those at the top but, for the unknown workers, there was a different attitude altogether.

Not that many knew about Genesis's abilities. Her life would be way worse if they did.

No wonder her sisters had taken off when everything had blown up. Too bad that hadn't been an option for Genesis. Besides, … she had responsibilities and nowhere to go.

With a sigh, she considered all the broken glass on her floor; maybe she shouldn't store her herbs in glass canisters. Maybe cloth bags or even tying them to hang down from the ceiling would be better after all.

For the rest of the morning, she puttered around her shop, happy to have it looking back to normal again. Then, needing to keep busy, she'd repackaged her herbs for most of the afternoon. By the end of the day, she was comforted to see that she'd actually accomplished a fair bit.

Yet she couldn't shake the feeling that something was off. Something she should know about.

Only what was it?

"What do you think, Remi? Any idea what's going on?" She laughed. As if he would answer. Still, if nothing else, the sound of her voice was comforting.

She wished for the millionth time that her sisters were here. This last year had been horribly lonely. Both had left—one to hide away and one to find herself. And exactly how did that make any sense? While Genesis, ever the homebody, had stayed to protect their heritage.

The three girls had been blessed beyond measure by the old woman who had taken them all in. That they'd remained together was an even bigger blessing. As the eldest of the triplets, Genesis had always been the quiet one. The one who'd stepped up in a crisis.

And, a year ago, a crisis had hit in the worst way.

Granny had died, leaving everything to the three girls equally. But what they'd inherited would send shock waves through the community—and potentially a horrific backlash. That was one of the reasons why Genesis had not brought out the documents to prove her claim at this point. Genesis didn't think she could handle it alone.

Granny had always been considered an odd hermit by the locals. And that was the kinder of the names. Caught up in their grief over the loss of Granny, none of the three sisters had worried about staking their claim. Granny's death had caused a vortex in their lives, and their personal relationships had gone off the wall as well. Instead of three potential weddings, there'd been none.

Inheritances they would have to fight everyone over hadn't seemed important at the time. Or since. Genesis had hidden away from everything this last year, only doing the bare necessities, when she could no longer ignore her inner proddings to check on the pools, the forests. She hadn't wanted to be left alone, ... but it was past time to mourn what was gone and to deal with the reality of what her life was now.

Growing up had been hard. They weren't like the other kids. They didn't have a "normal" family. They'd had trouble making friends, and they'd been the butt of many jokes, but that didn't matter because they had Granny. She'd been special. Like seriously special. And no one knew.

And most wouldn't believe it if they did.

Life on Glory wasn't the same as on other planets. And so very different from Earth. Some planets—like Glory—hadn't been as fully researched as others, before the emigration had started. The actual living conditions could only be surmised, but time had been short, and people had been anxious to get out. Sure, the planet had been examined, tested, and approved, but Glory was farther away from Earth than other options, making it the least popular and the least well-known location.

And, on top of that, it was an energy hot spot. Areas too hot to live in had been quickly segregated into energy reserves—a geographical truth that the settlers had found out the hard way. Now the towns existed on the edges of these special areas.

No one truly understood how the energy centers worked. Glory held massive forests, healing waters, and unique cave systems in each one. It was an ecosystem they all depended on for their own energetic systems.

There had been many energy problems in the beginning, but, over time, they'd learned. Initially no one had understood that recharging could be too extreme. Or that the forest needed to be cared for on an energetic basis, but then they'd come from Earth, where energy workers were rare.

After the first emigrants had arrived on Glory, energy abilities had started showing up in the population. Now, hundreds of years later, there were enough workers that they had their own Council, led by Matt Luker. As a relatively new leader, Matt was an unknown. Genesis had no idea what he was truly like, even though Genesis's sister Celeste had been engaged to him.

Before she'd left.

As she closed up the shop, Genesis remembered her plans to go to the caves. With all the weird stirrings in the energy field lately, she needed to. She had been remiss in her duties, preferring to ignore them rather than face her memories, her losses, her grief. But she couldn't any longer.

Besides, she had to return the chart she had with her.

The energy disturbances had been bad this last year, but they had gotten much worse this last week, ever since the break-in at her place. A break-in that should not have been possible. Not with the energy locks she'd used.

It was her fault. She should never have brought the star chart home to work on in her apartment. She'd known it then but had once again ignored the inner prompting. Her gaze strayed to the chart, the one she'd been working on for weeks, sitting atop the folder—not inside the folder. It shouldn't have been removed from the cottage in the first place. She had to get it back home. And fast.

Considering the break-in this morning at the shop, she

figured she was already too late. Someone knew. That meant she and her sisters were no longer safe. And neither were the documents—the proof of their heritage.

CONNOR BATEMAN QUIETLY approached the hidden cave entrance. He couldn't sense any disturbance. Couldn't see any signs of intruders. But, then again, that meant little around here. For someone like him, hiding his tracks was easy. Many people could move silently, not leaving even a ripple in the atmosphere to indicate that they'd come and gone. If he had full use of his abilities, he could likely see more. As it was, he could only investigate at a level slightly above a normal person. Except he had years of experience to draw on.

He studied the porous rock carefully. This reserve appeared to be the same as every other one he'd been in. They were amazing ecosystems that needed to be protected.

His job was to do just that.

Connor had only just returned to Little Glory for the first time in just under a year, thanks to a special request from Grandfather—although he was a distant blood relative to Connor, Grandfather just preferred to be called that by all. He was old but still active and powerful, although he was starting to show his years. Working for Grandfather, doing contracts for the Glory Energy Council as an investigator, he'd seen his share of weird sightings and events all over the planet.

But now, something was happening in the town of Little Glory. And Connor finally had a reason forcing him to come back. He'd been planning to since the day he'd left, but somehow the jobs close by went to other investigators. He had to wonder if Grandfather hadn't known about his relationship with Genesis.

If Grandfather had known, he would have sent Connor to the opposite side of the planet. Which was exactly where Connor had spent the bulk of the last year. But why had Grandfather brought Connor here now? Maybe Grandfather had realized they would need Genesis's help to get to the bottom of this disturbance and figured Connor would be the one to charm her into helping. If that were the case, Grandfather had seriously overestimated Connor's influence.

Murmurs of problems within the forest, disturbances in the pools, odd colorful flares in the sky. The reserve was under stress. The real question was why.

And that was what he intended to find out.

Connor had to find Genesis. At least, he hoped he would find her. Council leader Matt had told Connor that she was still in town.

But that didn't mean she'd be happy to see him.

A rumble reverberated under his feet, adding to his unease. Power had to be respected, controlled if possible, or it would blow like a volcano to release the pressure. They couldn't afford to have an eruption here. The town was close by. Maybe too close.

He needed to determine why the ecosystem was out of balance and to figure out how to return it to its normal state … and fast.

The dark cave appeared in front of him. He slipped inside.

CHAPTER 2

GENESIS DECIDED TO leave her car parked behind the shop and to hike to the closest cave entrance. She would cut through the cavern and be home at the cottage in no time. She no longer felt safe at her small apartment. And she couldn't rest until the chart was back where it belonged. That someone had seen it was bad enough. What if they had taken an image of it to show to other people? She knew her thoughts bordered on paranoia, but it was hard to ignore a lifetime of cautiousness. If someone were looking for it, that would explain the break-in at the shop. After the first break-in at her apartment, she'd made sure to hide the chart, so no one could find it. But that hadn't stopped someone from looking.

Remi raced around her, over and under the tree branches, bouncing up the trunks, then down again. She laughed. "We should do this more often."

She hadn't been in this particular area in a while. And that wasn't good, considering the changes she saw.

The bushes were smaller here, stunted. Their color, dull, instead of the rich green that they should be sporting. The ground crunched underfoot from the extreme drought as she walked, another oddity, given the groundwater levels here.

Twenty minutes later, she took the path to the left that led deeper into the forest. A slight breeze drifted in on the lazy afternoon, making the walk a step up from beautiful. There was no feeling like it. Green grass, healthy trees, and sunshine.

As she moved through this special area, she noted signs of a clearing, off to the left—where there shouldn't be a clearing. She stepped up to the edge and gasped.

Large trailers were parked at one end. Work trailers. And huge metal machines.

Except no one was allowed to build anything here. This land was sacred.

With a sinking heart, she realized just how long it had been since she'd come this way. She hadn't meant to neglect her duties. But, with Granny's passing, so many of the things Genesis used to do had fallen by the wayside. Unfortunately.

What she saw now was an obscenity. Skirting around the large machinery, she followed the path. It led away from the trailers and deeper into the woods. The underground caves had many entrances, but the one she'd always used was less popular. She wasn't antipeople, but, due to the work she did, she did it in private.

The sky was darkening, when she finally reached the entrance to the cave system. Pulling out the large flashlight she'd packed in her bag before leaving the store, she turned it on and highlighted the entrance. It didn't look as if anyone had come this way recently. Low-lying brush covered most of the entrance, and moss crawled up much of one side. Pretty and effective.

"Let's go, Remi." No answer. She turned around to search for him.

No sign. "Remi?" Damn. "Come on, Remi. I need you."

Instantly he raced toward her from out of the under-brush, his mouth open in a huge grin. She'd often wondered if he smiled at his prey the same way before attacking because that grin of his was sheer evil.

She laughed. "Come on, boy. Let's go."

He raced into the entrance.

She followed. Inside, the tunnels glowed a strange dull yellow. Genesis stared at her surroundings, as she walked past. The walls should have been bright with effervescence, not this sickened dark-vomit color. Something was definitely off. "What's going on here, buddy?"

Remi didn't answer. But he didn't run off again. He walked on his hind legs at her side, his own bearing one of curiosity and confusion.

"Not so sure what's happened, are you?" She kept walking. "That's okay. Neither am I."

A hundred yards down the path, she found gum wrappers. That pissed her off, but the liquor bottles farther down really upset her. Six months ago, she would have never found any garbage in the tunnels. So why now?

The problem as she saw it was complex. The thinner the energy, the more negativity could make its way in, making it harder to fix, since the more negativity there was, the thinner the walls became. The energy barrier had obviously thinned to dangerously low levels. The decline had been so slow that she hadn't realized how bad it had gotten and so quickly.

She'd first noticed it after her sisters had left, but it had been minor, so she'd considered it a normal ebb and flow of energy workers in the area. Now it was serious if it allowed for this activity. If the protective barrier were healthy, the equipment couldn't have entered this sacred space. Hell, the drivers couldn't have found the pools in the first place.

What kind of work were they doing in the forest? "Or," she muttered under her breath, "are they working down here?"

That thought made her go cold. No one, under any circumstances, should be doing anything down here in the
cavern's pools.

And then she realized she'd been walking parallel to a set
of wheel tracks.

Not truck tracks but wide and deep—more like heavy
equipment. With fear clogging her throat, she raced forward.
Large underground pools were up ahead. Pools and spaces
that were sacred to the reserve, one that provided life force
nutrients for the forest above.

Ahead was the return to the outside world and just like
that, she came to the end of the path. At least, as far as the
giant machine had made it. It was parked ahead in the
middle of the path, as if the driver had just walked away.

Fuming, she squeezed past the machinery. Having this
metal, this negative energy here, was obscene. That anyone
could be so careless of this spiritual space made her want to
weep.

And then she saw the broken stones beside the pools.
Someone had damaged the edge of the pool. There were now
steps that went into the pool on the far side. Steps that
hadn't been there six months ago.

Someone appeared to be trying to open access here—
possibly to commercialize the sacred pools.

And that couldn't be. No one had gotten permission.
From the community. From the property owners. She
should know. She and her sisters owned the land surrounding the entire forest, especially these pools, compliments of
Granny. Except nobody knew that, did they? The triplets
had avoided contact with any legal system here because of
the obvious prejudice against Granny and her granddaugh-

ters. But Genesis had spent a lifetime trusting in Granny, so Genesis wasn't about to lose faith in her grandmother now. If Granny said the documents gave them claim to the pools and the forests, possibly more, then she'd believe her. But what if no one else believed Genesis? *Then* what would she do?

CONNOR STOOD IN the silence of the cave and breathed in deeply the slightly mineral scent. The air, the energy, the space oozed with healing effervescence—something this area was famous for. Most people needed this air to heal. To feel good. But some of the special people, like Genesis, thrived on it.

In fact, he strongly suspected she and her sisters couldn't live without it. They certainly couldn't live away from such waters. He'd heard rumors of problems in the family in recent months but hadn't had a chance yet to catch up on the latest gossip. Not that he knew who to ask. Matt had been involved with one of the sisters, but getting the head of the Paranormal Council to open up on personal issues was a lost cause. Even though they'd been good friends once.

Connor walked forward, listening to the echoes of his footsteps, as the tunnel widened into a larger anteroom. Several sacred pools were underground, with corresponding sacred forests aboveground.

And in between them existed a complicated energy system that kept life flowing in abundance. The space was protected.

At least, it was supposed to be. Now he saw signs of heavy traffic down here. Traffic that didn't belong. At least he didn't think so. He hadn't asked Grandfather about this.

Of course Grandfather hadn't offered anything more than the bare minimum in information either.

It was no wonder no one liked the old man. He was a bull of a man, with an attitude to match. Connor had long been suspicious that he had plans. Big plans.

And no one would stand in his way.

CHAPTER 3

GENESIS FROZE, AS a weird tingle rippled down her spine. She wasn't alone. Reacting quickly, Genesis slipped into the shadows and waited. Remi sat quietly at her side. Footsteps approached. Heavy, male. A little hesitant. Someone unsure of the way.

Not many men could come down here at night like this. Unless he was part of the construction crew. Or maybe there was a security detail. After all, the equipment was likely valuable.

If she had anything to say about it though, that machinery would be gone immediately. It was an eyesore. An insult. The machinery clashed with the organic nature of this place. Its presence was simply not permitted.

She nodded her head firmly. They would be gone soon. She'd make sure of it.

"Hello?"

The quiet call surprised her.

She slipped farther into the shadows. The white-blue beam of a flashlight glowed in front of her.

"Anyone here?"

As if she would answer. The footsteps continued past. She held her breath, waiting. If he turned and came Like she would back the same way, he would see her. And then what would she do?

She couldn't squeeze back any farther. But, with limited options available, she had to try her whisper trick. Closing her eyes, she stilled and went inside herself. Setting up gentle whispers to float throughout the cavern, she sent out the message, *All is well. Everything is fine. No one is here.*

The stranger walked around the large pools, his flashlight scanning the water. He held something small and dark in his other hand.

She didn't know for sure, but it looked like one of those high-res guns she'd heard about.

Then he was gone from her view.

Listening for sounds of his passing, she smiled as his footsteps softened, changing from a hard stride to a casual stroll within seconds. Brilliant.

She usually needed to preserve her energy; using her abilities drained much of her resources. Down here though, she'd recharge almost instantly. So sending whispered messages was nothing. Her sister Tori could perform that trick from anywhere, but, for Genesis, it was harder, and she didn't have much luck in working on people with paranormal abilities. Besides, any man carrying a gun meant nothing good. And someone was doing something illegal down here. If he wanted to keep it a secret, her presence might cause trouble. How much trouble was the big question. These caves went on forever.

Someone who didn't know them well might assume they could hide a body in here. In theory, Genesis could get lost down here herself and could never get out. In theory.

The reality of the situation was much different. She could be lost down here for a while, true, but she had Remi. He would have her out in no time, and, even without Remi, Genesis would still get out on her own. It would simply take a little longer. There were a lot of passageways. She would need to explore to find the one that would lead to the surface. That wouldn't bother her. She was one of the few people who was comfortable here. But then she had an affinity to water.

She tilted her head and listened.

Blessed silence.

The intruder was gone.

Deeming it safe, she slipped farther into the tunnel, but her mind couldn't move past the obvious intrusion. What was the equipment doing here? What exactly was going on? It would only take the slightest of changes to destroy the delicate balance of the forest. Especially with her sister Tori pulling energy from the forest like she was. And that was yet another question that needed an answer. How was she doing it from a long distance? Doing so while she lived in town was normal. Natural. But now that she'd disappeared—and was still drawing strength from the same source—the balance here was shifting. It had to.

Tori was just as integral to this ecosystem as Celeste, the youngest of them, and Genesis herself.

Genesis needed to find her sisters and to help them heal. After Granny's death, everything had spiraled out of control. It was too much to hope they would return voluntarily, much less soon. If they did, the energy flares would calm down too. What a cosmic joke. The energy responded to major shifts in the owners' lives, yet did nothing to help the owners to heal.

Still, Genesis couldn't imagine that her sisters' energy requirements were the cause of the strange, twisted energy patterns going on in the forest or the ones down here. That didn't seem like a strong-enough reason. So just what else was going on?

Was her sisters' absence enough to cause this? Especially when combined with the loss of Granny's powerful energy? Instead of stepping in to fill the void, the sisters had scattered, and the energy barrier had thinned to the point of collapse. Fear spiked through Genesis. She was just as responsible. She'd been avoiding even thinking about what was going on here—and look at how well that had worked.

The darkness deepened ahead, and she shivered. With the deterioration of the energy field and the presence of strangers, she felt a nervousness here she'd never before experienced. Just then, Remi bolted.

"Remi?" Genesis called out, a slight tremble in her voice. "Stay close, please."

A slight scrabbling noise sounded beside her, as he returned. He placed a long-fingered hand in hers. "Thanks, buddy. I could use the help." She smiled down at him. He grinned that wide ear-to-ear splitting movement, which made most people back away, thanks to those major hooked teeth. Still, he would never hurt a friend. Everyone else was fair game though.

And he was highly susceptible to Genesis's moods.

And her people preferences.

Turning several more corners, she walked into one of the main caverns. Melancholy hit when she saw the worn spot where her grandmother had spent many hours—especially toward the end. It had given her great peace to be this close to the forest. Both directly beneath and also directly above the source. When her bones had ached, she would visit, and the pain would ease for days.

They had the cottage in the woods for just that reason. Genesis had often stayed there when she wasn't in town. The cottage had been Granny's home.

Wandering through the large cavern brought tears to her eyes. She missed Granny and her sisters, … and, yes, damn it, … she missed Connor. It'd been a very long year.

Granny had always told Genesis to pick wisely because heartache was sure to follow if she didn't. She'd met Connor soon after Granny's death, so the wise woman hadn't been there to vet her choice. The relationship had not lasted more than a week, but the heartache that followed—watching cool, capable, composed Tori have her life destroyed by a man and then Celeste go to pieces with her own horrible relationship experience—had made Genesis decide that relationships weren't for her.

She stared around the massive space, hating the sense of wrongness that permeated the sacred cave.

Remi chittered, his voice faint, farther up and off to the left. She followed the sound. "What's the matter, boy?"

His chitters turned to cries of distress.

Oh, crap.

She ran forward, trying to sort through the energy that had swelled up in front of her. She couldn't see much, thanks to the brilliant glow of energy in the space, but Remi was certainly nowhere to be found. That was normal and almost made her feel better. Almost.

But when he didn't come when called? That was a different story.

Quietly she checked out the corner and realized that the only place he could have gone was down a tunnel that lay directly in front of her. She frowned. Since when had that tunnel been there? She knew every nook and cranny of this cavern, and that tunnel hadn't been here before. She crept up to it, letting the waves of energy hit her full-on. "Remi?"

No answer.

Remi *had* gone down there. But why?

"Genesis?"

She hesitated, stumbling slightly, straining to hear what sounded like a familiar voice. Connor? No. Not possible. She paused, considering, then shook her head.

With a backward glance at the empty cavern, she followed her pet into the darkness.

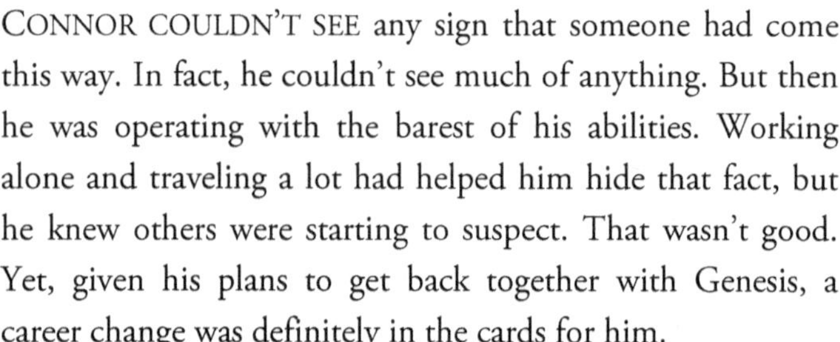

CONNOR COULDN'T SEE any sign that someone had come this way. In fact, he couldn't see much of anything. But then he was operating with the barest of his abilities. Working alone and traveling a lot had helped him hide that fact, but he knew others were starting to suspect. That wasn't good. Yet, given his plans to get back together with Genesis, a career change was definitely in the cards for him.

In the distance, he saw a glow, like a sweeping flashlight. Who could that be?

Instinctively he called out, "Genesis?" Then realized he had no basis for that assumption. With the machinery, equipment, and the signs of work going on, it could easily be someone other than her. The flashlight stopped moving. Then it winked out. In a way, that seemed to confirm it was her.

And, hell, she was still pissed at him. He agreed she had some right, but, damn it, he needed her to understand.

"Genesis, please don't take off. It's hard enough to see with a flashlight. Without it on, you're likely to get lost." The instant the words were out, he wished he'd kept his mouth shut. As if she could get lost. He could almost hear her disdainful sniff in the air. He rolled his eyes and walked toward where the light had been.

Only to find she hadn't stayed in one place.

She'd taken off.

Or hidden from him.

Either way, it was bad news. He stood here, his hand gripping his hair in frustration. "What now, Genesis?"

No answer. Damn it.

"Don't do this because you're mad at me. I'm not here to hurt you."

Still no answer. Now he was really pissed. He spun around, hoping she would step out of the shadows.

Nothing. Now what? What in the hell was going on?

"Genesis, can we talk? Please come o—"

Something slammed into the back of his head, and pain exploded in his skull. He collapsed to his knees, his fighting instincts warring with the pain. Training had him spinning to one knee and flipping back around to face his attacker. Half expecting Genesis, he was startled by the sight of a huge man wielding a flashlight as a weapon. Shit.

As the attacker lifted his flashlight for a second blow, Connor kicked his legs out from under him and pounced. His first punch hit the man in the jaw and the second one in the nose. The man bellowed, threw Connor to the side, and jumped to his feet. But rather than coming after Connor again, the stranger bolted into the darkness.

Connor scrambled to his feet. He could go after his attacker, but he didn't know his way around, and neither did he have a flashlight, like his opponent. Now that he realized Genesis wasn't down here alone, his first concern was for her.

She was here. He could sense her. He had always been able to know when she was close. He was grateful that gift hadn't diminished along with his other talents.

Had this guy found Genesis? Had he hurt her? Connor's head ached from the blow. Gently he touched the back of his head, swearing when his fingers came away sticky.

"Damn." He peered into the darkness. "Genesis, are you here? If you're hiding, please come out. The guy's gone."

No answer. Realizing she was so much more capable of being alone down here than he was, he slowly started back the way he'd come in. After several careful steps, he knew he'd lost his way.

He groaned, his head starting to pound.

He took another step. The cavern wavered. He blinked and tried to clear his vision. He staggered forward and fell to his knees. *Shit.* Blackness filled his mind, and he sprawled on the ground.

CHAPTER 4

GENESIS HADN'T GONE much farther in the dark tunnel when Remi came running toward her out of the darkness, squealing an alarm.

"Remi? What the hell happened?"

Remi chattered at her side, then grabbed her hand and pulled her in his direction. She went to step forward but Remi yanked her hand back, stopping her. "Remi?"

Then Remi started to tug on her hand some more. Backward. "You brought me down here in the first place. Now what?"

But he wasn't interested in anything but pulling her backward. She knew better than to argue. He didn't like something up ahead. Or was scared of it.

"Fine. Let's go. Lead me back then." But they'd walked most of the way already. She came into the large cavern where she'd seen the man walking and stopped. "Are you sure, Remi? What about that guy with the gun?"

Remi chattered. When she didn't move fast enough, Remi snapped at her, his tone more aggressive than she'd heard in years. "Okay, fine."

Giving in, she held his hand and let him lead her to the Center of the cavern she'd been avoiding.

Where she saw a man facedown on the ground.

"Oh no."

She raced over, dropping to her knees at his side. And realized in that second that it wasn't just any man. It was Connor Bateman. Her lost love. *Why? How?*

"Connor? Can you hear me?"

Her hands frantically searched his lean frame for injuries, her fingers slowing when she reached his hair and the sticky mess at the back of his head.

His pulse was warm and strong, and his chest rose and fell with a reassuring rhythm. But he was out cold. She dared not move him, not when he was injured like this. But she couldn't leave him either. And, on top of that, no methods of communication worked down here.

Genesis stared at him. What was he doing here? And why now? Now that she'd finally accustomed herself to his absence? She brushed his hair off his forehead and gently stroked his cheek.

If they could stay here, the energy of the cavern would help heal him. The pools would be better, but she could never carry him that far. The two of them would have to stay here until he woke up and just hope the man with the gun didn't return.

Hopefully Connor would wake soon. The longer he stayed unconscious, the worse the scenario.

The wound didn't look that bad, but head wounds could be tricky. "Wake up, Connor, please."

She continued to gently stroke him, easing his pain and willing the healing energy of the cavern to do its job. "Please, Connor. Please wake up."

Remi sat between them, one hand on her shoulder and one on Connor's. Granny would have said that Remi was completing the circle.

Granny was full of those little tidbits.

Connor shifted, rolling over. He groaned.

"Easy, Connor. You've got a head injury. You've been unconscious."

He groaned again and tried to sit up but collapsed onto his side instead. "What happened?"

Genesis rose and shook out her legs, stiff from sitting in the same position for so long.

"Either someone hit you over the head, or you fell." She squatted in front of him. "What are you doing here?" She frowned. "Did Matt send you here?" Her voice dropped. "Or Grandfather?"

Genesis watched as he blinked at her. Then saw her. Like, really saw her. And his lips slowly curved upward. A beautiful, caring movement that caught her attention and wouldn't let go. She sighed. He'd always had the power to move her, a sensuality that he never seemed to be aware of. He'd been quiet—reserved almost—when she'd first met him. It had been that very quietness that had attracted her. Always beautiful, this visible vulnerability was touching.

And she barely knew him.

On impulse, she dropped a kiss on the top of his head, surprising herself.

And him too. His gaze shot up to hers.

"Don't take that the wrong way." She backed up slightly. "I was just kissing your *owie* better."

His gaze shifted away from hers, and she wondered for a moment if she'd really seen a whisper of disappointment in it.

"You never answered my question," she said, smoothly shifting back onto neutral ground.

"I came to check out the pools, and … I came looking for you."

"Why?" She stared down at him curiously. "I'm fine. Did Matt send you?"

"He was concerned about you, yes." Connor struggled to his feet. "Only I'm the one who got beaned instead."

Once she was reassured that he wasn't in danger of falling over or collapsing, she stepped slightly away from him and searched the darkness. "Did you see your attacker?"

"No. I'd been calling out to you, when I got hit from behind. I fought back, and he took off."

The disgust in his voice said everything. But she had to study his features to see if he was telling the truth. Inside, her heart and mind twisted over his words. Why had he come looking for her? And why here? He couldn't have known she'd be here.

He took a deep breath. "Yeah, I feel like a stupid fool."

She winced inwardly. She would really have to work on her attitude when it came to Connor. "Do you know anything about the work being done here?"

"No idea. I hadn't heard of anyone doing construction here. I can see the public wanting to open up the pools to more people but ... not like this." He turned in a slow circle, surveying the cavern.

"And what about the simple matter of asking permission from the owner of the property? Or is this one of Grandfather's projects? After all, he wouldn't worry about a little thing like legalities, would he?" Despite her best efforts, some of her bitterness slipped into her tone.

"I don't think Grandfather has anything to do with this." Connor walked over to the closest wall and stretched a hand out to stroke along the smooth stone. "I thought this area was not deeded."

"Says who?" she snapped.

He glanced over his shoulder at her. "It's always been that way?"

She stared back at him. "Is that what Grandfather told you?"

Connor studied her face, then walked closer. "I heard you have a problem with him, and I'm sorry for that. He's not an easy man to live or work with, but he's not some common criminal."

He wasn't a common anything, she thought, but she managed to keep from spitting the words out. "*Hmm.*" She turned and started back the way she'd come in. "I don't believe you but no point in arguing. We'll never agree on that point."

Even his sigh spoke of his fatigue.

"Come on. Let's get you back to the surface. You've been down here long enough."

"I've hardly been here at all. An hour or two at most," he protested. "You've likely been down here way longer."

"I'm not injured." And knowing the words would hurt but not sure how else to say them, she added, "And my senses are all functioning properly."

He stared at her, his gaze dark, hooded. Silent. Abruptly he said, "I do know how to take care of myself, you know? This isn't exactly the first time I've been in a situation like this."

She shot a pointed look at his injured scalp. He glared back but kept his mouth closed. "Why did you come down here in the first place?" she asked him.

"I'm keeping an eye on the pools," he said.

She slipped across the open cavern, sliding along the walls. "And I'm looking for the reason why the forest is such a mess."

Having made her point, she led the way back to the tunnel. She didn't really want him using her private way in and out of the place, but it was preferable to meeting the guy who'd attacked Connor.

His color had returned with her comment on his missing abilities. Good. Yet maybe she shouldn't have mentioned it, but it wasn't as if he could hide it from her. She didn't normally take cheap shots, but it helped put some distance between them. Some necessary distance. She had no intention of getting back into an intimate relationship with Connor. He'd been her one and only love, and things had been unbelievably hot between them, which made his betrayal all the more devastating.

And that was *her* problem. He'd made no promises. He'd left that last morning, without waking her to say goodbye. And, foolish her, she'd been devastated. An idiot to think he would leave his job and would stay here for her. But she'd made the mistake of letting him in. He'd been the only man to stir her senses before or since.

That hadn't changed.

She just had to remember that he was here for a reason—and she wasn't it.

CONNOR HATED THE distance between them. Cordial friends. Polite enemies. But he grudgingly kept a huge space from her, when what he really wanted was to take her into the pools around the corner, strip the clothes from her back, and remind her just how good they were together. She'd been the hottest thing he'd ever experienced. Their week together had blown him away, and he'd never forgotten a single second of it. He couldn't get enough. Anytime.

Anyplace. God, he loved her and had since he'd first laid eyes on her.

He had wanted her to leave with him. He hadn't imagined that she wouldn't feel the same way.

He hadn't been raised here in town, and, as such, hadn't had the same prejudices that many did against Genesis's granny and, therefore, directed at her. Apparently her granny had been one short stop away from being loony. That the whole family line was unstable. And that nothing could come of a relationship with Genesis, long-term. Or, at least, that's what Grandfather had voiced loudly and regularly.

Connor refused to believe that. Then he'd believed she would choose him over her painful existence in this town. If she left with him, they could have a life together, a life without the mockery of the townspeople.

Only she'd refused.

Even the next morning, the heat of anger and rejection still fueling him, he'd left.

But, with every mile he put between them, he knew leaving had been a mistake. He should have stayed. Or better yet, he should have dragged her with him.

Instead he'd walked away.

He'd hated himself that day … and the next and every day that followed. And then, not long afterward, the hurt started. A slow bleeding ache that had never healed.

Knowing he'd wronged her but confused about his own feelings, he'd buried himself in work, waiting for his emotions to stabilize. And eventually they had—firmly on Genesis's side.

By the time he had sorted out his heart, months had passed, and he began losing his energetic abilities. Plus he'd just been assigned another major problem on the opposite side of Glory, even with his mental state in turmoil, even feeling like only half a man. Inferior. Damaged.

It was all he could do to cope with the trauma and still do his investigative work. He could have gone to Grandfather and explained.

But Connor had been too proud. And too worried.

He was a guardian. A protector. An investigator to keep the energy centers safe. He'd found his place here because of those abilities. Then, when he'd lost them, he'd thought it was just some fluke, a mere blip on the radar. He thought they'd return—any day now. And when they hadn't, he'd gone straight into denial. Until finally he accepted that this could very well be his future. He'd spent the last six months soul-searching, realizing that he'd lost more than just his abilities. He'd also lost Genesis.

He could cast his mind far and wide for a reason for the loss of his abilities. And Genesis, being an energy worker, had been put under the spotlight of suspicion. After all, they'd just broken up. Early on, still mired in pain by the fact that she wouldn't leave with him, he'd wondered if she might have taken away his abilities. To punish him.

That was an idea he'd almost instantly tossed away. It wasn't in her to do that. She was a healer, a woman who specialized in mixing herbs to soothe and to calm—not to hurt and not in response to anger. To hurt someone by removing their energy would be the antithesis of who she was.

He cast a look sideways, as they walked quietly. She was very powerful. And, at the same time, so gentle. He wondered for the hundredth time at the depth of her power and just how strong she was. She'd never shared any of that information, but he had his suspicions.

"Heavy thoughts," Genesis said lightly.

"Yeah." Talk about an understatement. He glanced around to note that she'd led him through a new tunnel, one he'd never seen before. Moonlight shone ahead and grew brighter, as they stepped out into the woods. "I didn't know about this entrance."

"It's not well-known. I didn't want to meet your attacker, so I chose this path."

"How many entrances are there?"

"We've never counted," she said, "but there are dozens."

As he watched, she came to a standstill and cocked her head, listening intently to something. He couldn't see anything wrong. Suddenly Genesis laughed, held out her hand, and then continued walking. He stared at her outstretched hand. Was he supposed to hold that? He wanted to, but he had the horrible feeling that she was already holding someone else's hand.

And then he remembered the talk about her. And her imaginary friend. At the time, he'd laughed. Like a fool. Spirit pets, some people called them. But since no one could see these pets but their owners, the stories were hard to prove. Energy workers saw them apparently, but Connor had been raised isolated, unaware of paranormal abilities. Puberty had changed all that, but he'd yet to see one of those spirit pets himself.

He stared at her now, her head tilted to one side, as if listening to someone who walked next to her.

Was it possible? In the last year, he'd heard about more people having pets no one could see. As if a mass condition of neurosis had hit Little Glory. But, if the others were all energy workers, what were the chances that those like him, with less-than-their-full abilities—or none at all—just couldn't see these animals? Not that he'd seen them before losing his abilities.

It wasn't impossible to have invisible pets. Glory held many wonders. They'd barely scratched the surface of what this planet could offer.

What had she called him? Rami? No, Remi. That was it. She said he was a rare plumer. Long furry body, walked on two or four legs, and made a weird sound when he cried.

It was one thing to slay a dragon you could see, but how could Connor open up to a relationship with an animal he couldn't see? It was hard to acknowledge that the damn thing even existed.

If it did, he'd like to see it at least once—to know for sure.

But, according to the lore, the plumers chose their owners, chose who could see them.

And he hadn't been chosen.

Something to do with energy readers and having an affinity for other energy workers.

Which he no longer was.

CHAPTER 5

GENESIS MOVED EASILY through the forest. She was a creature of the moonlight. And sunlight too really, but she had a special, unique connection with moonlight. She always thought of secrets, of healing, of sadness, when she walked in moonlight. As if something about it set off her emotions. Sunlight was different. It brought joy and laughter and exuberance to her world, whereas the moon was about inner quiet and introspection.

Having Connor beside her was both exhilarating and nerve-racking. Remi had walked up and grabbed her hand; Genesis hadn't thought anything of it. They were always together. But she rarely showed his presence to others by her actions.

Not that Connor would have noticed.

The pale, wan look on Connor's face spoke volumes. He needed to lie down and rest. And soon. She didn't think he was fully aware, but, for the last hundred yards, he'd been following her blindly. He'd spoken little before but even that had slowed to a mumble.

She didn't know what to do. If he hadn't been attacked, she would have taken him to the pools, but considering the attacker was quite possibly still around, that wasn't a safe option.

And Connor couldn't drive back. Not in the shape he

was in.

That left one place within walking distance. The cottage.

The fact that Connor didn't argue was troublesome too, as he followed her through the woods in the opposite direction of where he'd entered. He had to be hurting bad for this to happen. His eyes were half closed, and he held one hand out as if looking for support, but, at the same time, he kept putting one foot in front of the other.

Somewhere along the path, she'd slipped her arm around his waist, helping to keep him upright, his arm resting on her shoulders. She led him deeper into the woods. Most people knew nothing of this area, and the ones who did avoided it at all costs.

"How much farther?" he whispered.

The sound of his words were so faint that she had to lean in closer to hear. She shot him a worried glance. How badly injured was he? "Just a couple more turns." She picked up the pace slightly, needing to reach the cottage before he collapsed. He was too heavy for her to lift. She winced as more of his weight dropped onto her shoulders.

Catching sight of his face, she noticed the gleam of sweat forming on his forehead and a glassy, unseeing look in his eyes. "Shit." She tried to move faster, but she couldn't and still keep both of them on their feet. "Remi, can you help?"

A quiet, worried chitter sounded, as Remi moved to Connor's other side and held his hand. She bit back a laugh. "Thanks, Remi."

More chattering.

Damn, she was struggling with Connor's weight now. Then inspiration struck. "Remi, show me the way. A shortcut. Break a path for me to follow."

Remi bounded ahead to the left. Genesis corrected her

course and followed. She was small and lithe, although strong, yet supporting Connor made a big difference. He was now shuffling along, completely leaning on her, trusting her to take him somewhere safe.

For all their personal history, she could not let him down.

He was a wounded animal. And what was even worse, he got that way because of her. He'd come looking for her.

Remi burst excitedly through the brush, jumping up her legs and swinging from her shoulder onto Connor's shoulders. She took his enthusiasm to mean the cottage was just up ahead.

Just then, Connor stopped moving, swaying on his feet. *Oh, shit.*

"We're almost there, Connor. Just a few more steps. Come on, please. Take a few more steps." He struggled forward one more step and stopped. Genesis exhaled loudly, tightened her grip on him, and pushed him forward.

Alternating encouragement with shoving, they finally broke through the brush to see the cottage. Relief swept over her. As they walked closer to the building, a sound behind her caught her attention. She glanced back. The brush had already closed up, and the path had disappeared. Everything looked normal. Yet it didn't *feel* normal.

With a last wary eye at their surroundings, she nudged Connor forward. "We're here. Let me open the door." She leaned him against the wall beside the entry and, using Granny's energy twists, unlocked the door.

Home.

She turned to Connor and led him inside, directly through the small living room to another doorway. The pool room. Opening that lock was a little more complicated.

Once they were inside, Genesis took a deep breath and felt calm flow through her. These healing pools were connected. Taking care of them was vital for the community. However, the community didn't know about this pool. It was hers. Taking care of it meant it was always there for her.

Pushing Connor into a seat at the side of the pool, she bent to unlace his boots and tugged them off, followed by his socks, which she stuffed into his boots. His shirt slipped off over his head easily enough. Then came his pants. Crap.

"Connor, I need you to stand up, so I get your pants off."

He looked at her in confusion. Then blinked. "What?"

Not worrying about trying to explain, she tugged him upright and quickly opened the button and zipper and yanked down his pants, leaving his boxers in place. He stepped out and stood, shivering. The pool would warm him quickly.

At least she hoped so.

She urged him to the edge of the pool. "Connor, do you know what this is?"

"Healing pool," he whispered, "but I don't know this one."

"That's because it's mine."

A slip of understanding shone from his gaze, but it quickly vanished, as though everything happening around him appeared to be too much to comprehend.

"I need you to get in. It will help your head wound."

He stared at the pool, as if too much effort were required. She put her arms around him and urged him into the water. At the first touch of his foot in the water, it swarmed up his leg.

She gave him a gentle push; he stood off balance momentarily and then toppled full-length into the water. Instantly the water surged up, covering him, supporting him, helping him.

Genesis stepped back, confident that the waters would look after him, and returned to close the front door and to retie the locks. Now no one could get in without her knowledge. And Remi had other ways to get inside.

He didn't need doors.

She did a quick survey of the cottage, checking that all was as it should be. It appeared to be exactly as she'd left it. The man from the tunnel hadn't found it, nor had anyone else. Thankfully. She came here often; it was a special place for her and her sisters. It reconnected her to Granny's spirit.

Genesis walked back and took a quick look to see Connor floating in the pool, apparently unconscious.

As long as he was breathing, she'd leave him in place. She went to work and soon had a pot of tea steeping and an iron kettle of soup simmering.

He would need sleep after the pool session. Digging into the linen closet, she found the stash of towels. Taking several, she walked back to Connor.

He still floated, eyes closed, in the middle of the pool. Surrounded by natural rock on all sides, the water reflected off the bottom. Studying his color, she realized he needed to stay in a bit longer. She left the towels behind and returned to the soup and turned down the flame, then poured herself a cup of tea and sat beside the pool with it.

Having him here in front of her, in a place she'd hoped to bring him a long time ago, had an edge of incredulity to it. He'd been her ... everything. For one week she'd experienced heaven. And, when it had gone bad, it had gone completely and utterly bad.

She had never regretted those nights; she'd only ever wished for a different ending. She was the sister who couldn't leave. When he'd pleaded with her, she'd cried and explained that one of the three triplets had to stay. There was no choice. Then he'd made love to her, like he couldn't bear to part from her, and she thought he'd understood.

When she woke up the next morning, ... he was gone.

So what was this reunion about then?

Plus, ... up until tonight, she'd thought that seeing him here, in her home, would hurt. But it didn't. It felt odd, strange, and good. ... In a weird way, it felt right.

And that scared her even more.

CONNOR CAME AWAKE as gently as a breath blowing on the breeze. He sighed, a deep long last expulsion of old air, old emotions, and old hurts. He opened his eyes.

Except for the fact that he was in water, he had no idea where he was. He floated easily, loathe to get out, feeling calmer and more peaceful than he had in a long time. He studied the ceiling above him. A large glass dome let him see the starry night above, bright lights in a dark, blurry panorama. He tilted his head as best he could to see more. Small lamps created luminous golden pools around the room. And the water he floated in glowed with an unearthly light.

He turned his head to see a cozy room only big enough for this pool and a few chairs and a small table on the side. He swore he'd never been in this space before. Moving his hands slowly, he shifted enough so that he could turn around and see everything. And stopped.

Genesis sat at the edge of the pool, staring into a teacup, as if the answers to the world were there.

She looked so lost, so fragile, that his heart went out to her.

Slowly his memories filled in.

He'd been in the underground pools, looking for her. Matt had suggested that Connor find her and ask her if she knew what was happening to the reserve.

Instead he'd gotten his head bashed in without warning, and she'd found *him*.

He studied her bent head, wondering how someone so small could be so strong. She'd come from humble beginnings. Looked down on because of her ancient loony granny, Genesis then survived that loss of her grandmother and had watched the dominoes continue to fall all around her, as her sisters' love relationships broke up, with the two women leaving Genesis behind. Alone.

Just like he had.

He'd loved her before. But, it had been too fast, too powerful. And now he realized he had never stopped loving her, and he knew he would spend the rest of his days trying to convince her to give him a second chance.

Give them a second chance.

He had his head on straight now, and he knew what was important. As far as he could tell, they were alone here. And maybe that was a good time for his confession. To tell her what he'd done—and why. And what he was prepared to do to win her back. Which was … anything.

He took a deep breath and whispered in a gentle voice, "Hi."

CHAPTER 6

GENESIS LOOKED OVER at him, and her heart melted. That look in his eyes. As if she were the most important thing in his life. A look she'd always loved and had never thought she would see again.

In the same gentle tone he'd used, she whispered, "Hi back."

He smiled, a long slow smile that started with his mouth and moved to his eyes, spreading to encompass the room—with her in the center. She felt her resistance crumbling. She loved him so much. Always had. But how did one reconcile what they'd been through?

And did that matter? Maybe they should move forward as the two different people they were today. He'd dropped in and would drop out again just as fast. She could enjoy the moment the way she had last time. Only this time she was older. Wiser. She could love him and let him go. She had to. Because she wanted those moments—however fleeting—with him.

From the look in his eyes, he was willing.

Her heart beat out a resounding message, *Hurry, make the most of the moment.* But her mind, that part of her that knew what kind of heartache lay ahead, whispered, *Be careful.* Whatever happened, it would still hurt in the end.

"How are you feeling?" she asked, studying his face. His

color looked better, and he appeared rested. He looked relaxed and so at home. She deliberately kept her eyes on his face. He was lean and muscled, with tan lines that would have amused her if she'd been in the same place emotionally as the last time she'd seen them. That he looked equally well in a suit had made Grandfather happy to send him to the various elitist evening functions that she never could attend, not being one of that crowd.

"I feel"—he closed his eyes and released a heavy sigh—"at peace."

"Good. And the head wound?"

He reached up a wet hand and gently touched the injury, surprise lighting his face. "It doesn't hurt at all." He glanced around the small room. "Where am I?"

She hesitated, then realized it was too late to keep this secret. "It's my place."

His gaze zipped back toward her. "What?"

She raised an eyebrow and waited. He hadn't known about this place. She'd never shown it to him. Hell, she'd never brought anyone here.

His attention quickly searched the small room again, then zinged back to land and to lock on her face. His gaze narrowed. "Yours?"

"Yes." And she took a sip of tea, watching him over the rim. "And my sisters."

He sat up slowly. "When did you get it?"

"It was Granny's." She stood in a smooth movement and turned her back on him. As she left, she tossed back, "If you are feeling okay, you can get out whenever you like. The towels are on the side of the pool."

Back in the kitchen, she set the table with the light meal she'd prepared. Hearing the sounds of him moving around, she served two bowls.

Looking tired but more like himself, Connor stepped into the kitchen, instantly dwarfing the small room. Unconsciously she stepped back. "I don't have much food. I didn't expect visitors."

His glance encompassed the space, before coming to rest on the bowls on the table. He smiled. "I can't remember a time when I was quite so grateful to see a bowl of soup."

"Hungry?"

"Starved." He pointed to a chair. "May I?"

"Oh." She flushed. "Please, sit down." She hated the sudden awkwardness, the immediate retreat to polite formality. When communication broke down, politeness became the comfortable medium to buffer the widening distance between them. She took her seat and immediately apologized. "Sorry there isn't more."

He shook his head. "This is just fine. Thank you for bringing me here." He stopped and looked up from his bowl. "You took care of me and brought me to a spirit pool so I could heal. And now"—he smiled and waved his hand toward the food—"you're feeding me." He spooned up another mouthful. "And I am hungry."

"A side effect of the pools."

"Really?" His gaze pinned her in place.

She nodded. She didn't add that, if one appetite wasn't fueled, then another appetite became uncontrollable, until it was fed.

"Thank you." His quiet voice interrupted her reverie.

Taking another sip of soup, she said, "You're welcome."

She let the silence develop a little further. She could sense he was bursting with questions, but she had no plans to make it easy on him. Instead she focused on finishing her soup, while her mind filled with the issue of the oncoming night. He wouldn't fit anywhere in the little cottage. Connor was over six feet tall, and the bed in the spare room had been hers. Her granny's bed was bigger, as it was a full-size bed, whereas hers was from her childhood. At just over five feet, she'd never grown out of it. As long as her granny had been alive, Genesis had slept in the little bed. Afterward, she'd switched to Granny's bed. It felt slightly wrong to have Connor sleep there. Still, her options were limited. There were also her sisters' rooms, more like studios, but they were private.

She glanced at the moonlight shining into the kitchen; it was past bedtime. They'd stay here tonight, and, in the morning, she'd lead him back out again.

He pushed away his empty bowl. "That hit the spot." Then he yawned.

Genesis stood and collected the dirty dishes. "Bedtime."

"I'll help you clean up first."

She quickly finished up and turned to face him. He might have healed, but he appeared to be hitting the after-pool effects. All the pools had different aftereffects, depending on their spiritual level, but, at the same time, they had a lot of similarities. Her pool made one really hungry and really tired. "Come on. Let's get you into bed."

She led the way to Granny's room. "This is actually my room, but I'll sleep in the spare room, as that bed is too small for you."

"No." He shook his head. "It won't matter. I'm so tired, I'll zone out with no trouble, even if my lower legs hang off the end of the frame."

She led him to her old bed and showed him. "It's my old childhood bed." He winced and she laughed. "Come on. I'll show you the other one."

At the door to her bedroom, she motioned him inside ahead of her.

"Oh, wow. Just like in the room with the pool." He stood in the middle of the room, staring upward.

"Granny was a stargazer," she said, by way of explanation for the huge glass-domed ceiling.

"I didn't think we had any more of those."

She didn't answer. Tears collected in her eyes. He turned, as if sensing her distress, and walked over to her. "I'm sorry. I forgot."

Genesis swallowed hard. She smiled brightly at him. "I'm fine. It gets easier with time."

He gently stroked her arms. "Easier, yes, but we always mourn those we've loved and lost."

"True." She sniffled, swiped at her eyes, then motioned to her bed. "It's yours for the night."

Connor protested, but she wouldn't listen. "I'm too tired to argue over this. Go to sleep, and I'll see you in the morning." At the doorway, she turned back. "If you wake up in pain in the night, head to the pool."

"I will," he said. "Thank you."

And she walked away.

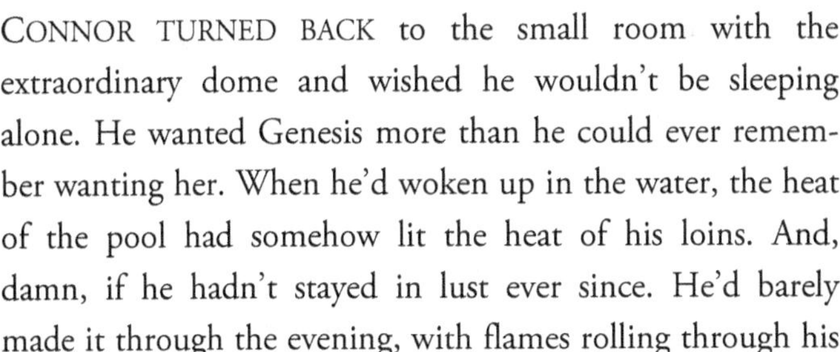

CONNOR TURNED BACK to the small room with the extraordinary dome and wished he wouldn't be sleeping alone. He wanted Genesis more than he could ever remember wanting her. When he'd woken up in the water, the heat of the pool had somehow lit the heat of his loins. And, damn, if he hadn't stayed in lust ever since. He'd barely made it through the evening, with flames rolling through his veins. Just seeing her in front of him, the way she'd sipped her soup, licked her lips, and shied away like a doe when he moved. Everything about her stoked the flames.

The thrill of the chase pumped through him, firing up his heartbeat. He'd closed his eyes, feigning exhaustion, when all he'd wanted was to lay her on the table and to make crazy passionate love to her right there.

He shuddered. He should have taken the small bed. He wouldn't get any sleep tonight anyway.

Throwing himself on the bed, he sighed heavily. The night sky stared down at him. Stars, millions of them, gleamed brightly in the sky. It made him feel small. Insignificant. He thought about Genesis's revelation—about her grandmother being a stargazer. He'd only heard of such a thing as an ancient art. Almost a myth now.

It was a skill that rulers once used to make the right decisions at the right time.

He couldn't imagine. Her granny had been looked at as a joke. A bit of local color most people had avoided. Including him, on the couple trips he'd taken to visit. He'd seen her at a store, one time in the park, and, like everyone else, he'd avoided her.

He remembered what Grandfather had said about the oddness of Genesis's family, remembered the mockery in his voice at the time.

It couldn't have been easy to be Genesis, growing up in that environment.

Connor hoped she'd had a loving and happy home. At least the four women had been close. And Genesis was special, so Granny had done a wonderful job. It said much about Genesis's upbringing, even if the townspeople wouldn't see it that way. Connor and Genesis had been so in love that her past hadn't reared its head during his time with her. And her past hadn't been important. Then.

Now he had to wonder.

That she'd chosen to stay here, rather than leave with him, had broken his heart. Had left him gasping with pain. He'd somehow thought it would get better. But all it did was highlight how much he'd missed her.

And still did. But now he understood. At least some of it. It wasn't so much that she hadn't wanted to leave, but that she couldn't. When she'd first told him that, he'd thought it was an excuse. Now that he understood more—Matt had helped with that—Connor knew that one sister had to remain here at all times. So, with the other two disappearing, Genesis had no choice but to stay.

No more misunderstandings. They'd take it slow this time. See what their options were. He knew one thing for sure.

He wasn't leaving her again.

He closed his eyes, at peace for the first time in months, … and fell asleep to thoughts of her soft skin.

CHAPTER 7

GENESIS ROLLED OVER and punched her pillow, closing her eyes for the hundredth time. She groaned. Damn it. Why? She was exhausted, her body worn out. She needed to be clearheaded tomorrow. She had so much to do. She desperately needed a good night's sleep.

But, at this point, she'd be nothing more than a baggy-eyed witch in the morning. She flopped onto her back. "Remi, could you just knock me out?"

He popped up beside her, his chatter fast and furious. "Yes, you're right. This bed is small, and he's in ours."

She sighed. She just couldn't seem to relax. That might be her answer. The healing pool. She could use it herself. The only hesitation was that she'd be nude in her own pool. And what if Connor woke up?

She'd told him to go into the pool, if he hurt.

Well, she'd have to deal with that when the time came. Once the idea of bathing was in her mind, the thought wouldn't leave her alone. She took a quick listen outside his door, and, not hearing any sounds coming from where he slept, she tiptoed to her pool. Closing the door, she slipped off her robe and stepped nude into the water.

Oh Lord, that felt good. Her heart ached, and, after finding Connor, along with the physical effort to bring him home, her body was sore and bruised. She stood waist-deep in the water and unbraided her long golden hair, using her fingers to untangle the wavy strands. Then she slowly sank into the warm blue energizing waters, until she was completely submerged.

After a moment she came up for air, took a breath, and floated on her back. Quiet moans escaped as she lay here, completely supported by the water. She focused on taking several deep breaths to release the stress and to heal the multiple aches and pains that had permeated her body so deeply that she'd almost accepted them as normal.

And that wasn't good. She couldn't work energy if her body was stressed. Or depleted. Hearing a sudden noise, she quickly rolled into a tight ball in case it was Connor. Peering over her shoulder, she searched to see if he had come into the room.

Instead she spotted Remi diving through the water like a seal. She smiled. His system healed here too. And maybe even more than that. It was a play area for him. Remi gave her an open-mouthed grin.

She laughed. "Yeah, I know. We should have just come here, when we first couldn't sleep."

She rolled over onto her back and floated, staring up at the glass ceiling above. The full moon shone bright overhead, its rays dropping to ripple across the gentle waves. Such a magical feeling.

Now, as the healing water soothed her skin and warmed her heart, she rolled over again and let the water bathe her face. She loved when she was completely submerged and floating in the middle of the water. Not everyone could float midway. Too often they sank or floated to the top. She loved to be completely surrounded, completely protected by the waters.

When her air ran out, she pushed her face to break through the surface and take a deep breath. And went under again.

When she came up several long moments later, Connor stood at the edge of the pool, standing only in his boxers. He stared down at her worriedly.

She curled into a ball, hiding her body from his view.

"I didn't mean to disturb you, but I didn't hear any noise for so long that I started to get worried. Then, when you didn't surface ..." He let his voice trail off. "Are you coming out?"

"Not yet." And she certainly wouldn't walk out of the protective water while he stood there. The chemistry between them had flashed over far less than this. She didn't dare. This was not the way she wanted to get to know him again. They'd spent all of their previous relationship in bed.

They'd only wanted each other.

And they'd had each other as often as possible.

Just because she'd accepted the breakup didn't mean she'd forgotten how combustible they were, given the right circumstances. Naked in a pool definitely qualified.

He picked up a towel from the stack and dropped it beside her.

"Thank you."

He nodded and turned away. At the doorway, he pivoted and asked, "Are you okay?"

She hesitated. Then she gave him a small smile and said, "Yes. Thank you."

"You could have come in here before, you know? You didn't have to wait until I'd gone to bed."

"I couldn't sleep," she whispered. "I expected you to sleep solid."

His lips twitched. "I thought so too, but dreams of angels danced through my head."

And he walked out, his boxers hugging those muscled cheeks.

Remi popped up from where he'd been lying on the side bench. Slipping into the water like an otter, he swam over to her.

"Oh, what am I going to do?" she whispered. "I miss him so."

***

CONNOR RECLINED ON his bed and stared up at the moonlight. Sleep couldn't be further from his mind. The naked nymph in the next room completely dominated his thoughts.

He loved her. She couldn't hide her response to him, even though it didn't make her happy. She didn't trust him. She hadn't forgiven him. Maybe she never would. He had to live with that.

And he would, if he could have her back. Determined to clear the air once and for all, he rose from the bed and walked over to the doorway of the pool room. Keeping his back to her, he said, "I didn't mean to hurt you."

Shocked surprise sat heavily in the air.

"Well, you did." Her tone was short, soft, and sad.

It damn-near broke his heart. "I know that. And I'm so sorry."

No answer.

"You hurt me too," he added hoarsely.

Still no answer.

He risked a quick glance over his shoulder. She was in the deepest part of the pool and up against the edge, her lithe body hidden from his view. He had made her uncomfortable. She meant too much to him for that.

But this seemed like too good an opportunity to pass up.

If she'd just talk to him.

"Genesis?"

"I'm here."

He ran his fingers through his hair. "I can't do more than apologize … and then show you that I'm different."

Splashing sounds caught his ear, then the soft slap of wet feet on stone. He turned slowly to see her wrapped up in a towel, standing several steps away from him. The towel end was tucked up under her arm, but wet spots were also developing in the most interesting of places. Her wet hair had been twisted into a rope that still dropped down her shoulder. His gaze dropped to her bare feet. And, damn, they'd always been sexy as hell. Petite and delicate looking, they belied the strength of the woman they supported.

Dripping wet, she left tiny footsteps on the stone floor. With a smile, she brushed past him and walked to her room.

"Please, Genesis, take your bed."

Startled, she looked back at him. "Why? I'm fine here. You go to bed and sleep. Your injury isn't fully healed. A good night's sleep is the best thing for you."

He reached out and grabbed her arm.

She froze, her huge blue eyes wide with shock, as she stared at him, waiting.

"The best thing for me is you."

CHAPTER 8

WELL. IT SEEMED that no matter how hard she'd tried, they'd gotten here regardless. She stared down at the hand on her arm in bemusement. He'd always been able to do that to her; one touch and she melted.

But melting was not on her agenda tonight. Or any other night. Sure, he'd obviously changed, and the good man had likely become a better one. That didn't mean he was the man for her. He'd *been* the man for her but not so much now. Why? Because he wasn't the only one who'd changed. Abandonment did that to a woman.

As did betrayal.

She didn't know if she could trust him again.

He slipped a finger under her chin and lifted it, so he could see into her eyes. She closed them, so he couldn't note the secrets in hers. "You don't have to do that. I can't read your eyes anymore." His bitterness washed over her, and she winced. "I've been slowly losing my abilities this last year. The doctors have no idea why."

"I'm sorry. That must be uncomfortable." And likely the reason for the big change in Connor, maybe even the catalyst for the rest. Losing one's abilities changed a person. Genesis only knew of one other who'd lost his, and he'd slowly gone insane, before committing suicide one night while all alone. As his behavior had become so erratic in his last months that he had hid away, and it had been days before his body was found.

A distressing time for all.

She stepped away from his hand, turned her back on him, and resolutely entered the small bedroom. She could be strong. She could avoid him. She could do this.

"I love you, Genesis," he whispered behind her. "I always have."

There was no artifice in his voice. It was naked, pained, defeated, with everything laid out in front of her. She hesitated. Maybe she couldn't do this.

Her heart was shaky, her stomach quivering, her mind in chaos. This was not what she expected.

She turned to stare into his dark-brown eyes and studied his intense gaze. He was willing to take whatever she dished out because he felt he deserved it.

"I'm so sorry for not believing you," he said. "For not understanding."

Damn. She dropped her gaze. He could bring her to her knees with just a few words.

"The bottom line is, misguided or not, I loved you back then, and I've loved you every day since." He turned and walked a few steps away. "I just wanted to say that, in case I never got another chance." And he strode into her bedroom, partially closing the door.

Leaving her standing here, wondering what to do.

And the way he'd left it, he'd given her a choice.

The door was still open.

If she wanted to walk through it.

Genesis moved until she stood in the open doorway, where he laid in bed and studied the energy of the room surrounding the bed. Confusion. Frustration. Pain. Sorrow.

Love.

She watched Connor roll over. She'd refused to study the energy of her friends before, unless asked. It was too intimate. Too personal. Invasive almost. Unless a person was sick or injured, she found it almost impossible to cross that line. Yet, as she stared at the man who'd broken her heart and who could very well break it again, she realized he was hurting too.

And that wasn't what she wanted. Yet she wasn't a healer of people. At least that wasn't her specialty. She couldn't just fix him up the way some energy workers she knew could, but she could weave light and peace into his soul and remove strands of pain.

If he'd let her.

Inside her, a thin voice whispered, *That is not what he wants. It's not what you want. You want to be with him, healing your hearts and bodies at the same time. This doesn't have to be forever. This is for right now. This moment in time. Take the moment. They'll be memories to make you smile after he's gone. Because he will leave. You know that.*

Genesis dropped her head. What she wanted to do didn't matter here.

That same voice said, *If not now, when does what you want matter? You need this. If only to say goodbye.* In a twisted way, that made the difference. She hadn't had a chance to say goodbye. For better or for worse, he'd left her with unfinished business.

And now she had a chance to fix ... something.

She walked closer.

He froze and stared at her, lightness and hope filling his gaze. "Genesis?"

By the time she reached his side of the bed, he was sitting up and staring at her. He opened his mouth. She leaned over and laid a finger against his lips. "No talking," she murmured. And, while he watched, she dropped her towel to stand in front of him, nude.

His gaze heated. He threw back the covers and shifted over to make room for her.

Feeling finally settled, feeling right, she slipped into bed and into his arms.

He held her close to his heart, gently rubbing her back. She smiled. He'd always been a tender lover. At first. She tilted her head back and gazed into eyes that had gone dark with need. As if in slow motion, she watched his mouth lower. Her eyelids closed, and she sighed seconds before he took her lips in a kiss that was both tender and hot. Full of forgiveness and heat. Full of regrets and promises.

The absolute tenderness of his touch brought tears to her eyes. He kissed them away and then dropped kisses on her closed eyelids.

The last of her doubts slipped away with the last of her tears.

He slid his hands through her long hair, holding her firm, and deepened the kiss. Gently, at first, as the tenderness in both demanded it, then harder. She pulled back slightly to smile up at him.

His lips curved. Then he lowered his head again and ravished her. Heat raced along her spine, as his hands slid over her cool skin, warming her inside and out. Their bodies knew each other. Recognized each other and instinctively remembered what the other liked. What the other needed.

When his hand slid up to cup her breast, she shuddered. When he lowered his head to kiss the place just above her heart, she moaned. Emotions swamped her. Memories overwhelmed her, even as his touch startled her. There'd been no one else for her. There couldn't be anyone else for her. He was, and always would be, her only lover.

The other half of her.

She gave herself to him, fully, openly, honestly.

He gave as much as he received everything. The tension in the room crackled, as he sipped, tasted, and enjoyed her. And she let him, lying on the bed, her hands clutching his head as he explored the body that had always been his.

Impatient now, her fingers were active, sliding over muscles and bone, scraping gently, before moving on to the next spot. He shifted restlessly under her touch.

He lifted his head and, when their gazes met this time, his dark chocolate met her sky blue both heated. Both aware.

His gaze deepened as he slid his hand down her hip and across her belly to slide through her curls. She shuddered and lifted her hips. He withdrew his hand, slid on top of her, and, when he took her mouth this time, she pressed herself against him.

Her blood pounded, matching the need driving though her. She twisted beneath him, sliding her feet up and down his calves. Then she slipped her hand between them to find him. Hard and smooth and … hers.

He groaned, hiked up her hips, withdrew from her touch, … and plunged.

She cried out.

He stilled. Effort for control in his voice, he whispered, "Did I hurt you?"

"No. It's just been so long." She twisted under him, feeling her body stretch, easing as if recognizing the invader. Then relaxed. She sighed, as the empty spaces inside filled and warmed.

She reached up and bit his lower lip, then slid her tongue to stroke just inside. He kissed her back, his hands reaching up to cup both breasts, kicking her temperature up again. With teasing fingers, he stroked and caressed until she squirmed beneath him.

When she shuddered, he shifted his position, grasped her hips, and plunged deeper. She gasped, but he didn't slow down. He drove her to the edge and held her. He filled her, swamped her, and flooded her with sensations.

Until she cried out, "More."

He hooked her leg over his arm and drove deep. And ground himself in place. Her eyes rolled up, and she cried out and went limp, her body exploding under his.

His hips pumped once, … twice, … and his cries joined hers.

When he collapsed beside her, she curled up close.

But the night had only begun. Insatiable, they teased and satisfied, explored and found, gave and received all night long. She gave him everything.

And received so much more. They only had a little time, and she wanted to experience everything again. She knew this would be only one night, and she was determined to store up every touch, every moment, every sigh and cry for later. She needed to slip him as deep into her heart as she could stuff him.

If there was a hint of desperation in her greedy touch, she could be forgiven. She'd loved him for so long. And to know she had tonight—only this moment—to soak up everything she could, she let down her guard as she never had before, and she went after him and let him have her without reserve.

Desperate to make the most of every moment, knowing

that time would march on regardless and would steal him from her yet again, they loved each other through the night.

Until the small hours of the morning, with dawn sneaking into the room, they collapsed, curled together, heart to heart, and slept.

CONNOR WATCHED GENESIS sleep. Deep circles bruised the skin under her eyes, and, although her skin glowed, there was a translucence to it that worried him. He knew little of her past, only that it must have been hard. And, more than that, she had to work her energy or suffer.

His talent had been different. He'd been developing highly skilled security instincts—reading people, intuition, a sense of awareness in a situation, reading the nuances off each one. He could see where a problem was coming from, but his skill had stopped just short of giving him details.

And then, within a week of being with her the last time, his abilities had slowly faded.

He shuddered. That week, his entire world had begun to fall apart.

But today, he'd found the most important part.

Bending over, he kissed the tip of her nose. There'd been an odd note in her actions tonight. Almost a finality. A loving and letting go. Fear burned an icy spot into his heart. He couldn't let it. He hadn't realized himself how very important she was to him—until he'd found her once more.

He didn't dare lose her again.

Regardless of what she felt or thought, he was here for the long haul. He just had to prove it to her.

Tugging her close, he drifted off to sleep.

CHAPTER 9

GENESIS WOKE, TEARS sliding down her cheeks. Her night with Connor had brought back powerful memories. And powerful hurts. She slipped out from under the covers and walked to the pool. Her body ached with delicious sensations. She slipped into the waters and lay down, sighing happily as the aches and pains eased.

The long night had woken up areas of her body she'd forgotten existed. Floating in the healing waters, she closed her eyes and picked up several strands of droplets from the surface of the water. She laid them across her forehead, letting the strands weave into her own energy, easing the sadness that threatened to overwhelm her.

She refused to regret the night in his arms. It had been as exquisite as their last night one year ago.

Except it was morning. And she had no intention of holding on to him. He needed to move on. Their breakup had held him back. She understood. Her life had been on hold for a long time too.

That was what last night had been all about.

Saying goodbye.

And, if she repeated those two words enough times, she might even believe it. She didn't want to say goodbye. But no promises were made. No reconciliation. Just a letting go.

And she would be an adult about it. Do the right thing.

Let him leave. It was better this way.

She rolled over in the pool and let her tears mingle into the water, healing her pain and easing her grief of what was to come.

A warm hand landed on her shoulder. She jerked and lifted her head. It could only be Connor, but she hadn't expected him here. With her.

Her first instinct was that this was her space. Private. And that was just stupid, after the hours they'd spent reacquainting with each other's bodies in the most intimate of ways.

He knelt beside her and tugged her into his arms. And just held her.

The tears wouldn't stop. She snuggled against his warm chest and hung on.

Wafts of steam rose around them, hugging them, healing them, even if they weren't aware of it. Genesis understood the effects of the healing water. However, she'd never been in the waters with another person.

"Why the tears?"

She swiped her eyes and went to sink back into the water. Instead of releasing her, he sank down with her, carrying her in his arms, as they floated.

"Talk to me."

She closed her eyes and rested. She had no answer. But her eyes burned, and her heart ached.

With grief.

"Please, sweetheart." He shifted back slightly, so he could look down into her face. "Why are you so sad?" He dropped his lips to her forehead. "Please, tell me."

Instead she could only look up at him as big fat tears continued to roll down her cheeks. He pulled her closer and just held her.

"I wish I could go back in time. Take back everything I did and said that hurt you."

She shook her head. "It wouldn't matter."

He stopped for a second and then shook his head. "I don't believe that. I won't believe that."

"It's better this way," she whispered.

"And that's where you are wrong." He brushed her cheek with his finger. "This? … What we have here is right. It's important. We are important."

She smiled. He believed what he was saying, but he didn't realize that nothing had changed. She did. She reached up and brushed her fingers through his wavy hair. With a sad smile, she stood and climbed out of the pool.

Too emotional, she pulled back inside, desperate to hold it together. To get through this as an adult. He was a good man. Just not her man. And that wasn't his fault. She walked to the window and stared out as the morning sun drifted across the bushes. A still summer morning.

A beautiful summer morning.

She sensed more than felt him behind her.

"Please, give me a chance," he whispered.

"I can't." She wiped her cheeks. "Nothing has changed."

The words exploded from him. "Everything has changed. We're here together, aren't we? That's change."

She gave a broken laugh. "That was just sex. We never had a problem with that."

"It was not just sex. Don't go there. I love you. I always have."

Her heart ached. She turned, hating to look but needing to see the truth or the lies on his face. She carefully studied his features, reading deep in his energy. Could she trust what she was seeing? She had before. And he'd let her down.

As if sensing the change in her, Connor grasped her arms in his hands. "I was wrong. I shouldn't have walked away from you. If I'd known what I know now, … I wouldn't have. And that is something I will regret for the rest of my life."

She shook her head. "It wasn't about making a choice." She stopped. "It was about not needing for there to be a choice in the first place."

"We were young," he murmured. "And what we had was hot."

"Too hot apparently."

"I don't think that's possible."

She stared at him. "Besides, this isn't the time."

The water beside them gurgled, almost angrily, reacting to the tension in the room.

"I'm not following you. Explain?" He stared into the water that rippled uneasily.

She motioned to the pool. "They wouldn't have behaved like that before. Whoever started that construction in the sacred pools knew that the forest power was low. Knew that they could go in and could rape the land without fear of reprisal." She took a deep breath. "The real question is, did that person who is damaging the pools do something to hurt the forest, and did they do it intentionally?"

He stared at her. "I have no idea who is building there."

"Not many companies are big enough—or ballsy enough—to try that."

"You're thinking Grandfather?"

Her gaze slid toward him, then away. "I don't know. I would hate to think he'd do that level of damage to a necessary energy source for the people. For his community."

"I can't see it either."

But she heard the doubt in his voice. The pain of the possibility. "It could be someone else, but they must have deep pockets."

He shrugged. "Many have that."

She nodded and hardened her resolve. "Whoever it is, I have to go after them."

He stared. "Why?"

"Because no one else will. This is my forest. My reserve. I'm one of the guardians, along with my sisters." She sat on the edge of the pool, swishing her hands in the water, as she tried to organize her thoughts. "I can't let it die. That will kill all of us."

"How can such a responsibility be yours alone?" He slumped backward.

Genesis sighed softly. He needed to understand. He was a powerful investigator, well respected both personally and professionally. She needed him on her side. She also needed his help. But only if he was on her side. She took a deep breath. "It is definitely that bad. Especially for me. Things have started going very wrong. This is my place in the heart of the woods. I have to protect my heritage and my granny's."

He shrugged. "Okay, I can see that. But why not the Paranormal Council? They are the ones ultimately responsible."

"Sure. Except your Grandfather has a lot of influence. Granny hated the Council and refused to have anything to do with them. I'm not sure anyone on that Council will believe me. And …" This was where it got very dicey. "If Grandfather's involved in the damage in some way …"

"He has influence but not that much. Matt is doing a

hell of a cleanup job there."

She stared at him. "Really?" At his nod, she raised an eyebrow. "I hadn't heard."

"You isolated yourself for a long time. A lot has happened in a year. The Council elected Matt to take over. Not that he would have allowed any alternative."

"How could I have missed hearing about that?" Had she been so oblivious, and how much did it matter? Granny had trusted Matt, but he'd broken Celeste's heart.

"Maybe you didn't want to know."

More than a little stunned, she wondered at the totality of such a mind-set. Had she been so hurt that she'd kept everyone from her old life out of her mind just because of Connor? Apparently so. "Then you'd better catch me up."

He shot her a questioning look, but, at her nod, he gave a quick rundown on the forced takeover of the Council, and the motions that were passed, limiting Grandfather's influence. She'd heard Matt ran the Council now but hadn't understood how he'd gained control. It couldn't have been easy going against Grandfather. As she listened, she realized how much she'd refused to see.

She'd had other friends. Other people who might have believed in Granny. She'd turned her back on them too. Without an explanation. They might have understood, but she hadn't given them a second thought. Or a chance to help.

All this time, she'd been so busy hating Connor and his family that she'd not once looked at her own actions. Now that she had, she didn't like it at all. She tugged on her robe.

Silently she stared out the window. Damn. How had she gotten so far away from herself? Had her pain kept her so focused on staying away, staying hidden, staying separated?

And now she'd been brought back. Expecting, thinking it would all be the same as when she'd left it.

But time had marched on.

She'd marched in her own direction, and the rest of the world had gone in the other. She felt out of the loop. Part of her wanted to hear every little detail and to catch up, yet another part wondered if that was the same for Connor. Did he feel like he wanted to know everything about her life? Had he felt so cut off that, when they'd come together, there was a thirst for so much more?

But the forest was her priority.

"I have to find out what's wrong in the forest with the pools." She turned to face him. "There could be more happening down below as well."

He'd stepped up behind her. "Then I'll go with you."

It would hurt him to hear these words, but she needed to remind him. "It's dangerous for you without your senses."

"I still have common sense, experience, and lots of other skills. I can protect you. I may not have any of my paranormal senses, but I am not useless."

True. She studied his determined features and realized arguing would do neither of them any good. "Fine. I want to leave within the hour."

He paused. "Now? Today?"

"Yes. We have no time to lose. Whoever attacked you last night reported it to his boss. We need to get in and to go to the caves below. Find out if there are more problems that we don't know about. See what's going on."

"Let's go."

As if not sure whether to believe him or not, she said, "You realize it'll be someone you know?"

"And also known to you."

"Maybe, but I'm not as attached to the people here."

"You are. You've just forgotten about them. Now that you've remembered, you realize the bonds are still there."

"Maybe, but we don't have time for a philosophical discourse on that right now." She turned away, her mind already on what she needed to do.

He grinned. "As long as we pick it up later."

She rolled her eyes. "Whatever. And I need to know that your head is fine. I'm not taking you into the caves if you have any vision trouble, headache, or any other symptom. You know that down there your normal senses will be completely whacked."

"Until yesterday I'd never been down there, at least not in that area."

She stared. "Really?"

"Really." He shook his head. "Most people don't even know about it. They weren't raised by a stargazer Granny."

She laughed. "True. But Granny had a lot of respect for those caves. She firmly believed in the connection of Mother Earth and the rest of the universe. She wouldn't go down into the caves unless she had to."

"She had no trouble navigating?"

"None at all. She'd been going down there for over a century."

He paused midway through the doorway. Stepping back into the pool room, he stared at her. "Did you say a century?"

She brushed past him, deliberately letting her breasts brush against his bare chest as she moved through the doorway. "Yes. Surely you knew she was old?"

"Old is one thing. If she'd been going into the caves for that long, she was ancient." He grinned. "And she looked damn good for her age."

That brought a laugh out of her. "You don't know the half of it."

CONNOR DRESSED QUICKLY. Now they were getting somewhere. He'd been down a few levels of the caves years ago, but he'd had his abilities back then. That had given him a certain level of immunity. Many had none and went anyway. Always curious groups of daredevils, partiers, and then the just plain stupid had entered the caves.

Every year there were several deaths, despite all the warnings, news articles, and safety meetings. It was sad in a way. The locals knew the rules, but always the new arrivals would be lured to the caves by the locals, just to then steal everything they had and leave them there.

For the first time since Connor had started working for Grandfather, Connor's life felt incomplete. Wrong.

Somehow going into the cave … felt right.

As long as he stayed with Genesis, he'd be safe. But, more important, as long as he stayed with her, she'd be safe.

And he didn't dare let her get hurt.

"If you take any longer getting ready, it will be tomorrow already."

He spun around, only just realizing that he'd been standing here, staring out the window. "Do you have anything for breakfast?"

She grimaced. "There isn't much. A few granola bars."

"It'll do." He motioned back to the kitchen. "We'll take them, and I'll treat you to a full meal when we're done."

"Sounds good." She walked into the kitchen and rustled in the cupboard, turning to hand him several bars. "Breakfast is served, my dear."

"I'll eat while we walk."

With a quick nod, she filled several bottles with water and led the way out of the cottage. Outside, in the early light, he stopped and stared at the calm, cool paleness of the morning. "I've never seen anything like this."

"No, and you won't again." She started forward.

He fell in behind her. "Unless I come back here."

"Which you can only do if you are with me."

"And why is that?"

She never broke stride. "Because this space, the cottage, is hidden. Only my family can find it."

The brush started closing in behind her, and he hurried to catch up. If he wasn't careful, he'd lose her and possibly become completely lost. They walked steadily in silence for twenty minutes. He surveyed the area. He would swear he hadn't seen this part of the woods before. He was as familiar as many others with this general location, but this area? … This area was very different. The plants were lusher here. Greener. Thicker. If the rest of the forest was some semblance of normal, then this area had been coddled, pampered. Protected.

A special place.

He felt like an interloper.

No, that felt too negative. Maybe a visitor. An honored guest.

CHAPTER 10

GENESIS WALKED IN silence, listening. To the forest. To the energy. To the animals. There'd been little change here. At least on the surface. But underneath, she sensed a rumbling, a shadow of something else.

No. Not even a shadow. More like the hint of a shadow. As if it could become a shadow, if it were allowed to develop enough. And she had to ensure that it didn't get that chance.

If she could only figure out the problem.

As she approached the back entrance to the caves, she held her finger to her lips.

Connor nodded and stepped up beside her.

Motioning to a cliff wall up ahead, she ran forward. When he didn't follow fast enough, she gestured more insistently. With a warning look at him to stay close, she walked parallel to the wall, one hand sliding on the stone as she went. An outcropping of darker rock appeared in front of her. Good. She peered around the side, relieved to see the entrance was the same as the last time she'd been here.

After finding the construction at the pools, she wasn't sure what—if anything—she'd find now.

This was one of Granny's entrances. Genesis had hoped it would be pristine. That would make her trip easier.

With Connor on her heels, she crossed to the far side. With a quick check around, she started down the carved stone steps. Some of the entrances went down for miles, before you reached the main caverns, twisting and twining as they went.

Granny's entrance, on the other hand, was one of the straightest and the most direct routes.

As well as one of the most dangerous.

"Remember. Stay close to me."

"I'm right here." He stared down into the blackness. "I didn't know entrances were over here."

"Entrances are all over this place." She turned, walked a few steps inside, then stopped to look at him. "This is one of the steepest pathways. If you fall, it could be difficult."

"I won't fall," he replied.

"Stay close anyway." She turned and headed into the darkness. There wasn't a sound for the first couple dozen steps. Then she heard the first musical notes of running water. Like water gently splashing over a wall. Not like a waterfall but a slow-moving river, flowing over a smooth rock.

The walls of the cave gleamed, as the moisture in the air thickened. The noise built the lower they went. After twenty minutes, the rumble of the water drowned out any other sound. She kept glancing at Connor to confirm he was still with her. The steps were choppy and uneven.

"Stay focused. I'm here. I'm fine."

The slight sharpness in his tone made her realize she was hovering.

And he would find it insulting. He was a protector, after all. Without a word, she decided to trust that he'd be fine and now focused on getting to the bottom safely.

She stopped on the last step. Weird incandescent green light hovered, like a low-lying cloud, giving an odd glow to the cavern and tunnels ahead.

"Uh, what's with the light? The weird color?"

"It's a result of the mineral composition mixing with the normal light of the caves and the energy of the healing waters," she answered absentmindedly.

"That color has no relationship to healing anything."

She laughed. "This is the normal color."

"If you say so," he replied.

She stepped into the fog, unable to stop herself from glancing back to make sure he followed. The green fog wallowed around his legs. He kicked at it, sending clouds to one side, then the other. But it always returned to hug his legs. He glanced up to find Genesis watching him, laughing at him. "Are you done?"

He grinned. "Sure."

She rolled her eyes and turned away to study the narrow tunnels. So far, this area all looked normal. If she could determine how far the problem went, maybe she could find a solution to keeping it contained. Rot like she'd seen could completely take over a space like this in no time, especially if left unchecked. Granny had been gone for a year and her sisters slightly less. The troubles had started around the same time.

Apparently Matt had taken over the Council about then too. More changes that would affect the energy of the area. She asked Connor, "What modifications has Matt made in regard to this area?"

"I have no idea. He'd had doubts about how effective the support work has been to date as it is. I would expect him to have increased the checks in order to pinpoint the state of every forest."

"If he was doing every forest, then it would take a long

time, if he had the same team doing the assessment."

"I think he has several teams."

"Can you contact him and find out?"

"Yes, when we return to the surface."

"We aren't going back the same way. I have a trail through here that will take us to the other side. Hopefully this way I can see where the damage is."

His eyes lit with understanding. "Smart."

She stopped and studied the multiple tunnels that appeared in front of them. "Interesting."

He stepped up and studied the faint tracks through the green fog. "Others have been here."

"Apparently." And that was not good. This area should always be deserted. She knew of no one else who would come this way. Unless Matt had sent them.

"We need to approach the Paranormal Council in private." And, boy, did she have something to say to them.

"Private?" he asked. "Are you asking to meet Matt?"

"That might be the best avenue forward." Talking to Matt might be the only way to get to the bottom of this. She didn't know him personally, but Granny had believed in him. That meant a lot to Genesis. Granny had always been spot-on with people. Genesis could only hope that, once she placed her trust in Matt, he would not let her down, the way he had her sister. And Genesis certainly didn't trust the rest of the council. She didn't know any of them.

"The annual meeting is happening today. So Matt will be a little busy."

Right. The two men she'd seen in her shop yesterday. "Who all is here for the meeting?" she asked.

"Everyone who matters. The Portmans, father and son, are here. The Coulsons. McDermidts." He shrugged. "As I said, everyone."

She nodded, trying to keep her feelings buried. The men in her shop had been the Portmans. Granny had always liked Portman Senior.

Remembering the older man's stern countenance, Genesis had to wonder why.

Still, that wasn't today's issue.

She studied the three paths in front of her. The energy was the strongest on the left and the faintest in the Center. "Let's take the Center passage. It's shorter and less widely traveled."

Silence reigned as they hurried down the tunnel. The energy here was flat, still. The color should be almost thigh-high here, circulating as it met up and mixed with hers and Connor's energies. Instead it lay around their ankles, almost lifeless.

And that was bad news. Genesis couldn't help the fear building inside her. She hadn't even made it to the main caves yet, and other energies were here. Other people. Nonenergy people, plus a few energy people. None she recognized. None she liked the look of. She couldn't see the same negative energy down in the caves as she'd seen up top, but, regardless, this energy didn't look good. Yet she couldn't explain it.

She had a horrible feeling she wouldn't like what she'd find up ahead. And, despite her caution, she started to run.

As quickly as they'd raced forward, she came to a grinding halt. She threw out both arms to the side to stop Connor from moving past.

In a harsh, shocked whisper, she said, "Look."

CONNOR QUICKLY ASSESSED the situation and stepped in front of her, carefully keeping her hidden from view.

Several men lay collapsed on the cave floor in front of them. Instinctively he pulled on his damaged abilities, feeling them ineffectively spout and jump. While it wasn't anywhere near what his abilities used to be like, it was the first time he'd felt even that much activity in a long time. With relief and hope surging through him, he narrowed his gaze, as he studied each body, their condition, their features.

"We have to help them." Genesis stepped around him. He moved in front again, effectively blocking the way. "What are you doing?" she hissed. "They need our help."

"They're dead." Hard and cool, he had no doubts. Blood pooled on the side of the closest man. He couldn't see an obvious injury from where he stood but was inclined to presume a small caliber gun had been responsible. Or one of the new stunners on the market. But then a lot of blood was on the ground to come from one of those.

"Are you sure?" Genesis peered around his arms, then glared up at him. "If they are dead, I can't do anything to help, but at least let me make sure."

Having already determined that the men had died several hours ago and that it was safe now, he lowered his arm so she could pass.

"Thank you," she muttered. Dropping beside the first man, she checked for a pulse. No way would she find one. The man's skin had a bleached, chilled look to it. "His skin is cold," she said in surprise.

Connor didn't bother answering; he stepped over to check out the second man. "Yes. This likely happened hours ago." He lifted a corner of the man's jacket and studied the nice neat hole through the chest area. "Shot to death."

"But nobody uses blasters."

"I do," Connor declared, his voice coming out hard and cold, despite his best efforts, "when there is no other way." He felt her hot questioning gaze on his back, but he was focused on the contents of the man's wallet he'd found. "Jeb Burrows." He turned to look at her. "Do you know that name?"

She frowned. "No, I don't think so." She walked closer and stared down at the man at her feet. "I'm not sure, but I think I've seen him before."

"Where?"

She shrugged. "Or maybe not."

"Where?" He took a deep breath and told himself to be patient.

"It almost looks like the man from the cave yesterday. The man who attacked you."

CHAPTER 11

GENESIS WALKED BACK to the first man, her mind churning, trying to pluck the one or two fragments from her memories. Was it only yesterday she'd seen him? Now look at him.

This couldn't be a coincidence. Could it?

"Well? Is it him?"

She shook her head. "I can't be sure."

"We need to get a hold of Matt." He tugged her back and pulled her up against him. "We need someone to cart these men out of here."

"Do you think the men were involved in something down here, or were their bodies just dumped here?"

"If they were involved, then they must have come here willingly and been shot," he said, staring down the tunnel. "No one will carry these men this far from the surface. They're just too big and heavy. The only question remaining is if their assailants have left."

"Only one way to find out." She walked over to the cave wall and made a notation on the stone with her finger; a weird softly glowing green ball formed and stayed on the wall in that same spot. "This will give us the location of the men, so they can be found."

"Right. I don't think I've ever seen someone do that." He marked the location on his navigator.

As she stepped back to study the light-green glowing mark, she said, "Tricks from Granny."

"Ah."

She waited for him to say more, but he never did. "Right. Let's get moving then."

He took the lead, setting a fast pace.

She smiled. *Interesting.*

"What are you smiling at?" he asked her, without turning around.

She gasped and hurried to catch up. "How did you know I was smiling?"

He snorted but didn't slow down. "I know you."

Apparently. And, for some stupid reason, that brightened her mood.

He reached out, wrapped an arm around her shoulders, and tugged her up closer to his side.

She wanted to laugh but knew it was hardly appropriate. But maybe, just maybe, … he did care.

And, if so, how did that change anything?

They turned the next corner, when Connor shoved her behind him again.

"Stop doing that," she hissed.

Then she heard it.

Voices. *Shit.*

"We can't just leave them down here," said a young-sounding male with a whiny voice. "It's not right."

"It was the job. Remember?"

"I know," said the first man. "Still doesn't make it right."

"You idiot. We agreed to do this. If we don't, we'll end up lying right there beside them."

"No way. We did the job. Now I want to get paid and to

get the hell out of here. We came a long way for what was supposed to be big money. Like hell I'm sticking around here."

"I thought you were worried about leaving the bodies here."

"Well, now I'm worried about my body. And anyone who would leave bodies lying around like this has no respect for anyone. That means they have no respect for us or our work. And that means …"

"That we're likely to end up buried down here ourselves."

"That's right. Dead men don't talk."

At that moment, Connor stepped casually out of the shadows, a gun in his hand. "But live men can talk, so talk. Who hired you to kill those men?"

Genesis's jaw dropped. Where had Connor gotten that gun? She was sure he hadn't had it on him when he'd been injured. But neither had she checked his clothes to make sure.

The two men stared at Connor in shock. Their gazes shifted to her, immediately dismissing her, and returned to Connor. "Hey, who are you? What the hell are you doing down here?"

"I could ask you the same question." Connor held the gun low, his body vibrating with readiness. His aura, the deep blue of the protector, was snug against his body. Ready for action.

She shifted her gaze to the two other men. Their energy had scattered. They hadn't expected to see anyone here and didn't like the sudden turn of events. She waited to see who was the dominant of the pair.

The bigger barrel-chested male, only slightly older than

his cohort, grinned. "But I'm not answering." He started backing up.

The second man was a skinny stretch beside his buddy, but there was power in those long, lean arms. She studied his energy, looking for signs of what his talent actually was, and she couldn't understand what she saw.

Could drugs be the reason for the sluggishness, the darkness she noted? She hadn't spent much time in the last many years healing, an area in which her grandmother told her that she would excel at with more practice. However, from the looks of the second man, he was almost past her assistance. To her, that made him more dangerous than his aggressive partner.

"Where do you think you are going?" Connor asked, his voice sharp.

"Anywhere we want." And he turned and bolted, his skinny partner hard on his heels. Connor raced after them. Genesis didn't bother. As the skinny male departed, he'd thrown out an arm to disperse a black cloud of energy. She heard a small pinging sound but couldn't see what was responsible. It effectively blocked their energy trail. Genesis figured she could go through it and find other traces of where they'd gone, but chances were the skinny guy had a way of dissipating his personal trail in the meantime. Not that it would stop her.

Connor burst through the blackness, coming to a stop in front of her. Frustrated anger twisted his features. "Damn, we've lost them."

She looked at him quickly. He ran his fingers through his hair, as he glared into the darkness.

How had he lost his abilities? She wished now she'd been around at the time. She didn't try fooling herself into thinking that she could have done something about his loss back then, but the possibility had been there.

And, if she couldn't have done anything to help, even a stay in her pools would have prevented a complete loss. That no one had thought to help him in such a way bothered her. A lot.

"What do you know that I don't?" Connor stood in front of her, his hands fisted on his hips.

"I know that the second man is either very sick or is under the influence of something that is hurting him. He threw out black energy to hide his tracks, but I doubt he has the strength to do much more."

"But that black stuff is thick."

"No, it only appeared to be that way. It was just dark." She stepped through the darkness to the other side and stopped to search the tunnel. The other man's wisps of black clouds dotted the area. "I won't have any trouble following him."

"Those clouds aren't normal, are they?" He groaned, his hands clenching.

"No. Not at all." She didn't add that seeing them wasn't normal either. So were his abilities coming back, or did they still flicker slightly? It appeared that something was changing. Maybe being in her pool had helped, or this could be the result of the latest head injury.

They walked steadily for another ten minutes, listening carefully, but the only sound was their soft-soled footsteps.

"I assume you weren't expecting to see anyone down here?" he asked her.

She glanced over at him in surprise. "I didn't expect to see dead men or their killers, that's for sure, but I was just thinking that it was awfully quiet with only the three of us down here." She flushed and instantly corrected her mistake. "Two of us."

And she walked away from him, hoping he wouldn't ask her about her error. If he could see the black energy, why the hell couldn't he see Remi?

As if she'd spoken his name aloud, Remi raced over and climbed up her leg to ride on her shoulder. He chattered quietly in her ear. She hadn't seen him around the dead men, but then he'd been smarter than her; he'd taken off and disappeared. She would have liked to do the same.

With him back, she relaxed a little more.

A split second later, the cave shifted into complete blackness.

Not a gloomy dark of night happening, but a blackness that allowed for no light whatsoever. They were completely surrounded.

CONNOR REACHED OUT to grab Genesis's arm. He tugged her close against him. "What the hell just happened?" he whispered.

"I'm not sure," she murmured. "I've never seen this before."

"Could it be from the caves themselves?"

She paused; he almost heard the wheels turning in her mind. Then he sensed her shaking her head. "I don't think so. Even if the pools were completely dried up, there should still be enough light from the walls and the energy itself to give us some illumination."

"So that one male is potentially causing this?"

"Possibly. But that would be incredibly strong energy."

"But not impossible," he persisted. He studied the absolute blackness, never having seen anything like it in his entire life. Even outside on a moonless night there were shades to the night, degrees of darkness. Here, there wasn't even that. So how could that be? His analytical mind kicked in. It couldn't exist. Therefore, it wasn't real. He stepped forward, tugging Genesis with him, knowing that this blackness was an illusion.

Three steps forward and the tunnel cleared completely.

And they stood, staring at the same two men as before.

"Jesus, Bernie. You said they couldn't come through that."

"I didn't expect them to." Bernie scratched his chin. "I told you that I wasn't feeling well. I need to recharge."

"Well, if you can't recharge down here, something's wrong with your recharger."

Bernie slid him a sideways glance. "You don't mean that, do you, Charlie?"

Charlie growled. "Shut up! Don't use my name, you fool."

Connor slid his phone from of his pocket. Even though it wouldn't get any reception down here, it would take pictures of the two men just fine. But he had to get close enough. And that was a different story.

"Give it to me." Genesis slipped it from his hand.

He waited. But no flashes came. Did she know how to use the camera? They would only have one chance. When that flash went off, the men would run after them to get the photos.

Just as he was about to ask for it back, the flash came, followed by several more. From opposite sides of the room. As the men spun around, the flash kept going off, always from different directions.

What the hell?

He looked down at Genesis to find her grinning. In a low voice, he said, "Care to explain what's going on?"

"It's Remi. He loves toys."

Remi? Oh. Right. Her invisible pet.

CHAPTER 12

WELL, IT WASN'T the way she'd planned to have Connor acknowledge Remi's existence, but, as far as being effective, she couldn't have come up with anything better.

Dare he doubt her now?

She couldn't stop grinning. The two men were trying to find the source of the flashes, but they were just too slow. Each time the flash had stopped blinding them, Remi had already moved.

Finally the men stopped, chests heaving, to stare at the two of them.

"What kind of trickery is this?" Bernie asked, wiping his brow.

Sweat beaded on his forehead, too heavily to just be the result of exertion. Genesis studied him with concern. He did not look well. The caves were not the place for a sick man. Now they had two dead and one needing medical attention.

Remi returned to Genesis's side.

"Camera, please."

Remi chattered at her.

"Remi, now."

With a disgusted sound, he dropped the phone into her open hand.

One eyebrow raised, she returned the phone to Connor.

He took it silently and then peered down where her hand had been, before shrugging and pocketing the phone.

She turned to face the men, catching a glimpse of them racing away into a tunnel gone black. "Do we go after them?"

"No. I'll send the photos to Matt. He can take care of it from there." He turned to study her. "I'd like to get you out of here though. It's too dangerous down here right now."

"It's always dangerous," she said, absently studying the space where the men had stood. "It's just different now."

"Different in any other way beside the obvious?"

She shrugged. "I can't explain it. Let's keep going."

With a quick glance at him, she led the way into the next tunnel. It appeared deserted and untouched. As did the next and the next. When she came to the last, a wave of wrongness hit her. She stopped and held up her hand to Connor.

He peered around the corner. "Shit." He raced forward, and she followed. Charlie lay out cold on the ground. Connor bent to check his pulse. "He's alive, but he doesn't look too good."

"Where's Bernie?" She searched the small cavern but found no sign of the second man. Black wisps of his energy dotted the area but in a straight line, as if he'd bolted and didn't look back. So what the hell had happened to his buddy? "Any idea what happened to Charlie?"

"None. No apparent sign of an injury," Cannon replied.

She shook her head, as she turned her gaze to the prone man. "His energy level is dangerously low. He must be injured internally. There's no other possibility."

Connor did a quick search of the man's body, then sat back on his heels. "I don't know. Maybe he's got a concussion." He glanced up at her. "Or maybe Bernie found a way to drain Charlie's energy to use for himself?"

"Regardless he needs help. Now we really have to get to the surface. This has gone too far."

Connor stared at her. "And finding the dead men didn't say that to you before? You needed to see another injured man to become worried? We need to talk. Your priorities are so screwed."

She glared at him. "The men were dead, so we didn't need to worry about them. This guy needs help."

"Ah, remember. This guy is the one who killed those others. Why does he deserve more attention than his victims?"

Mouth open, she could only stare at him. "This is a stupid conversation."

He shook his head. "What is the fastest way out of here?"

Relieved about the change of topic, she turned around to orient herself. "Not far up ahead is one of the entrances into the middle of the tunnel."

He nodded, bent, and lifted the injured man. "Lead the way."

She ran ahead. She hadn't expected him to bring the man with them, but, considering how long it would take to bring help back to Charlie, it only made sense.

The tunnel was deserted. She came to the turnoff and stopped. Bernie had continued down into the main caves. A part of her didn't want to leave the other man down here.

"Which way?" Connor asked.

She glanced back at him, noted his corded forearms and the tightness around his lips, and realized that Charlie was as heavy as he looked, and she was just standing here, gawking.

"Sorry. We're going this way."

She led him back to the surface, trying not to continuously look back to check on Connor. Once on the surface, she took several deep breaths, filling her lungs with fresh air. Connor lay Charlie on the grass and fished out his phone.

He reached Matt immediately. Genesis tuned out much of the conversation, until she heard her name. She spun around and watched. Connor's gaze was locked on hers as he said, "Yes, she's here with me. She says something is wrong in the caves. She needs to talk to you." Connor was silent for a moment. "Fine. We'll be here."

He closed his phone and put it away. "He's coming himself. And he wants you to be here when he arrives."

Genesis nodded. Inside, she winced at the wording. Maybe she should take off instead of talking to him.

"He needs to talk to you. About a lot of things apparently." Connor looked at her in question, curiosity in his gaze.

She refused to open the discussion. The Council had had a huge problem with Granny. Genesis herself had little to do with them. And she preferred it that way. Then again, she might not have a choice anymore. This energy reserve needed help way more than her need to stay out of the limelight. "So will you take Charlie out of here and then come back?"

He shook his head. "No. I'm staying. Matt's sending a craft to pick up the injured man."

She raised one eyebrow. "Nice to have money."

"The Council always has money."

"Yeah, they just don't like to spend it on necessities."

"More to the point, they may not know what those necessities are." He gave her a pointed look. "Now you will get a chance to tell Matt what they are."

She snorted. "As if he will care."

"Don't tar Matt with the same brush as the others."

"Maybe, maybe not. And how come you're so sure?"

"He's a friend. I've known him a long time. The man comes from heart. Although I will admit I haven't had as much to do with him in the last few years."

She rolled her eyes. "Right. So it's not that he's honest and moral and cares about the forest or any of us who work that energy, but that he's an old drinking buddy. Got it."

"Hey." Connor's voice was sharp. "He's anything but a drinking buddy. And he does care. If you can read energy the way I remember you can, you can check him out when he arrives."

"It's not allowed, remember?"

"Bull. You do it all the time. I don't mean an invasive reading but enough that you can see who he is inside."

"Why would I believe that? Many are talented enough to hide who they are inside."

"Damn, you are stubborn."

She offered a grim smile. "Lessons learned and all that."

She turned her back on him to study the prone man. He was in a bad way. She didn't want to do too much, as she could cause more harm, but her granny had always said that energy work, done with the right intention, could never hurt anyone.

She got to work. She started pulling away the black strands of energy from his system, flicking them to the ground, where they wallowed for a few moments, then slowly sank.

CONNOR WATCHED GENESIS work. He used to see much of what she was doing, but, right now, it was as if she were pantomiming in front of him. He wished Matt would hurry up. His new hovercraft was damn fast, but he still had to get to it and get it in the air. Thankfully it was big enough to carry several people.

Just as he turned back to Genesis, he heard a high-pitched whine. That had to be Matt.

The whine came closer, and, just when he thought the noise would overwhelm him, it shut off, and, right beside him, the hovercraft lowered and parked.

"How did he know where to find us so fast?" Genesis asked softly. Connor wondered the same.

Matt strode over. Two other men, carrying a stretcher, raced to arrive first. Genesis stepped back and let the others work but hovered, as if unsure of their skill level.

Connor held out his hand to greet his old friend, a man who appeared dark and imposing to others, but Matt threw an arm around his shoulders and squeezed. "A hell of a mess."

"True." The three watched as the injured man was loaded up and carried back to the craft.

Matt waved them off. "They will come back for me." As soon as they lifted off and the noise level settled down, Matt turned to study Genesis.

She walked over to stand beside Connor. "I hope he'll be okay."

"So do I," said Connor, staring at her, but for a different reason. "I want to know who the hell he is working for."

"We also need to find the second man," Matt said. He stepped forward and held out his hand to Genesis. "I'm Matt Luker. Nice to finally meet you." She stared at it, then at him.

Connor held his breath.

CHAPTER 13

G ENESIS DIDN'T KNOW what to make of Matt. A definite large-and-in-charge type of man. And they needed that right now; yet she knew some of his history from her sister. She shook his hand, sliding a sidelong glance at Connor. "You can breathe now," she muttered. "What did you think I would do? Hit him?"

"You can hit me anytime." Matt laughed. "As long as we are being friendly, maybe you can fill me in on what the hell is going on."

She scowled. "As if I know."

Connor sighed. "But you know more than most."

She shrugged and explained what little she knew.

"Construction at the healing pools?" Matt frowned. "That will nullify the actual healing energy."

"Exactly. But I doubt the person who is building there cares. Likely a for-profit project." She shrugged. "Like so much in life, people are greedy, and, if they think they can lock up the healing pools and charge for entrance, they would."

"The forest is for everyone," Connor said.

Matt shook his head. "There's long been an argument on that point." He studied Genesis.

To avoid his piercing gaze, she turned to study the foliage around them. This conversation needed to change and fast. "Are we ready to go back down there?"

"I am," Matt said.

Connor frowned at Matt. "Do you not have a security team coming?"

Matt shook his head. "A little difficult to know who is trustworthy these days. I've done a major house cleaning but haven't finished the job. I'm waiting for a couple members to play the next hand, so I can ascertain how far the poison has spread."

Genesis could understand that. And, with every word he spoke, she started to like Matt better and better.

She turned to lead the way back to the caves, taking the same path as she had before. The men fell into step behind her. As she walked, she listened. This was one of Connor's friends. A man Connor both liked and respected. Did Matt know about Connor's missing talents? If the two men were close, Matt should.

At the tunnel opening, she glanced back to see if they were following. They were only a few feet behind, but they weren't paying any attention to her.

She started down the narrow trail. The blackness enveloped her immediately. She stopped, panic filling her lungs. What the heck? She spun around to retreat when she realized she wasn't alone.

And the person with her wasn't Connor or Matt.

She froze, letting her senses come alive. This was the same sort of blackness that they'd dealt with earlier. And it was an illusion, nothing more than energy. And she could work with energy.

Blindfolded.

And that was a good thing because that's how this space made her feel.

Heavy breathing somewhere very close by brought up her flight response from inside, and she wanted to shove down the energy and bolt for the surface. She had to count on the fact that Connor was somewhere behind her. In fact, that heavy breathing could be him.

But it didn't feel like him.

And he'd had no chance to get ahead of her.

Remi, where are you? A tiny hand slipped into hers. He was here. And not happy about the situation.

As the general location and timbre of the stranger's heavy breathing hadn't changed, she had to wonder if the worker was blinded by his own energy. Could he not see her? Or the men? If so, what good was a talent that blinded everyone? But his talent didn't look normal. The blackness was unwholesome. Tainted.

That's what it was. His talent had become corrupt. Diseased, maybe. Not having seen anything like it, she didn't know what to call it. But it seemed unnatural—as if it wasn't the same talent he'd been born with. Had he done something deliberately to change it? Or … she had heard rumors of some people going insane by running too hot. Something that could have happened long ago, when this planet was first inhabited.

But surely not now.

As she studied the cloying blackness around her, she wondered why anyone would willingly change their energy, their talent.

Surely they were all doing fine without interference?

But that blackness said something else altogether. Drugs maybe? Earth problems had quickly become Glory problems, even with all the restrictions and regulations in place.

Exhaling so gently that her breath wouldn't raise any

waves of the blackness around her, she pulled her own energy forward and wove the strands into a secure netting around both her and Remi. She would have included Connor and Matt if she could, but she couldn't tell if they were anywhere nearby.

As the energy built up protectively around her, she could see through the darkness.

Bernie stood at her side, his chest heaving, his hands fisted, blood dripping down his legs.

Then he collapsed. On her.

She went down, crying out for help, as she tried to support the injured man. She couldn't grab him, her hands slipping as they quickly were covered in blood. Using her energy, she shoved back the blackness and called out, "Connor, help."

Silence.

She twisted so she could look behind her and found both Connor and Matt collapsed on the trail above her.

CONNOR WOKE TO a splitting headache. Genesis was at his side, her back to him. As he rolled his head over to stare at her, she turned around.

"Hey," he murmured. "What happened?"

"An energy overload." Relief filled her expression, her gaze intent as she studied him. "You look better."

"Was Matt knocked out?"

She nodded. "Yes, he was. And that's exactly the first question he asked me about you."

A grin pulled briefly at his mouth. "Yeah, he would."

"How's the headache?"

"Unbelievable." His eyelids drifted close. The headache

eased, then eased some more. He opened his eyes to find her moving her hand over his head. "What are you doing?"

"Moving the black energy away from your head. That's causing the pain."

"Oh." He let his eyelids drift closed again, welcoming the easing of the pounding tempo in his head.

After a few minutes, it felt as if a cool cloth had been placed on his forehead. He opened his eyelids again to find her moving back to sit beside him. And then noted he was lying on a bed in an unfamiliar room. He lifted his head. "Where are we?"

"At the Council headquarters."

He fell back. "Interesting choice."

"Not mine. Matt's men ordered it. I could hardly leave you alone, so I had to come. Although it would be better if I had stayed back there. At least there I had options. Here, I'm stuck," she said, a note of bitterness in her voice.

"Not really," he said carefully. "Matt's men would take you where you need to go."

"But the truth is, she wouldn't go without you." Matt spoke from the doorway behind him.

With effort, Connor rolled over to find Matt walking toward him. His gait was a little unsteady, and he looked like Connor felt. Or had felt, before Genesis fixed his head.

"You look like shit," Matt said good-naturedly.

Connor grinned. "But you feel like shit. Genesis removed my headache, so, although I'm not vertical yet, I feel much better than you do," he said cheerfully.

Matt glared at them both. "That's cheating."

Genesis rolled her eyes. "Hardly. You weren't here to work on. Sit down, and I'll remove the black from your head too."

Matt obediently sat in a vacant chair. "Is that what's causing this pounding?"

"Yes."

She quickly plucked out the largest of the black strands twisting through his head.

Instantly Matt groaned with relief. "Oh God, thank you. That feels so much better."

She smiled down at him and continued to work.

After a moment, Matt said in a quiet voice, "You are a miracle worker. Thank you."

"You're welcome." She stepped back with a smile, but then her expression flattened. "Where are the two injured men? And will they be okay?"

"One is likely to survive, but he's not conscious as yet. Neither is the other one. They are both in bad shape."

"That's too bad. We could use some answers," Connor said, sitting up. He swung his legs to the floor and stood. The room twisted slightly as he stabilized, but it was better than he expected. "I feel much better." He turned around to stare at the other two. "So now what?"

Genesis stood. "So now I return to the caves and find out what's going on."

"Not alone."

"You've been injured. Again." She stared at him, a serious tone in her voice. "I think you should stay here."

Matt was already shaking his head. "No. You can't go alone."

Connor snorted. "And I'm not staying here like an invalid. I'm going with you. Matt can get answers from Bernie."

"Bernie?" Matt glanced from one to the other. "Was the other man Charlie?"

"Yes," Genesis replied, surprise on her face.

"Why?" asked Connor.

"They are imported muscle. I've heard their names kicked around."

"They killed the men in the caves."

"Speaking of which, the crew should be back soon." Matt checked his watch. "I sent them to retrieve the bodies."

"We also need to find the murder weapon." Connor didn't like not having an answer to that question. The first group of men had been shot. He understood that Bernie and Charlie had been responsible. Yet he hadn't seen a gun on either of them. How did that work? Connor had been the one down there with a gun. All he could figure was the two muscle men had thrown away their guns. Good luck finding them then. Those caves were vast mazes. That evidence was likely gone forever.

"Regardless of these men, I still need to find out if there has been some damage to the ecosystem. Bernie's energy is not normal. Drugs might explain the changes, but I think something is going on in the caves, close to the core, that caused it. And is likely causing the damage to the forest."

"Like what?" Matt asked. "And how was his energy affected?"

Connor watched the two stare at each other. "I know I don't have your abilities, but that blackness was dangerous."

"You do have *your* abilities though," Genesis said calmly, "but you're right. That energy is dangerous. I'm pretty sure Charlie was adversely affected from just being around Bernie. Bernie finally succumbed to the overload, when he fell on me." She faced Matt. "I don't know what they are doing down there, if anything, but something is out of whack in the caves." She shrugged. "Maybe it's nothing. Maybe it's man-made. Maybe someone is trying to change the healing balance of the waters. I don't know."

Connor tried to listen, but his mind had stalled at her initial words.

He cleared his throat. The other two looked at him. "What was that about having my abilities?"

She stared at him. "Your abilities are there. As if you've just found them after a long time and are still disconnected."

His throat closed. "What?"

"Remember in the caves, when you sensed me there, but I was behind you? Remember the bits of black energy that you saw? Not all of it but the little tufts of it?"

He frowned. "Yeah, and?" She smiled. He glared at her. He hated feeling like he was missing something. He turned to look at Matt, one eyebrow raised in question. "Do you know what she's talking about?"

Matt grinned widely. "I just might." He walked closer to Genesis. "Are you sure?"

The air whizzed around him. Connor wanted to snap at them to be serious. To explain what the hell was going on. "Genesis?"

She fisted her hands on her hips and glared at him. "You don't have to believe me. It's your damn abilities, not mine."

"I have no idea what you are talking about. Why would my abilities be disconnected? I don't feel like they are back. Besides, where could they have gone? It's not like they are a set of keys that I've lost for a year and just found," he said in exasperation. He really hated this.

To make a statement like she'd done, she must have some proof. He'd been in hell. Not just pain but a living hell, day in and day out. His abilities had been with him since birth. A part of him as comfortable and as familiar as his arms or hands. The loss had crippled him. And it had taken him months to adapt to the loss. Damn it.

Genesis shook her head. "I can't see all the layers, but you are using your abilities, even though you aren't aware of it, because you're just using a little of it so far. As you reconnect, everything feels normal because it's supposed to be normal. They've been there all the time. You just were separated from them, maybe not by choice."

"How is that possible?"

She shrugged. "I don't know. Maybe the fact that you are back here again at the same place where you lost them is the key. Two parts of a whole pulling together."

"Wow," Matt said. "Can you see that happening?"

"Because his energy is strengthening as it comes together, I can see some bits and pieces."

Matt stared at her in surprise. "Are you serious? Are you saying someone did this to him?"

"Maybe." She took a deep breath and added, "Maybe not. Maybe he did it to himself."

Connor would never do that to himself. Therefore, someone else had. Connor spun on his heels and strode over to the window. Everything inside had clenched up tight. Locked down. A single word whispered over and over in his head.

Betrayed.

CHAPTER 14

GENESIS WATCHED CONNOR grip the windowsill until his fingers turned white. She'd given him a hell of a blow. And it wasn't over. The only way that energy could have been laid down so heavily and for so long was if he'd allowed it. Meaning he'd known and had accepted the other person's will—so someone close to him. Yet, as she studied his complex energy, and, understanding humanity as she did, she wondered if he hadn't done this to himself as some sort of punishment.

Then again, he was a hell of an investigator. Top of his class. Graduated first at the academy. He'd been so good. And had made a lot of enemies. Had this been an act of jealousy? Or rage? Or just because someone could?

Looking around at Matt, she found him assessing Connor, but his gaze had changed. She stepped back and looked from a different angle and realized he was studying Connor's energy. Matt was a man of power. She knew he was the head of the Council but hadn't heard any specifics. She walked closer and murmured, "Can you see anything?"

"Lots." He glanced at her. "Connor, may I do a full scan?"

When Connor stiffened, Genesis cringed. After a moment, he relaxed. "Go ahead. It'll be just like in the old days."

That didn't sound so bad, but she didn't understand the undercurrents. And she wanted to.

"It's all right, Genesis. This is harmless. I once did a scan of him way back when." Matt's voice trailed off and his eyes defocused, as he studied Connor.

Connor picked up the story. "I damn near killed him for crossing the line."

"You tried. I had the best of intentions though." Matt's voice was light, glib.

She couldn't imagine, but neither man continued this story. Unable to curb her curiosity, she asked, "And … what happened?"

"We had a good dust-up, and the girl that he was checking my energy over—to see if I really loved her—chose someone completely different. A third man."

She giggled. "Really? You couldn't resist finding out if he loved her?"

Matt grinned. "Hey, anything for love."

"Yeah," she joked. "Was that for love of a girl or for your best friend?"

"Both," said Connor, his shoulders relaxing. "And the irony is, Matt didn't give a damn about her after all. He had a new girlfriend within a week."

"And you did too," Matt noted.

"We were so young."

"Yeah, and how young were you?" Genesis had to know now.

Both men answered together. "Twelve!"

She started to laugh. "Oh my God. That's priceless."

Connor turned to face her, a lazy grin on his face, and leaned against the window. "Those were the days."

"They can be again," Matt said quietly, the tone of his

voice changing instantly.

She studied Matt's face, wondering at those undercurrents in his voice.

Connor stepped forward. "What are you talking about?"

"We always worked beautifully together. Remember? All the time we were partners, we were good together."

Connor tilted his head. "What exactly are you saying, Matt?"

"Come work for me. For the Council. I need someone I can trust. And trust is a little hard to find these days." He spread out his hands. "I mean full-time. Not working Grandfather's contracts. Help me run the Council. It would mean less traveling. You'd get to stay here most of the time."

A hell of a good idea on many levels, Genesis thought, her heart jumping at the possibility, but she wasn't so sure that Connor was ready to deal with upheaval in his life. Then again, his world had completely changed just in these last few days.

In a move that startled her, Connor started to laugh. "You weren't checking out my energy because of the suppression you mentioned. You were checking out my integrity."

Matt grinned. "Well, I couldn't do it without your permission, and, since I had a great reason to go in in the first place ..." He shrugged. "And now I know. You haven't changed a bit."

"On that level."

Matt reached out a hand. They shook hands, while Genesis stood and watched, knowing she'd just witnessed something special.

"Come work for me." Matt dropped his hand. "We need you."

"It could get sticky."

Matt nodded. "It will. But that's not a bad thing."

"And my abilities?"

Matt grinned. "Oh, don't worry. I'll be happy to help you figure this out."

She watched the understanding grow between them. She wasn't privy to everything, but, with Connor's connection to Grandfather, well, things could—would—undoubtedly get very sticky. If he walked away from Grandfather, his loyalties would be called into question.

But Matt seemed able to handle the shifting strands of power. And no doubt Connor was one of the best to stand at his side. If he could retrieve all his abilities, the pair of them would be unstoppable.

She couldn't help but feel that something monumental had just happened.

A far-reaching change that would impact everyone.

About damn time.

CONNOR NEEDED TIME to sort through the emotions and the thoughts that dominated his mind. He couldn't even begin to sort out who or why someone might have done this to him. And, if someone had, what else had they done? And how had that affected his behavior? Affected who he'd been?

He wanted to say no. But he looked at Genesis and thought about the conversations they'd had when they'd been together.

His jaw clenched, and an anger he didn't recognize rose up in him. He felt his energy shift, power reawakening from sleep. Still a ways to go yet, but at least he sensed a renewal. For that, he was grateful. But to think of all he'd been through this last year. ... He wanted payback from whoever had done this. He wanted them dead. No. He actually wanted ... He shook his head and glanced down at his bare hands. ... He realized he wanted to kill this person himself.

Waves of newly released energy sprung forward. More bonds broke in an escalating cause and effect manner. He stood in place, shuddering. He raised his tortured gaze to stare at the two most important people in his life.

He hated the fear in his heart. The suspicion. The doubts. God, that hurt. He'd never wanted to hurt her. But he had. He closed his eyes and bowed his head.

He'd failed her.

"No, you didn't."

He opened his eyelids to stare at her. "Did you read my mind?"

She snorted. "No. You said that out loud."

He shook his head. "I'm a mess. I can't tell what's real and not at the moment."

"That's because the bonds holding back your talent are breaking. As one breaks, it weakens the others' ability to hold on, so more and more are breaking."

"And ... when the bonds are all gone?"

"You tell me."

"I've never been a strong talent, so maybe the adjustment won't be that bad."

"I've got news for you. I suspect you're a very strong talent. There's a good chance that you've been suppressing your own energy for a long time."

"But why?" Bewildered, Connor couldn't think of a single reason to limit his abilities. "It's not as if I'm a danger to anyone."

Matt tilted his head for a closer look. "But not having

been raised in an energy environment, you could have easily suppressed the scope of your power to appear more normal. Also, you're a protector, with strong intuition and an awesome bullshit meter. Maybe someone is protecting himself by keeping your energy repressed."

At the *bullshit meter* comment, Genesis laughed.

"And," Matt added, "up until a year ago, you'd been telling me how much stronger that was getting. Said you could practically look at someone and see that they were up to something."

"Which means that," said Genesis, "whoever did this to you might have known that and thought they had something to hide."

"I don't know anyone like that," Connor exploded. "None of the work I've been doing had that level of subterfuge to it. Or people with that kind of ability." Both Genesis and Matt simply stared at him. He shook his head. "You have to be wrong."

"Another question to consider," Genesis said. "Is there any correlation between the damage to the forest and your energy suppression?"

Both men stared at her.

"How likely would that be?" Matt shook his head. "I can't see it."

"But something is going on. And by taking out one of the best bullshit meters, something else was allowed to take place. And the only type of activity that makes sense in a case like this is an illegal one."

CHAPTER 15

A T GENESIS'S INSISTENCE, they'd flown back to the same spot, then hiked down to the caves from a different entrance, cutting their travel time in half. She hadn't expected Matt to return with them, but, as Connor had refused to stay behind and was still incredibly off-kilter, they'd all agreed to come.

Genesis rubbed the side of her face. And stared at the bloodstain on the cave floor, the only sign of violence left, after Matt's men had removed the bodies.

She averted her gaze and walked past the evidence. They needed to pick up the pace in order to get to the main caverns soon. In silence, they passed where they'd found Charlie, then the tunnel turnoff where Bernie had found them.

After entering the main tunnel, she lifted her nose experimentally. A heavy mineral essence drifted toward her. The descent deeper into the cavern started soon afterward.

Within minutes, she reached the cut stairs. One of the miracles of this planet, so like Earth and so unique in its own way here on Glory, was the energy system. Caves fed the underground pools that fed the next level of pools that then fed the forest up above, which recharged the atmosphere and the people. Not to mention the animals. Except the animals had a more organic system going on as well. People weren't the natural inhabitants here. They'd only been on the planet for a few hundred years. Long enough for them to see it as theirs and long enough to adapt—although they'd lost many early on.

Once they understood the energetic system of the planet, people had thrived. But now, with this forest issue, they'd come up against something new.

And she would bet the problems were human in nature.

People just never learned. Their planet Earth was healing, but it would be centuries before she could be inhabited again by the masses. Scientists and students lived there in a roster system, studying the damage and the effects and the speed of the healing. They'd all cheered when they realized Earth *was* healing, but it had been a sober realization, as everyone had looked to their new planets—ten so far—and realized they could damage their new homes if they didn't change their ways. So far, Glory had done well with her new animal species.

Behind Genesis, she heard Matt and Connor quietly discussing matters. She'd tried to give them a bit of privacy. Something she could use herself. She was a little overwhelmed with everything that had happened too.

She considered the possibility that someone had affected Connor to the point that he'd changed his core personality. She'd been a mess back then, and now she had to wonder how much of her own life had been affected by this asshole because of what he'd done to Connor.

Would she be happily married now? Maybe even have started a family? Families were encouraged here on Glory; the population was still too small now.

The cut stairs ended. She stopped at the bottom to survey the massive cavern and one of many in the long string of healing pools. The opaque blue water rippled with a nonexistent breeze, as if alive. Which, as they'd come to understand, was more true than false. The pools shifted at a higher vibration energy that allowed the people, who had much lower vibration energy, to heal when submerged in the waters.

She strolled down the side of the first pool and marveled at the clear color. So beautiful. So simple. And so treacherous to the unwary. That was why no one could come down here on their own. It was too dangerous. Almost everyone knew that.

Even getting to the caves was dangerous. The paths were often dark, with uncertain footing, and, once down here, it was easy to get lost and to become disoriented. A fair number of people had been found, curled up in a ball, beside the pools' hypnotic waves.

With the men still talking and walking behind her, she strolled toward the next pool. She couldn't see anything wrong here. It looked the same. It felt the same.

Each pool was lower than the other. The water came from both an underground spring and from surface water. It was as if the lake system here had a natural recirculating system. A team of scientists constantly monitored the system, watching and trying their damnedest to understand. But, so far, the actual "how the system worked" was beyond them.

What they had learned was that any attempts to change the system actually damaged it. Hence, Genesis's belief that the problem from their forest originated down here.

Somewhere.

She continued down the same direction. The next pool looked normal. As did the one below that. Granny had always said, the lower the pool, the stronger the energy and the better the healing abilities. The ones at the very bottom couldn't even be approached because they resonated at such a high level.

As she continued to walk, Connor called out to her, "How much farther, Genesis?"

"Another seven pools, I believe. After that, I have no idea."

"That's as low as I've gone," said Matt. "I've heard another dozen are at the lower levels."

Genesis nodded. "Granny said as much. I know she'd been down another four or five below where I've been. She would never let me go down with her though."

"She's probably the only one to go that low and survive."

"Maybe. She said the energy from the lower pools is partly what kept her alive so long."

"And that keeping-her-alive part is what would kill most other people," Connor noted.

"Or be something other people would kill for," Matt added.

They were both right. These pools were sacred and inherent to the survival of the people of Glory. It was suicidal to even come down here, unless you were a strong energy worker.

"Have you ever considered blocking off access to these caverns, Matt?" she asked him. Genesis hated the idea, but, if people were messing around in here, then something would have to be done. Although she'd vote for an energy seal rather than a real lock-and-bolt type any day.

"It's been brought up and dismissed repeatedly over the ages. There's never been any real need to consider it," Matt said. "Almost impossible to do with so many entrances, most we don't even know about."

"Until now."

They passed another pool and then another. By the time Genesis had reached the lowest pool she'd ever traveled to before, she was energized and ready to kick ass. It was a side effect of the pools. She knew most people's energetic systems couldn't handle being here, but, for her, that was a different story. Her body thrived on it. The triplets had done many overnight vigils down here with Granny, bringing small amounts of food and extra water for an extended stay.

Genesis hadn't realized how special her upbringing really was. It wasn't the easiest at the time, dealing with all the mocking and the disparaging remarks regarding Granny, and Genesis had allowed herself to be influenced by that for a little while, until she'd gotten her head on straight. Once there, she would never make that mistake again.

She stopped at the edge of the next pool and looked down. This one, shaped like a kidney bean, was smaller and more brilliant than the others. She remembered seeing it before too. She wandered closer.

"Careful."

"I'm fine. I know this one."

"Let's go as far as we can to confirm we aren't missing something down here."

She nodded and turned to continue down the path. The air had thickened with the humidity, and her lightweight shirt clung to her back and shoulders. The water looked incredibly inviting.

She resisted the urge to dive in fully dressed and carried on to the next pool and the next. Each one wound deeper into the mountain. With the men's breathing heavier behind her, she kept walking. She was almost light-headed. Definitely happy, but heading toward dangerously delirious.

As soon as she recognized it, she wove several layers of energy around her body, distancing herself from the pools' effects. She spun around to glance at the men. Instead of a glorious happiness, they looked fatigued, as if every step were too much, the weight of their bodies too heavy to carry any farther.

Genesis had never been down here with anyone other than Granny. It never occurred to her that the men would have a different reaction than she was having. And her reaction was normal for her experience. "Matt, is this how you felt when you came down here before?"

He looked at her, a slight confusion in his eyes, appearing to take time to consider what she was saying, then frowned. "I don't remember. I don't think it was this far or this hard to breathe."

"It's not supposed to be. At least, I don't think so," she said. She stopped in place and watched as the men approached. Sheer guts kept them on their feet. She'd never seen anything like it. "I'll go down alone. You two need to stop here or, even better yet, start back up. It's too much for you."

They both opened their mouths to protest, but she shook her head. "No. Assess rationally what's going on. For some reason, the pools are affecting you very differently than they are me." Most likely a result of her affinity for water.

"It doesn't matter. We are coming."

Connor stubbornly jutted out his jaw. Matt was no different; he'd already started to walk again, even though it appeared to be painful for him. She wondered why for a moment and suddenly remembered that she'd isolated her aura from the pools' effects, so maybe she could do the same for them. Quickly she wove a protective blanket and wrapped it around both men in a single cocoon. They both stopped struggling to breathe, and then they stood straighter, as if throwing great weights off their shoulders.

Connor looked at her. "What did you do?"

She smiled sheepishly and explained, "Sorry I didn't think of it sooner."

"Thanks for thinking of it now," Matt said. "I feel much better."

"I wish I knew why you look like you could dance and sing, and I still feel like lying down and having a nap," Connor said.

"It might be because of my energy vibrations, and it could be due to Granny. And"—she shrugged—"as Tori has an affinity for the forest, I have an affinity to water. Whereas in your case, the pools are making it more and more difficult for you to go any deeper."

Matt asked quietly, "And Celeste, what does she have an affinity for?"

"Animals," Genesis answered shortly. Granny had collected animals of all kinds. Lost, hurt, ailing animals in both spirit and physical form.

"You think the pools have a protective energy going on to stop intruders?" Connor asked.

Genesis nodded. "That is a good way to look at it."

"Or to protect the visitors," Connor suggested. "They are healing pools. Not murdering pools, after all."

Genesis smiled. "True. They are protective. Of themselves and others." She turned. "I'll keep going down." And she continued to walk. The air felt good to her. Heavy and humid, but her skin loved it. Her lungs couldn't get enough of it. She wanted to skip down the path, as her body and soul reveled in the experience.

She came to the next pool to find the water vibrating at a darker, deeper color level. The vibration was slower—not sluggish but heavy with meaning. It was fascinating. After a quick glance behind her to make sure the men were still fine, she turned and carried on. She would love to get to the last pool, but who knew how many there still were to go? And, if any problem was at the lower levels, it should have shown by now. Yet she couldn't bear leaving without knowing for sure. She picked up her pace. She would make a quick trip down and back. At least as far as she could go.

The next several pools had a different blue color. She'd never seen so many different hue variations as she reached each pool. They were stunning. If she were a painter, she'd love a chance to recreate them.

As she walked to the next pool, she skirted the edges and gave it a quick glance, enough to see that it was fine. She did the same with the next one. Her breathing started to get rough. Heavy. As if the air was warning her. *That's far enough. Go back.*

She didn't dare.

She had to find out for sure. Focusing on her breathing, she kept to a steady pace downward. Behind her, she heard Connor call out, "Genesis?"

"I'm fine. I just want to check out these next ones."

"Be careful," said Matt.

She waved a hand but didn't turn around. The pools and pathways curved around in a circle, so the men could keep an eye on her from where they stood. She could see them, but she couldn't risk looking at them. She didn't want to lose her focus. The high humidity down here made for slippery steps. And, with each level down, it was getting worse.

She'd lost count of how many pools she'd passed. As she looked over the edge of the next one, she noticed something disturbing down below. Strange waves were forming. Water that should have been calm as glass was undulating unnaturally.

She quickened her pace and suddenly felt as though she were walking in molasses. Her footsteps were almost impossible to lift and to land. She managed another dozen and realized she might not make it. But she had to. She stopped in place, shuddering. Sweat rippled down her spine and pooled between her breasts. She swayed in place.

"Genesis?" She heard the men's voices as if from a long way away.

She stared at the dark at least a full level below her and couldn't make herself take another step.

Then a small hand slipped into hers.

Remi.

She turned to smile down at him. He chattered at her anxiously for a bit, and she squeezed his fingers. He climbed up her hip and then sat on her shoulder. Within minutes, her anxiety eased, the heaviness lifting. Not gone entirely but down to manageable levels. "Remi, are you doing this?"

He rubbed his paw against her head, soothing, easing her.

She reached up, grateful for his presence. Grateful for his support. His love.

She took a deep breath and let it out. She took another one and felt much of her own anxiety unknotting inside.

She'd taken on the dark waves. Instead of being protected from them, she'd accepted them into her space. Somehow. She didn't understand. The energy hadn't affected Remi either. She didn't know why, but one important difference was that he was of this planet, and she, as a human being, was not. His system knew more than hers did apparently.

She took a moment and wove more healing energy through her own. Protective energy.

Remi started to bounce on her shoulder, chattering in an agitated manner. "What's the matter?" He bounced harder. Genesis frowned. "Something's wrong, but what?"

Suddenly she knew. She stopped what she was doing. She was weaving the energy from this place into her own energy. She was giving the black energy access. To her body. To her. Because it was the same energy. Her body accessed the energy because it was of the same blend. That it was dark and nasty looking didn't change the fact that it was of the same vibration. She'd allowed it.

She swallowed the knot of fear that had appeared in her throat. "Remi? What do I do?" She reached up to pet him, and sparks flew off his fur. "Whoa!"

He reached out and grabbed her fingers. There was another spark, then it calmed. As if he'd grounded the sparks. He used energy instinctively, like most animals on Glory. It seemed only people made things difficult.

And, if Remi could handle this energy easily enough, maybe she could too. She absorbed some of her pet's energy and spread it thinly around herself. Then she took a little more of his and did it over again.

Remi murmured gently in her ear, the sound soothing and comforting. She took that as a good sign and repeated her actions several times. Each layer made her feel fresher, stronger. Happier. That was when she knew she was fine again.

Keeping a hand on him, she walked down to the damaged pool. She saw more pools below, darker, more badly injured. This one was as far as the energy had moved up. She had to stop it from going higher yet again but how? After she'd figured that out, she had to find a way to heal it and the ones below. From this vantage point, she could only see two more pools. And both were dark to the point of being black. A match to the blackness from the one man—Bernie's—energy.

Were they connected?

How could they not be?

She ventured slowly but surely down the steps, finally discovering the bottom pool—at least that she could see. She heard the men calling out to her, but she didn't bother waving. She stayed focused and, with a shudder, she finally reached the lowest of the pools—the source, the origin. And the massive swirling darkness that blanked out everything inside.

Except one thing.

CONNOR STARED IN horror as Genesis approached the blackness. From where they'd finally been forced to stop, he couldn't see where the blackness ended. His heart slammed against his chest, as waves of black slowly enveloped her. She disappeared without slowing down.

"Oh shit," Matt said, beside him.

"What is she doing?" Connor asked.

"I don't know. And I don't like it." Matt added, "She's approaching the core of the mist." He paused. "Now she's in the center of the darkness."

"Jesus. Why?"

"She feels she has to. Because she's the caretaker of the

pools, the forest."

"We're hardly in the forest."

"No, but I think she'd say that the forest problems originate here." He sighed. "And I think she's right."

A horrific wash of fear slammed into Connor. He had no idea where it came from, but he knew what it meant. He'd just forgotten.

"She's in trouble." He gasped, his mind racing for a solution to get in and to get her out. He couldn't see any way. If he tried to go down there, he'd be lucky to make it ten feet.

"I can see that. Is your talent coming into play? And, if we are that lucky, can you use it to get her out?"

Connor stared at Matt. "I have no idea."

Except he did. But ... he stared down the edge of the blackness. If she was in the core, it was as if she'd been completely absorbed by it.

Taken over.

Now he panicked. "We have to help her."

Matt had his phone out. "Damn. I knew there wouldn't be any reception. We're too far below the surface."

Connor started down the path.

"Connor, wait! You can't go down there."

"No choice." Connor struggled to take his sixth step and realized no way he could get to her. Not like this. Not alone.

A faint sound reached his ears. Somewhere, in the distance, he heard a dog bark. He turned to stare at Matt. "Did you hear that?"

Matt frowned. "Hear what?"

"A dog. That barking sound."

"I didn't hear anything. Look. Maybe you shouldn't go any farther. It's too dangerous."

"I have to." Connor stared down the path, wondering

briefly if the energy here made him hear things. As if his thoughts of the sound prompted it, he heard it again. And it almost sounded familiar. But he didn't know many dogs. And he hadn't owned one for decades.

Damn. He closed his eyes and reached out to Genesis with his mind. And his probe was intercepted by … Remi!

No. Way.

He instinctively stepped forward. And found he could. So he took several more steps and then more again. He could walk. Somehow. The lead weights pulling him into the earth had fallen off. Inside, he heard multiple popping sounds, as if more of the energetic bonds inside him were snapping. He straightened, feeling freer than he'd ever felt before.

And he bolted toward Genesis.

CHAPTER 16

G ENESIS REACHED INTO the water and retrieved the black stone at the bottom of the shallow pool. Surprise rippled through her at its coolness.

Was this causing the problem? Something so simple? She studied the rock. It didn't feel any differently. It didn't look any differently than a million others she'd seen on the surface.

But it was.

It was energized—charged with a specific energy vibration that had changed the charge on it to a negative one.

Deliberately? It would have to be. At least she couldn't imagine any instance in which the charge could have happened naturally. The trouble was, she had no idea why anyone would do that.

Or why they'd put it in the pool.

She heard footsteps coming up behind her. She started to turn, feeling as though she was moving through sludge, as if the stone now affected her, like it had the pools. Even as she pivoted away, she thought she noticed a change in the color of the water. The deep ugliness lightened to something more like a dark gray. Somehow she knew, now that she'd removed the taint, the pool would heal itself. And within a very short time too. That's what the pools did. ... They healed.

She needed to get this stone out of here. Get it locked up somewhere safe.

She just didn't know where that was. Matt would know.

"Genesis?"

Connor. She looked up through the soup surrounding her to see Connor running easily toward her.

She laughed. "Wow, look at you."

Then his face changed as he caught sight of the rock in her hand. "Jesus. Put that thing down."

"Can't. It's what poisoned the pool. Look at the water. It's already starting to heal."

"But that rock could kill you." His gaze went from her to the rock to her and back again. "I can see it. Oozing blackness. Can you wrap it up, cover it in something to reduce its power?"

"Working on it." And she was wrapping it up as fast as she could, but it was damn hard. Remi reached up and placed his hand on the rock. His voice rose, as he chattered excitedly. She watched in amazement as the power of the stone calmed down. Leashed.

By her pet.

She stared in shock at Connor. "Remi stopped it."

Connor's gaze went from her to Remi and back again. "Wow."

"You can see him now? About time." She gave a weary laugh. "You have your abilities back."

He gave her that same lazy smile that always made her heart race. "It seems like it. I'll have to try some tests to see, but they're mostly back, I think. At least down here." He slipped an arm around her shoulders and tugged her close. "Now do you think we can get back to the surface?"

She beamed. "Absolutely." Feeling overjoyed, she started

her return trip. She took several steps and, without warning, collapsed to the ground.

BY THE TIME Connor reached the first of the blue pools, Matt raced toward him. "Let me take her," he said, holding out his arms.

Connor shook his head. "I've got her. Let's just get the hell out of here."

They had a long climb to the top. It was a good thing Genesis was a small slip of a girl. Although, with Connor's abilities surging through him, he barely felt her weight at all.

"What happened down there?" Matt asked.

"Look at what she's holding in her hand." Connor shifted her weight slightly, so Matt could see her hand.

"Is that a stone?"

"Yes. It was in the lowest pool, and, as soon as she removed it from the water, the pool started to heal. I don't sense any energy coming off it now, but I did when I first arrived. Nasty energy."

"Interesting. Did Genesis say anything before she collapsed?"

"Outside of saying it's what poisoned the pools, not really. I did see her pet for the first time though. She called him Remi."

And, sure enough, at the sound of his name, Remi showed up on Genesis's belly, riding the easy way.

Matt laughed. "Yeah, Remi is a character."

Connor shot him a disbelieving look. "You can see him?"

"Sure. Remi also communicates with Darbo."

"Darbo?" Connor wondered how many other people

had seen Remi but hadn't mentioned it to him. When Matt didn't answer, Connor turned his head slightly so he could see his face.

And came to a dead stop. Matt, big, tough director of the Paranormal Council, had a baby lemur sitting on his shoulder, one hand clutching Matt's ear.

Connor damn-near dropped Genesis. Shifting her more securely in his arms, he narrowed his eyes accusingly at Matt. "Darbo?"

Matt gave him an embarrassed grin but reached up to pet the tiny thing. "Darbo, meet Connor. Connor, meet Darbo."

CHAPTER 17

G ENESIS WOKE TO bright light and clean white sheets.
And Connor by her side. On top of the bedding. As if he'd been watching over her and had finally collapsed himself.

She slipped out from under the covers, surprised to find she only wore panties. After a quick trip to the bathroom, she ran back to slip under the covers and into the warmth of the bed. Her folded clothes lay neatly on one side. She looked around for Remi but found no sign of him. He'd probably gone on the hunt for food.

Her own stomach started to complain, after being empty for so long. From the clean elegant bedroom, she surmised that maybe they were back at the Paranormal Center.

Connor shifted, stretching an arm across the bed.

Smoothing a hand over his arm, she gently massaged his shoulder. She smiled at the moan that erupted from him.

When she stopped her hand movements, he murmured gently, "Don't stop."

"Good morning."

"Is it morning already?" He didn't lift his head, and his words were more of a mumble than anything else.

She leaned over and dropped a kiss on the top of his head. "Actually I have no idea what time it is. I just woke up myself."

He propped himself up on his forearms and studied her face. "You look much better."

"A good sleep rejuvenates almost anything."

A warm light shone in his eyes. "Really?" He dropped his gaze, interest heating his face.

She followed his gaze and flushed. She tugged the bedding higher up her chest. "Did you undress me?"

He smiled. "I figured you'd rather it be me instead of Matt."

That she did. She wrinkled her nose at the look in his eyes. "We have to get up. Solve some really big problems. Remember?"

"Oh, I think we have time." He reached out and pulled her down beside him. "Actually I'm sure we have time." And he kissed her.

She sank into his kiss, loving the moment. Joy slid over her skin, and she pulled back her head just enough for her laugh to escape.

He grinned.

"I'm ahead of you." Her busy fingers went to work on his shirt buttons.

"Nice." He reached up to cup her breast, gently caressing the soft skin. Her breath caught in the back of her throat, as she managed to get his shirt undone; she spread the shirt wide, leaving his heavily muscled chest open and available. She sighed as she stroked both hands over his smooth ribs, before sliding her fingers through the soft chest hair to rub over both nipples. "So beautiful," she murmured.

It was his turn to laugh. "So not."

She placed a finger against his lips, then leaned over to trail baby kisses up one side of his chest, then back down the other. She reached his navel and dropped a kiss into the center. She slid one hand up his thigh to stroke him through his pants.

He shuddered under her ministrations. When she went for his top button and slowly undid the zipper, he moaned.

"I might need your help getting you out of these clothes."

"No problem." He bounded out of bed so fast, tearing off his shirt in the process, that she had to laugh. His shirt went to the left, his pants dropped to the floor, and his boxers were kicked to the right. He hadn't been wearing socks. For some reason, that made her smile.

He flipped the bedding back on his side and came down beside her. "My turn," he growled.

"Happy to share," she murmured. Then she couldn't think. He stroked and teased, tasted and devoured, until she twisted and arched, as heat burned through her.

She pulled him over her, sliding her hands up either side of his face, tugging him down for a kiss.

When he finally slipped inside her, she cried out. He held her close, as pleasure swamped her, made her ache with joy.

Then he started to move, gently at first, sliding a hand over her hip, repositioning her higher, and plunged deeper. Gentle, yet strong. He filled her until she felt she couldn't take any more, and still he kept up the steady pace.

"Please," she cried out, as her blood heated and her body twisted once again, looking for release.

"You're mine," he murmured against her neck. "Now and forever."

She couldn't say anything, as wave upon wave crashed through her.

"Say it."

She opened glazed eyes.

He plunged then pulled back, waiting. "Say it," he urged.

She smiled, her gaze locked on his. "You're mine. Now and forever."

And he plunged, crashing them through the waves to the glorious safety on the other side.

A few minutes later, Genesis opened her eyes to the same room, the same bed. Even Connor was the same. But she was different. Inside. Warmer, lighter, … happier.

"Are you okay?" Connor murmured, cuddling her close.

She would have answered if she had the energy. The thoughts swirling through her were taking it all. It felt momentous. Like a promise. A commitment.

"Heavy thoughts?" He stared at her a little worriedly.

"Maybe. Did you mean it?"

He frowned and shifted, so he could stare down at her. "I always did. Before and even more so now."

And the worry that she hadn't even recognized inside her had eased.

Then she heard that same worry in his voice. "Did you?"

She reached up to stroke his cheek. "I always did. Before and even more so now."

He closed his eyelids and dropped his forehead to rest on hers. "God, I missed you."

CONNOR SAT ON the edge of the bed. He hadn't felt this good in years. He had Genesis back. He had his abilities back, at least most of them, and, for the first time, he felt complete.

"Connor, time to get up." Matt's amused voice came

through the door. "Sorry, buddy, but we've got a meeting in an hour. Breakfast is ready."

"We'll be there in ten." He heard Matt's footsteps fade away. Genesis came into the room, her wet hair hanging down her back, an incredibly tiny towel wrapped around her body—a towel that was still too damn big from his point of view.

"Did I hear voices?"

Connor stood and reached for his clothes, regrettably telling his body to behave. "That was Matt. We have a meeting in an hour." He dressed efficiently, with his back to her. When he reached for his shirt, warm hands slid around his chest, and she hugged him from behind.

He shuddered. "If you don't want to end up back in that bed, I'd suggest you get some clothes on."

"And if I do want to go back to bed?" she asked, sliding her hands down to the opening of his pants and slipping one hand inside. "Since when do you not have time for a quickie?"

He groaned, spun around, picked her up, and flattened her on the mattress. He was inside her in seconds. The shock on her face said she'd not been expecting it quite so abruptly. But she locked her legs around his hips and arched, as he slammed into her. Once, twice, … and they both shuddered with joy.

Seconds later, he dropped his head on hers and said, "I will always find time for you."

And he shifted away from her, leaving her sprawled on the bed, the towel under her, and a lazy look of satisfaction on her face.

He grinned. "Now, if you don't want us to be late and for Matt to know the reason why, I suggest you get up." He buttoned his shirt. "And if you need a little more attention, I'm sure we can excuse ourselves for a nap this afternoon."

She rolled her eyes. "Ha." She hopped off the bed and walked to her stack of clothing. "How come you're so energized?" she muttered. "I feel …" She stopped.

Uh-oh. He stepped up behind her. "Are you okay?"

She turned. He opened his arms and hugged her close. He closed his eyes, knowing they were out of time, but she needed him. "Are you upset about Matt knowing about us?"

She shook her head. "No. It's just … everything has changed so fast. I'm still adjusting."

"You aren't alone anymore." He tilted her chin up. "And won't be ever again."

"Promise?" she asked, the look in her eyes breaking his heart. He had much to make up for. A lot of hurts to kiss better, a lot of trust to reestablish. But he could start. Here and now.

"I promise."

CHAPTER 18

THE PARANORMAL CENTER was a huge complex, as it needed to accommodate all members whenever there was a large gathering. Thankfully breakfast was in a small dining room, the perfect size for the three of them. Matt was already there and waiting.

Connor pulled out a chair for Genesis, then sat down at her side.

Matt motioned to someone behind them. Immediately coffee was served. "How are you feeling, Genesis?"

The concern in his voice reminded her that she'd blacked out yesterday and had to be carried out of the caverns. "I feel good. A little tired but, other than that, my energy has recharged." She poured cream into her coffee. "How did I get here, by the way? I don't remember much of what happened."

"You collapsed just after you picked up the rock."

Her eyes lit up at the memory. Right, that damned rock. The waves coming off it had been so incredibly powerful. "Do you know what was wrong with it? Why it was so damaging?"

"Our scientists are looking at it." Matt stopped, his lips quirking. "We might need your help. You wrapped it up so tightly that they can't undo your energy knots to study it in-depth."

"I barely remember, but I think Remi helped," she murmured. "It sent out horrific waves of need ..." She shrugged. "It sounds stupid, but it was evil. Diseased, maybe."

"It was certainly putting out a lot of negative energy." Matt picked up his coffee and took a sip. "However, a tech went into the caves this morning, and the pools appear to be healing nicely."

"Oh, that's wonderful." If the pools healed, then the waves of healing energy would carry upward to heal the forest. "That will help turn the cycle back the way we need it to go." She paused. "Especially if we can get the construction stopped."

"That's major if someone has gone ahead without permission." Matt stared down at his plate. "Ownership of that area has always been an issue."

Connor's fork stopped in midair. He stared at Genesis.

She could hardly breathe. Thankfully Connor asked the question forming in her mind that she hadn't been able to get out.

"What kind of issue?"

Matt looked from one to another. "It was deeded centuries ago to one of the caretakers. But with that person's death, the ownership was supposed to be handed down to the strongest energy worker in the line, one who was willing to devote time and effort to keeping the forest whole."

"So where's the problem with that?" she asked mildly.

"We don't know who has ownership now. No one has come forward with proof, although many insist it is theirs." He sighed. "I have to be honest. There have been grumblings that the pools need to be made more accessible for everyone, not just those who can make their way there."

An uncomfortable silence settled over their table.

Genesis caught Connor's questioning look. What did he know? How could he know anything? Should she say anything or not? She had Granny's proof. But was it good enough? She dropped her gaze to her plate and forked up more scrambled eggs, while she chewed on the problem.

"Am I missing something here?" Matt asked, his gaze going from one to the other. "Do you know something I don't?"

Connor put down his fork. "I think you should trust Matt," he told Genesis.

Genesis gasped, then frowned at him. "And why is that?"

"Because we need his help."

She motioned toward Matt, who watched them with interest. "It's rude to talk about a person as if he isn't here."

"True." Matt grinned as both Genesis and Connor glared at him. "So, fill me in. What's going on?"

Genesis opened her mouth, then immediately snapped it shut. She'd been alone a long time. It wasn't easy to open up to a stranger.

"Genesis?" Connor's voice gentled. "You can see that he's trustworthy."

"And I won't break a confidence," Matt added, "if that's the only way you'll tell me whatever is bothering you."

Did she want to? She studied his energy. Calm. Decisive. Steady. She took a deep breath and blurted out, "The forest and pools are ours. The three of us inherited it from Granny."

CONNOR WATCHED AS surprise, wonderment, then a bit of regret washed over his friend's face.

Then Matt spoke in a gentle voice. "Are you sure, Genesis?" He reached across the table and picked up her hand in his. "Your granny wasn't the most …" He shrugged, as if at a loss for words. "She wasn't the most stable personality."

Genesis smiled at him, her expression somewhat wry. "No, she wasn't in many people's eyes, but she was to me."

Matt studied her carefully for a long moment, then patted her hand and settled back.

Connor breathed easier. He didn't know what he'd been expecting, but he was happy to see this.

"Tell me about the proof."

In a quiet voice, Genesis explained.

Connor listened in, keeping a respectful silence. He finished his breakfast, while the discussion whirled on around him. Just as he lifted his coffee cup again, his phone rang. He took a quick look at the display. He had no wish to speak with the old man, but, at the same time, he couldn't avoid him forever.

"Connor, do you need to leave?" Genesis asked him gently.

"No. I'm not going anywhere."

Her expression was knowing. "But you must face him one day."

"And that day is not today."

"We must see the construction and then on to Genesis's cottage," Matt said. "I need to verify the documentation she has. It would be wonderful if she has what she believes she does. It would also solve many problems."

"And put a stop to anyone trying to take over the forest," Connor added, a little grimly. Lord knew that whenever something was worth acquiring, some people were desperate to acquire it. By whatever means necessary.

"What about the stone? Do we know who put it in the pools? Was it Bernie?" Genesis asked Matt.

"Maybe, but we can't question either of them yet. We're working on it." Matt pushed away from the table. "First on the agenda is that rock. We'll go to the lab, and hopefully you can unwrap the stone enough for the scientists to do their thing, and then we'll go to the caves and the cottage." Matt stood. "With the new transport, we'll be there and back in time for lunch."

"I'm surprised Grandfather doesn't have one of those hovercrafts," Genesis mused.

"Oh, he's trying to get one," Matt said, with a frown. "Then again, it's low on his priority list, with all the other things he's trying to acquire."

Connor stopped and turned. "What else is he trying to acquire?" When Matt didn't immediately respond, he added, his tone harsher than he intended, "Matt?"

Matt sighed. "He's trying to *acquire*—take over, in a legal sense—the Paranormal Center. And my job specifical-ly."

"*Ugh*," said Genesis. "That can't be good. He owns al-most everything else. Why would he want that too?"

"Because the Center has a lot of power. And the director has control. He wants to control all things paranormal."

Connor snorted. "As if that'll happen."

Matt smiled. "I was hoping, with you at my side, we could shut him out."

"So to the lab first?" Genesis asked.

Matt smiled. "Yes." He walked toward the door. Connor waited for Genesis to follow, then watched, with a flash of amusement, as she took a last look at the table, spied the plate of muffins off to one side, and snatched a couple to take along.

"Hungry?" he murmured.

She laughed and batted her eyelashes at him in fun, easing the tension inside him. "I did work up an appetite this morning. Besides, these trips never go as planned. And I don't want to end up trying to feed three of us on the meager offerings in my cottage."

"Oh, good point." Remembering yesterday's breakfast, he walked over to one of the staff who was clearing the table and asked him to bag the plate of muffins. When the man returned a few minutes later with a larger bag than expected, the waiter explained he'd added some sandwiches to round out the snack to a full meal.

The look on Genesis's face when he walked up to her with his big bag was priceless.

She repeated his earlier question, "Hungry?"

He couldn't help his answer. "I'm planning to work up an appetite later." As pink rolled across her cheeks, he laughed, wrapped an arm around her shoulders, and tugged her forward. He'd worry about Grandfather later.

Damn, but life was good.

CHAPTER 19

GENESIS HAD BEEN in the Center once a long time ago, but she'd never been privileged enough to see the floors below the main one. The labs were down there. The archives were even lower. And she really wanted to see the rooms below that, where the private museum was housed. Life on Glory had been an interesting ride for the humans so far, and one of the main ways to survive was to identify and to study anything not normal. Which was the purpose of the Center itself. Things were happening on Glory that no one understood, and that meant, when something unusual was found, it was brought here to be studied.

And the really weird and wonderful were kept in the museum.

Like that damn rock.

But to add more pieces to the puzzle, the inhabitants of Glory themselves were changing. Every generation adapted to life on the planet more than the one before. And considering that energy workers had been on Earth since time began, albeit often living secret lives, they were here too, and they were changing along with everyone else.

It was an exciting time to be alive.

And, as Genesis had found out, it was also incredibly dangerous.

Matt led them through a series of locked doors, until

they came to a large storage-vault type room. The vault was on the left, but several men, all dressed in white, stood around a white table, studying the rock.

Her rock.

She recognized the energy she'd woven around it, with Remi's help.

She walked over and, after a questioning look at Matt, picked it up. The men in suits all took a step backward.

In a simple motion, she unwrapped the top layer of energy from the rock. She didn't remember putting multiple layers on the thing, but the evidence was before her.

"Matt, how much do you want me to unwrap?"

He stepped forward and spoke quietly with a man standing off to one side, who appeared to be taking images and documenting the process as she worked.

After a moment, Matt turned to Genesis and said, "Take another layer off, please. We're looking through the camera to see the changes in the rock as you work. We need it uncovered enough to study, but not so uncovered as to make the situation unsafe."

Made sense. But how they could determine that fine line, she didn't know. She unwrapped another layer and waited. The rock warmed in her hand, and she sensed the energy inside seeking a way out, like a caged animal sensing freedom around the corner.

She pursed her lips, as she studied the energy rippling in her hand.

If she unwrapped too much, the negative black energy would easily overwhelm the lab and everyone in it.

But if she didn't open it up enough, then no one could study it or could do any tests on it.

Turning slowly, she studied the contents of the lab,

looking for an alternative. And found it in a large clear glass box with various tubes and pipes attached to it. She walked over to it, checking to make sure that it was empty.

"May I use this?" she asked Matt.

He nodded in response.

Genesis placed the rock inside the box. Then she closed the lid and lifted the container, moving it onto the table in the middle of the room. "Now if I unwrap the rock, can you deal with it inside here?" she asked.

The group of men nodded.

Connor asked, "But how can you unwrap it, if there is a barrier between you and it?"

"Watch." She smiled, turned back to the rock, reached for her energy, and mentally called it back to her. "Energy has no rules and restrictions, like your mind does," she said, keeping her attention on the container. "It can go through the glass if it's instructed to."

As she watched, her energy slipped through the cracks, taking the path of least resistance, and settled back around her. Once released, the energy of the rock swarmed around the inside of the container, like a swirling angry cloud of black and gray. Gasps and exclamations of surprise echoed throughout the room.

Genesis watched as the blackness tried to slide out through the cracks in the corners like her energy had, but she'd left just enough behind to create an airtight seal.

The scientists and technicians all slowly approached the table.

"What the hell is that?" asked one of them.

"No idea," Genesis said, with a shrug of her shoulders. "I think it's up to you folks to figure that out."

"How come it cannot leave the container?" Connor

asked quietly. "Like your energy did?"

She explained the safety precaution she'd made in leaving a little of her energy behind.

As she stared at the swirling morass of darkness, she had to wonder if it was enough. "It's as if an emotion, a person, is attached to that energy. Because, right now, it looks and feels incredibly angry, like it needs something very badly."

Connor stepped to her side, sliding an arm around her shoulders. "I don't like the look of it at all. I'm so very glad it's contained." He turned her around and led her away from the stone. "Now that it's secured, and you've done your bit, we're leaving."

"Oh, but," she protested, "some great things are here. I want to look around."

He gave a short laugh. "We'd never get you out of here. You can come back. Later. Right now, they have to look after this rock, and we have a full day planned already," he reminded her.

That brought back the morning's conversation. Right. The construction and then the proof of ownership. "Tomorrow then. I want to come back tomorrow."

On their way back upstairs, Matt smiled at her. "I promise that you can spend time down there. If we can get your membership lined up, then you can be a regular visitor. You have serious skills. We can use you."

"But not today," Genesis said in understanding. "We have too many things to do. Right? Let's go."

Connor led Genesis back outside to Matt's hovercraft, laughing at her childlike delight when she saw the Razor. Its shiny black exterior and hooked nose gave it a hawklike appearance, as it hummed softly, floating just a few inches off the ground. "We're going in that?"

"We are," Matt said, coming up behind them. He tossed Connor the keys.

Connor unlocked the back door and helped Genesis into the backseat. Matt walked around to the passenger side.

As she buckled up, Connor got into the driver's side. Without warning, he gave the craft more power, and it quickly and smoothly rose into the air. Connor chuckled at Genesis's shocked gasp.

"Wow."

"It's quite something, isn't it?" Matt twisted to look back at her.

"I'll say." Genesis watched the scenery go by below them, too enchanted to say much more. It was fascinating. A number of various hovercraft and personal aircraft were used on Glory, but Genesis hadn't had the opportunity to ride in either before.

"Let's take a look and see if we can spot anything important from above," Connor said, as they headed toward the tree line.

They flew over the forest and made a circuit around the construction area, before landing in an open space close to the site.

Connor turned to Matt. "Did you see anything?"

The other man shook his head. "Other than the signs of heavy equipment? No."

Connor released the door hatch on his side. "Then let's go take a closer look."

Genesis unbuckled and hopped out joyfully. "It took only ten minutes to get here," she marveled, still in awe of the flight. "That was great."

Connor grinned. "That's Matt. Got to have the latest of everything."

"Ha. It's not just that. It's for the benefit of us all. Besides, what if we lost all communication with the other planets—forever?"

"What does that have to do with having a hovercraft?" she asked.

"It means, we have to develop ourselves and must keep on top of the latest technology, not sit about, waiting for the others to show up and to hand it over."

That made sense.

"Well, I'm glad you have one, if it means I get a chance to travel in style." The last words came over her shoulder, as she led the way down to the construction area. Matt went silent, as the heavy equipment came into view.

"THIS IS NOT good," Connor said, a tinge of anger in his voice. He stared at the broken trees, where the machinery had trampled its way through, the damaged wall where stone had argued with steel—and lost. The man-made clearing that had been created with no thought to the delicate balance of the area.

The place was quiet. It was late morning, but no one appeared to be around. "I don't know if a security guard is on watch today as well," Genesis said. "The other one wasn't in this area but inside, farther down in the caves."

Matt walked around one of the machines. He pulled out his comm and relayed the serial number to someone on the other end. Then he walked to the other machine and reported it as well. After he ended his conversation, he motioned to Genesis. "Which way to where you saw the guard walking around?"

She nodded and took the lead again, heading toward one

of the passage entryways. "He was down here."

They walked down the passage in silence for several minutes. Then Genesis raised a hand in warning. Shadows flickered on the cave walls ahead. Remi appeared in front of her, chattering madly. "Remi is warning us."

"About what?" Connor asked.

Matt answered, "Men are up ahead."

"Good," Connor said, striding forward. "I owe someone a knockout blow."

"Whoa, there could be several men," Genesis said, running to catch up, her voice low and frantic.

"Even better." And he took off without looking back.

Connor couldn't wait to find the assholes ruining the forest with their mindless destruction of the area, as they opened up access to the sacred pools. Big money was behind this construction. Big money wouldn't take being shut down well.

He wanted Genesis out of this mess, safe and sound. The minute anyone heard she was the owner of the forest, all hell would break loose, even if she couldn't prove it. Just the hint of her having ownership would put her in danger.

Ownership of the forest was worth so much more than money. And he knew plenty of greedy bastards who would do her in for the price of a coffee. She wouldn't be safe again, until her deed could be legally registered. He had one goal in life right now, … to keep her safe.

CHAPTER 20

GENESIS RACED BEHIND Connor, concerned about his angry determination. Surely he wasn't in any shape to pick a fight. One man maybe, but, from Remi's chittering, she got the impression several men were up ahead.

She careened around the corner, and Matt passed her with a burst of speed.

Up ahead, she heard voices and slowed, expecting to find Matt and Connor stopped. Instead, there was no sign of them.

Shit.

She barreled forward and came up against Remi, almost screaming in panic. She bent over, gasping. "Remi, what's the matter?"

Remi raced up one side of her and down the other. She went to take another step, and he jumped on her leg to stop her.

That message was clear. She peered around the corner but couldn't see anything. Still, she trusted Remi. If he said something was up ahead, then something was up ahead.

She took a deep breath and assessed her options. She heard several voices now, but two of them were likely to be Matt and Connor. She glanced down at Remi and whispered, "Are they up there?"

He didn't answer. But Remi had known enough for her

to not go any farther, so there had to be a reason. And she needed to know what that was. Suddenly Remi moved, disappearing around the corner. Literally. Genesis watched as his energy slipped away. Hadn't she wished forever that she could do the same?

Wait. Maybe she could.

She could certainly wrap herself up in energy, weaving a blanket around her. Like the rock, it would likely protect her, but she didn't know that it would save her in the event of a bullet. But could she make the energy hide her? That would be illusion energy. And she wasn't an illusionist. But Remi could do it. Could he do it while she held him? And would that make her invisible too? No, that couldn't work. She'd had him on her shoulder when he was invisible before, and she hadn't been affected.

But what if she wove some of her energy into his aura, would that extend the invisibility? She'd tried when she was younger to do something similar but hadn't managed it. Her granny had just laughed and said she'd been trying too hard. That it was easy to do but wasn't something one could be taught. One just learned it by doing.

She closed her eyes and whispered, "Remi, come here."

A small paw slipped into her hand. She smiled. In her mind's eye, she wove bright sparkling healthy energy from her aura down into Remi's aura.

And found her energy was already there. Of course it was. They were already bonded, had been for a lifetime, so of course her energy was there.

She quickly reversed the process and extended his energy that was part of his invisibility, wrapping herself in it. She grinned madly as her feet disappeared under the lower wrapping, until that extended up her legs to her torso, until she was completely covered in a blend of Remi's and her energy. She was here, yet behind some shimmering layer.

It was both beautiful and exhilarating. She'd done it. With Remi's help.

But having done it once, like wrapping the rock, she thought she could do it again.

Now to see what was going on. With Remi at her side, she peered around the corner again, this time leaning farther out. Matt and Connor were there, surrounded by a group of five angry men.

She stole a look at Connor's face and realized he was beyond being just angry. His cold, lean face promised retribution. Matt was trying to talk reason into one of the men, but, as she got closer to them and heard the discussion, she realized that no one was budging. The men hadn't planned on anyone being here.

And they weren't happy to have company—especially these visitors. She walked right up to the first man and stood in front of him. No reaction. She grinned. She walked up to Matt and Connor and bit back a laugh when she saw Matt's gaze widen. He opened his mouth, then shut it. She nodded approvingly, and he nodded back, the tiniest of motions. Connor, on the other hand, showed no reaction.

His abilities were returning, but not enough for him to see her. She slipped a hand into his, feeling his start of surprise. He glanced at his side and frowned.

She squeezed his hand. Hesitantly he squeezed back. Now that he knew she was there, she searched for a way to change the status quo.

"Quit talking. What will we do with them?" asked one of the men behind them.

The man who'd been talking frowned. "We'll have to

call the boss."

"Better you than me," snorted another man. "Why don't we just get rid of them both? Likely get a bonus for it."

"I'd be careful with that thinking. One is the head of the Paranormal Council, and the other is Grandfather's employee. There will be repercussions if both go missing."

"So take out one and put the other in a coma." That brought out several guffaws.

Genesis couldn't believe what she heard. These guys were prepared to commit murder to get out of this. So no one could know who had been down here. *Shit.*

She released Connor's hand and slipped around to the big machinery. Good, the keys were in the ignition. She jumped up and turned the key. She popped the thing into gear and yanked the wheel so it faced the men. The men turned at the sudden noise, then scattered, yelling.

"What the hell?"

"Who's driving that thing?"

"No one. It's a runaway. Someone jump in and stop it."

The shouts came at her from all sides. Genesis might be invisible, but she was solid, and, if anyone hopped up, they would collide with her.

She jumped down and raced in the direction of the second vehicle, repeating her actions. Once it started moving, she hopped off and raced toward Matt and Connor, hiding behind the third machine.

"Let's go," she yelled at Matt.

"Where?" Matt said. "They've got the exit blocked."

Genesis turned to find three men standing in the entrance to the tunnel. But they didn't know about the other opening. And it was just a little farther down. "Follow me."

She turned and ran. Matt followed her, with Connor

close behind. She dashed into the cave and the hidden entrance, behind one of the jutting stalagmites.

Within minutes, she raced to the surface.

Sunshine beckoned. At the last minute, it disappeared. She was going too fast and barreled straight into whatever was in the way.

The solid thing gave a grunt and fell to the ground. Matt was on the man in minutes. Connor, the last out, asked, "Genesis, are you okay?"

"What the fuck hit me?" snapped the man, struggling to his feet.

Matt grinned. "A secret weapon."

The stranger stared at Matt. "What the hell are you talking about?"

"We should be asking you the same thing, Peter," Connor said, his face thunderous. "You're involved in this destruction?" He waved his arm. "You're the one developing the pools?"

"I might have known about it, and why not?" Peter blustered. "No ownership here. The pools should be for everyone."

"You might have known about it?" Connor snorted. "And maybe a little more than just known about it, huh?"

"What do you know? You and your cushy job. Go and try to make a real buck in this town. If you don't work for Grandfather, you don't work. And, if you do work for him, you only ever get paid what he deems appropriate. No one will blame me for taking on a side job." He broke off and narrowed his gaze at Connor. "What's it to you anyway?"

"This isn't your property. You can't just steal it."

"I'm not stealing it," Peter protested. "No one has legal rights to it."

Genesis gasped. This was all about ownership of the forest. She needed to get to her cottage and get the deeds safely into her own hands.

Connor shook his head. "And the goons working down here? Are they working for you?"

Peter shrugged. "Sure. We had to import them though. Good local men are hard to find." He glanced from Matt to Connor. "Why? Did they rough you up a bit?"

"On top of that, they were trying to figure out how to dispose of us," Matt said smoothly. "Thankfully we got away."

Peter grinned. "They were just joking."

"No, they weren't. Likely they know more than you do." Genesis said, suddenly appearing beside Connor.

Peter glanced at her suspiciously. "Where the hell did you come from?"

"Me?" she asked innocently. "I've been here all along. Now, if you don't mind, we're late. And we have to get moving." She turned and strode back to the hovercraft. She needed to get home.

With or without her escorts. That damn paperwork needed to be found.

It was the only hope of saving the reserve.

CONNOR HAD A million questions to ask. Only Genesis had raced so far ahead that he couldn't ask them. Matt wanted to question Peter, and that was just fine by Connor. He wanted to know who had put those two men into the hospital and then find the person who had placed that rock in the pool. He doubted his cousin was capable of that type of energy work, but Connor couldn't say for sure. He was a lazy opportunist but not a hard-ass. And what he'd said about Grandfather was correct. But something was definitely wrong. Peter had no money to speak of, so just who was bankrolling his operation?

Matt nudged Connor forward. "Come on," he said in a low voice. "Let's catch up to Genesis."

"What about Peter?"

"A team is coming to round up all six men."

Connor nodded and followed Matt back to the hover-craft, where they found Genesis waiting. "How is it you could see her before?"

"Before?" Matt asked, sounding preoccupied.

"Yeah. She was invisible. I swear she was holding my hand, but I couldn't see her."

"She *was* invisible to most people." Matt made an impatient movement with his hand. "Rather, she did something with her energy so she couldn't be seen. But she was still solid." He laughed. "That was a cool trick with the machinery. If she'd been truly invisible, then she couldn't have turned on the machines. She wouldn't have had a solid hand to turn the keys."

"Yet you could see her?" That rankled. Connor had felt her hand but hadn't seen her. That had to do with his damn talent again; it was improving but obviously wasn't nearly good enough yet.

"Sure, I see energy." Matt grinned, as if suddenly realizing what the problem was. "So do you. Remember?"

"Obviously I don't see enough," Connor muttered. Damn. He hadn't even been sure it had been her when she had grabbed his hand.

"It will take time. Seeing energy is instinctive. You're so used to not seeing it now that you have to retrain your mind to see it again."

That sounded stupid. He wanted to have everything integrated now. But apparently it wouldn't happen on his schedule.

"Nice trick," Matt said admiringly to Genesis, as they approached.

"Thanks." She smiled up at him. "I had to do something to change the status quo."

"And speaking of that," he lowered his voice, "I can't tell you how important it is that you bring me proof of your claim—like today."

"We'll retrieve it now," she said, and she got into the back seat of the Razor.

Connor wordlessly climbed into the driver's side. He caught her curious glance in his direction but chose to stay quiet. He didn't know what to say. Or how to feel. So he said nothing. But inside, he was pissed. She'd been in danger. Hell, they all had been. But Genesis had saved them. She hadn't needed his help; he'd needed hers. Not only did that make him feel useless, it reminded him that, although he was healing, he wasn't whole. And might not be for some time.

Matt turned to Genesis. "Now where to?"

She turned a serious face to Connor. "Home."

CHAPTER 21

WITH A FEW quietly relayed directions, the short trip was fast and uneventful. Genesis watched the ground below to make sure they weren't being followed. "Can we be tracked in this?" she asked.

Matt raised his eyebrows at the question but answered readily enough. "It's possible. It would be foolish to think otherwise, but someone would need to be in a position to have that kind of technology. I'm highly doubtful that others have the means. At least not locally."

She nodded. "True, but a couple of those men weren't local. And, if they weren't, how many others aren't?"

He spun around to look at her, an assessing look on his face. "Good enough for me." Matt pored over the dash and adjusted some of the dials. "If we're being tracked, we should see a signal of some kind show up."

There was nothing. Satisfied, Genesis sat back and relaxed. At the cottage, Connor did a low-flying sweep before bringing the craft to rest behind the cottage.

Genesis quickly opened the front door. She let the men inside, then went in and set up an energy barrier to alert her if unwelcome company approached. When she was done, Matt said, "You're really worried someone will find you here?"

"Yes." She didn't elaborate. She walked into the small

kitchen and put on the teakettle. She hated to admit it, but her nerves were rattled. She set out the muffins snagged from the Center earlier, choosing one for herself, and took a big bite. She opened the bag of sandwiches and arranged them on a plate too.

Remi raced around the room. She opened a box of treats and handed him one. Then, as an afterthought, she held one out to Matt. "Can Darbo have one?"

Matt grinned. "Why don't you ask and see?"

She reached up and held the treat in front of Darbo's nose. His nose quivered, and very slowly he unhooked one hand from Matt's ear and reached out for the morsel. She'd been surprised to see the little guy with Matt. She knew Darbo of old. Celeste had been so careful with him. Genesis had no idea how Matt had ended up with him but knew it must have had something to do with Celeste's departure. Genesis smiled. "He's adorable. So tiny."

"Thankfully, considering where he likes to hang."

"Surely he doesn't sleep there?"

"No." Matt shook his head gently. "He has a bed at home that he loves, but he's always with me, if we aren't at home."

She nodded. The teakettle chose that moment to whistle. Enjoying the soothing routine, she made a small pot of jasmine tea and carried it to the table. The plate of muffins were half gone already. Only a couple sandwiches were left. She eyed a second one and decided she was too tired. She sat down and rubbed her face.

"Are you okay?" Connor asked gently. He stood behind her and massaged her shoulders.

"I am. Just hadn't realized what was happening here while I wasn't looking," she muttered. "Like a year's worth of not looking."

"But you are now," Connor said. "And this is all fixable."

"As long as I can produce the proof."

He winced. "I hate to admit it, but it does boil down to that." He paused and then added in a diffident tone, "Do you have it?"

She took a sip of tea and sighed. "Sure. I just have to find it."

The hands massaging her shoulders stopped. "You don't know where the documents are?"

Matt froze, then leaned in to look into her eyes.

"This was Granny, remember? She was paranoid about everything."

"But you've seen these documents yourself?" Connor asked hopefully.

She stood and walked over to the cupboard that appeared to be part of the wall. "She hid so much stuff in here. I'll start with this mess." She proceeded to haul stacks of documents to the table. "Give me a hand, please."

With raised eyebrows, Connor and Matt helped sort through the stack as she went back for another one. Then she sat back down and took another sip of tea.

Matt held a large document in one hand, his eyes wide. "These are star charts," he said, his voice awed.

"Many are, yes."

There was reverence in his touch, as he took a closer look. "I'd heard rumors but hadn't seen any of her work." His head shot up, and he pinned her in place with his gaze. "Did she teach you?"

Genesis hesitated, then shrugged. What the hell. With a sideways glance at Connor, she nodded. "Somewhat. My training wasn't complete when she passed away. Celeste is much better at this than I am. I drew a chart that, when it didn't come to pass, made me realize I would never be like Granny or Celeste, and I walked away from it."

As she had walked away from so much back then.

Connor studied her face, but she avoided returning his look. He could think what he liked. Nothing was easy in what she'd gone through to learn her grandmother's skills and to realize she didn't have that same magical touch.

Connor dropped the topic, as his fascination with the charts took over. "These are incredible."

"She was very gifted." Genesis watched as Connor and Matt sorted documents into stacks. Charts and not charts. Then Connor went to work on the nonchart stacks.

And she let them. Picking up her tea, she tried to remember what her granny had said. Something about keeping the documents safe. That she should never let anyone see them. That they were more precious than anyone realized.

Now that Genesis understood what men would go through to get the forest, she understood her granny's paranoia. It saddened her that so many had thought her granny was mentally unstable. She'd been many things, but insane was nowhere on that list. Being a stargazer meant she spent a lot of time in the stars, studying the meanings of star transits and how they applied to life here. To the people here. Some showed events. Other charts were about specific people. There was a chart for everyone in the area. Genesis had never read them but imagined they'd make interesting reads to someone. Genesis knew that. She'd tried to learn but hadn't picked it up very quickly. She'd wanted to though.

Granny had said it told her destiny as she'd seen it. And that destiny had blown up. Now, in hindsight, that destiny didn't look all that bad. Granny had said Connor was her partner. Then again, she'd been reading star charts and hadn't known Connor. When they'd broken up, Genesis had tossed away all her beliefs about such things.

After all, Granny had been wrong.

So wrong about an area that was so important to Genesis that she'd been completely disillusioned. If Granny, a stargazer, had read the stars and had been wrong, then what chance had Genesis to get it right?

She'd been lost for so long. And now?

"What's this?" Connor lifted a leather packet with leather ties. And she suddenly remembered seeing it before. "That's it!" And Genesis realized that maybe, just maybe, some of her life was coming together—at least some of it. "That's it. At least I think it is." She laughed and held her hand out for it. "I remember that satchel."

Connor handed it over. She felt like a little kid, getting a present. She opened it and pulled out several sheaths of paper. Some of the papers were old beyond imagining. She laid them on the table and carefully unfolded the top yellowed piece, which almost didn't even seem like paper. She took a closer look. "I think this is canvas. Or some kind of cloth."

Matt and Connor crowded around her.

"It's vellum," Connor whispered in an awed voice. "This is absolutely ancient."

"I know," she whispered. "It's precious."

"And very valuable in itself," added Connor. "What does it say?"

Genesis started reading, struggling with the old script, when Matt raised his hand. "May I see it?"

Genesis leaned back in surprise. "Sure." She shifted to

give him room, surprised that he could read the old script.

He studied the document, running his fingers under the words but not actually touching the paper. "We must take it to the lab."

She shook her head. "I'm not ready to do that."

Matt stopped reading and looked at her curiously. "Do you think you can keep it safe?"

She thought about it. "I think so. But if this needs experts to verify its validity, then I suppose it will need to leave here anyway."

"Can you read what it says?" Connor asked Matt. He leaned over Genesis's shoulder.

"I can read bits and pieces, but the script is difficult to decipher, and some of the words are faded," Matt said reverently.

Genesis smoothed her fingers over a star symbol in the upper right-hand corner. "It's a stargazer registry document."

"And that makes it an incredibly important artifact." Matt straightened and shook his head. "I had no idea documents like this were here." He pointed to the other documents beneath the open one. "It looks like she has several more, as well."

"These documents have been in my family since forever. Generations and generations have passed them down." Genesis settled back in her seat and carefully closed the open document. She moved it off to one side and pulled up the next one. It appeared to be just as old and was as equally difficult to decipher. She shook her head, after staring at them for a few moments. "Okay, we'll need an expert."

She went through the same process with each of the other documents. The last one appeared to be more recent, written on paper. When she opened it, she gasped. "Oh my.

It's a letter from Granny." And it was addressed to her. She read it silently.

Dearest Genesis,

If you are reading this, my life has finally come to an end. Don't be sad, child. I'm ready to go. I'm more than ready. I've lived longer than anyone should. But you?... You have yet to live. And you need to. You need to return to your roots and find yourself again. Find that beautiful soul that lives inside. That soul who got hurt once and then ran. You can't run from your destiny. You can only hide until it finds you again. Inside you know this. Inside you understand this. Inside you are this.

Be strong. Life takes much from each of us, but it also leaves much reward. You have lost much in your short life. But you have also been given much.

It's time to see the good and to let the rest go.

You were always special. Now go forth and lead that special life.

To that end, being the last one of three stargazers, I pass to you the heritage you were born for. You were already given the biggest part on my death, but now, with these precious documents, you have the rest.

Use it wisely.

With love always,
Bellini Mercy, your beloved grandmother

When Connor stroked her cheek, Genesis started, as he wiped away a tear she hadn't been aware of shedding. Silently she handed the letter to him. He read it quickly, raised one eyebrow, and said softly, "This is beautiful. Documents to prove these are all yours."

He handed it to Matt, who was almost rubbing his hands together with joy. He looked down at Genesis, then said, "Considering all the problems we're dealing with, I'd feel better if we got all this back to the lab and under lock and key." He nodded to the leather documents. "We'll bring in an expert to translate these."

She nodded and carefully packed up the satchel, but something inside her felt very, very wrong. She didn't want to remove the materials from the cottage. "I feel odd taking this away. It feels like a mistake. Like it belongs here." She struggled to verbalize the emotions screaming at her in warning.

"Can you protect it?" Matt repeated his earlier question. "How about we take it to the lab, copy it all, and get it translated, so you know what you have, and then you can keep the copies while we keep the originals where it's all safe?"

She paused, considered his suggestion, then shrugged. "I have to keep the documents here. That's all I know. They have to stay with me, and they have to stay here."

"So we can't take them to the lab?" Connor asked. "Not even for a few hours?"

She frowned and turned the bag over and over in her hands. It would be foolish not to get this information translated, and keeping copies made perfect sense, ... but something about it felt wrong—as if the materials were tuned to this house. She couldn't let the bag leave. "I hate to say it. I'm not trying to be difficult, but the documents have to stay here."

"How is that not being difficult?" Connor groaned.

"It's not me," she said. "It's the documents. They can't leave here."

Silence. Matt and Connor looked at each other.

Connor ran a hand through his hair. "So bring the equipment here?" he asked. "And the expert?"

"Yes." She smiled brightly. "That's perfect." She felt her whole system relax, as the tension in the room eased.

"Fine," Matt said. "I don't like it, but let's get this done." He stepped back and pulled out his cell phone.

Connor moved behind Genesis and tugged her into a hug. "Are you sure?"

She tilted her head back, so she could look into his face. His dark-chocolate-colored eyes stared into hers with such warmth and acceptance and understanding that she felt herself trying to explain. Not that much to say.

"I've never felt surer of anything in my life. These documents shouldn't leave here." She frowned thoughtfully. "In fact, I'm not sure they *can* leave."

A FEW MINUTES later, Connor listened in, as Matt made the calls. It took some logistical arguments to sort out bringing the equipment and experts here. And they weren't allowed to know exactly where they were going, in order to protect the documents ... and Genesis.

"This had better be the real stuff," Matt growled, when he disconnected.

"It's real enough," said Connor. "And no doubt these are stargazer documents."

"That alone makes it worthwhile." Matt sighed. "Why can't they come to the vault where they'd be safe?"

"Genesis isn't convinced they'd be safe there." Connor paused, then added quietly, "She's also not sure that the documents can physically leave the cottage. It's some kind of protective portal."

"Don't use the term *portal*, please," groaned Matt. "That brings all kinds of complications to mind that I don't want to even contemplate."

Connor hadn't considered the ramifications of the word when used in conjunction with Genesis's cottage. Matt was right. That conjured up all kinds of things. And he didn't like that Genesis would be in the middle of it. Cautiously he said, "I don't think she meant in terms of doorways."

"Good. But I'm not sure what other ways there are to consider."

Connor shrugged. "She's looking for more documents. This house is a mess of hidden closets and cupboards. Some of this house is older than anything I've ever seen."

"Let's go in and look too," Matt said abruptly. "This entire cottage should be part of the archives."

Connor walked back to the kitchen, where Genesis sorted through another stack of documents. She looked up at the two of them. "And?"

"My staff isn't thrilled, but they are coming with equipment." Matt twisted his lips in a wry grin. "Expect Fenwick to try and change your mind."

She nodded but had already returned her gaze to the material in front of her. She paused and lifted up a yellowed sheet of paper. "Oh my God."

CHAPTER 22

GENESIS STARED AT the aged agreement in her hand. It was a legal adoption by her granny of Genesis and her sisters. But the names on the agreement blew her away. The names on the document weren't her parents, or the people she'd thought had been her parents. They were her parents' best friends. This was a formal agreement with a cash amount listed for the transaction.

She'd been sold.

Back to her own blood. She only had dim memories, but she knew Granny was hers. Her mother had been Granny's only child. And she'd been old enough when she'd given birth.

Genesis could understand them not wanting to take care of triplets, but to be paid to let her and her sisters go back to Granny? Now that was just wrong.

The amount of money was also no small peanuts. Granny hadn't had any money. At least, not after she'd bought back her granddaughters. Genesis couldn't imagine where Granny had gotten that money from in the first place. Genesis shook her head. What the hell was wrong with people?

Silently she handed the paper to Connor and reached for the next in the stack. DNA results. Times three. Proving Granny and the triplets were related. In a way, although

Genesis would have said instinctively that she was Granny's relative, this bit of proof made her feel better. Then again, Granny might have done it to make sure she was the same blood before she handed over the cash. She might have been considered odd by the community, but she was very sharp in understanding humanity.

Silently she handed over that paper too. She might need it to prove her inheritance. At the very least, it removed the doubts.

She went back to the next stack until the silence in the room grew to the point of being unnatural. She studied the darkening of Connor's features and asked gently, "What's the matter?"

"They sold you?" Connor asked incredulously. "Back to your own grandmother?"

She looked at Matt, his eyebrows raised in question. Matt shrugged and rifled through the papers in his hand. She grimaced. "Yeah. You do recognize the names, right?"

He looked back down. "Grandfather's sister."

"Figured they had to be blood, given the money-grabbing tendency."

Connor stood and stormed around the small room. "This is wrong on so many levels. These people are respected members of the community."

"Just like Grandfather is, right?" she asked.

He glared at her. "How can you be so calm? These people used you. Probably put a second in-ground pool into their house with this sale. If they had sold children once, maybe they'd done it again?"

"Maybe they did. That's something you can take up with the law." She nodded at the papers in Matt's hands. "The proof is there."

She looked around the room thoughtfully and added, "I owe them thanks for their greediness though. If they hadn't sold me, if Granny hadn't bought me, I might not have the rights to what I have now. If these people"—she tapped the sales agreement—"had any idea what I stood in line to gain, … do you really think they'd let me have it?"

He stared at her in shock and then sat, as the truth sank in. "Jesus."

"We will launch a full investigation," Matt said quietly. "This is not acceptable behavior."

"Exactly. So nail them on child trafficking and move on." She tried for a flippant tone, but, at the softening of Connor's features, she figured she hadn't quite pulled it off.

He reached out, snagged her chin, and lifted her face for a warmth-drenching kiss.

The fireworks spread, heating up all the chilled spots inside that had formed when she'd learned the terrible news.

"Uh, do you think you can hold off on that please?" Matt said, his voice teasing. "My old heart can't take it."

She laughed.

Connor smiled down at her. "People who think like that will never be rich," he said, not caring that Matt was still there, listening. "This, what we have together, that's wealth."

Unbidden, tears came to her eyes.

She leaned into him. Needing his tenderness. His understanding.

And felt him stiffen.

A moment later, she heard the sound of the hovercraft.

Matt said, "Company." He walked out to meet them.

Genesis sighed, looked at the heaps of material they still had to go through, and said, "Give me a hand to lay this out on my bed, will you? I need to sort it and don't want strangers seeing these."

He grabbed a stack of star charts and carried them to the head of the bed, then came back for another load. Within minutes she had the bulk of the paperwork out of the kitchen. She left the satchel and the two most recent documents. The hovercraft crossed overhead again, and she realized she'd have to open the energetic alarm system. She crossed to her door and changed the energy so that the cottage would become visible.

Matt watched. "Did you cloak the entire cottage?" he asked in shock.

Her shoulders sank. She turned to face him. "Yes." She took a deep breath. "I didn't want anyone to find us."

"Yeah, well, that will do it." He turned back to staring up at the blue sky on his way to the front door.

Just then, a hovercraft came in low and loud and landed beside theirs. She couldn't imagine a whole fleet of these cars appearing.

Matt and Connor walked out to meet the men. Genesis went back inside and worked on clearing away more mess.

FENWICK, THE RESEARCH head, was the first to hop out, his white hair slicked back against his skull. "Damn, this place is hard to find."

Matt shook his head. "You have no idea. Genesis made it even harder."

Fenwick's gaze sharpened, and he looked like he wanted to ask about Matt's statement, but he stayed quiet. Several other men climbed out of the hovercraft, and one of them opened up the rear hatch. Within minutes, the researchers had unloaded several large pieces of equipment.

Connor didn't know how this would work. He led the way back to the house to find Genesis standing in the doorway. She smiled at Fenwick, as he studied her small cottage. "Thanks for coming."

"We had a little trouble finding the place, or else we'd have been here sooner."

She smiled brightly, disarmingly. "Sorry about that. It is hard to find."

Matt rolled his eyes at her good-naturedly, muttering as he walked past her, "Yeah, sounds like we need to talk about that."

"I'll think about it." She stepped back to let the other men inside. Connor remained in the doorway.

Genesis turned but didn't know where to go. Three additional men and her kitchen was full. "Excuse me." She wove her way to the table. Under watchful eyes, she carefully opened the satchel and brought out the stacks of documents.

Soft gasps echoed behind her. She took the top document, carefully opened it, spread it out on the table, and then stepped back.

"Good Lord," said Fenwick. "Are those for real?"

She looked at him. "Isn't that the reason you gentlemen are here?"

CHAPTER 23

I T WAS IMPOSSIBLE to wait patiently, while the men put on their protective gloves and commenced their in-depth analysis and study of the documents. She paced the living area, and, when that didn't help, she returned to the bedroom to keep working on that mess she'd dumped in there. She'd only started when she found something so old and so much Granny, she couldn't stop a sob from breaking free.

"Genesis?"

She shook her head and wiped her cheeks. "I'm fine."

Connor waited in eloquent silence. When she could, she turned to smile at him. "I'm okay. Just bringing up memories." His smile warmed her heart.

"Then rejoice in the memories." He nodded at the document in her hand. "Is that something you need the experts to look at?"

She shook her head quickly and refolded the odd material just as fast. "No. It's not." She turned away and busied herself with rearranging her stack of documents. "How are they coming along?"

"Besides lots of exclamations—including lots of colorful language—I'm not sure."

That startled a laugh out of her. "I can imagine."

She kept working quietly, sorting the stargazer charts by year into stacks, and Genesis suddenly remembered that boxes of similar charts were in the attic. She slipped into the pool room and crossed to the far side. The towels were stacked below the built-in ladder. She cleared the lower rungs and climbed up, struggling to open the door.

"Here. Let me help." Connor's voice came from behind her.

"I'm fine. Been up here many times before. Although I was usually hauling boxes at the time."

"You mean more documents are up there?"

She groaned as the attic board shifted to the side, and then she coughed several times, as dust came down on her head. When it cleared, she put her head through the hole and looked around. "Oh yeah, it's all full."

Connor grabbed her by the waist and lowered her to the ground. "Let me."

"You won't know what boxes to bring down."

"What's in them all?" He stood on the ladder, half in and half out of the attic. He bent down to look at her, a stunned look on his face. "There must be hundreds of boxes here."

She nodded. "Most are star charts."

The look in his eyes made her realize what a gift her granny had left behind. "Do you want to keep them here or have them taken to the vault, where they can be studied? The knowledge preserved. Used for everyone?"

It was his last words that made her realize how much truth there was in that. Her granny's life work needed to be preserved. Needed to be utilized as it was always meant to be. For the people. Otherwise what was the point?

"Maybe the vault." She knew the doubt showed in her voice. "But I can't hand them over blindly. I want those cataloged and the boxes checked to see what else could be inside. Granny hadn't been the most organized."

Matt spoke from behind her, his voice gentle and caring. "So how do you feel about living at the Center while you do the sorting and cataloging?"

She turned to stare at him, hope blossoming inside her at the idea of a compromise. "I might like that."

Connor ducked down again. "And you might need a bigger vault."

"It was Granny's life's work," Genesis whispered, feeling the emotions clog her voice.

"And she was the last stargazer," Matt said. "The last of her line." He broke off and looked at her intently, one eyebrow rising. "Or was she?"

Connor went silent.

She looked from one to the other and then shrugged. "Honestly, I don't know. I was learning slowly but hadn't finished my training."

"It's not in the blood?"

"Yes." She nodded her head and added, "Yes, but it needs instinct and … maturity."

That brought a surprised laugh from Matt. "That makes a lot of sense. So we have a new generation stargazer. You have no idea how happy that makes me."

"I wouldn't get too excited. I'm really terrible at it. My sisters are much better," she muttered. She turned back to Connor. "Can you bring a few of the newer boxes down? I dated them before they went up."

Connor nodded and disappeared into the attic.

Matt reached over and squeezed Genesis's shoulder. "You have given the world a huge gift."

"Maybe and maybe not." She nodded as the first box came down. "There's a lot of material to go through." She glanced up at him. "I want to number and write down the boxes as they come down. They can't all go in one trip. I also don't want the boxes to just go straight to the vault. I need to sort through them first."

"I understand. We'll take it slow."

She sighed in relief. Thank God.

After a few minutes of traveling back and forth to her bedroom, Connor stopped and looked at her. "These ten boxes are all from the last couple years before your grandmother passed away."

"That's where I'll start." She walked to the bed, realizing this mess needed to be cleaned up first. "Matt, how are the experts coming along?"

"They're in awe. And they want more time to study the documents. They want to take them back to the Center."

She spun around. "No. Those ones aren't leaving."

"I thought you were past that." He frowned at her. "You did say the star charts could go into the vault to be studied."

"Yes. But those are not star charts." She reached across the bed and picked up a stack to show him. "These are star charts."

"And the documents that the experts are assessing?" he asked, as he accepted the stack. "What are they then?"

"They are stargazer registry documents."

"They appear to be many things," one of the men from the Center said, stepping into the doorway. "But we have no time to sort it out. They must go back to the vault. They must." He stared at Genesis. "It is not right that they should be here." He didn't say *with you*, but the words hung in the air nevertheless.

Genesis stared at him and felt her anger building. If she didn't know better, she'd say her granny's wrath was inside her. "It appears you misunderstood me. Those documents will *not* be leaving my home. You, however, can leave—*now.*"

"Uh, Genesis—" Connor began.

She held up her hand and cut him off. She glared at Matt. "Let me be perfectly clear about this. It is purely on my goodwill that you are even seeing these documents right now. After you leave, they will be hidden where none of you will ever find them again. Do you understand me?" she said, her voice rising with determination. "They are mine, not yours, and they do not belong to you." She glared at the offending scientist.

"Easy, Genesis." Matt stepped forward, his hands held up in a peaceful, placating manner.

Didn't matter. She wasn't fooled. Granny had been dealing with men like these supposed experts for a long time.

"I appreciate what you are doing," Matt said. "We do need the documentation for your landowner rights."

"No." She stopped him. "You need to see and verify. Possibly have a copy in some form or other, but you do not get the original deeds."

He took a deep breath. "Correct. But we can't verify that these are the deeds if we can't have time to study …" He stopped talking at her emphatic headshake.

"These are the deeds to the caves and healing pools." She walked to the bed and picked up the large piece of paper she'd been crying over earlier. She held it up for Matt to read. When the same man rushed over to also take a look, she glared at him until he backed up.

"You may look. Not touch," she snapped at Matt. "And only you."

Connor's hand landed on her shoulder and squeezed.

"Easy, Genesis. He may have gotten a little zealous in his eagerness to have a chance to study these rare documents, but they aren't going to steal them from you."

She turned to look at the man who'd pissed her off. "He looks like he's thinking of doing that right now."

All three men turned to stare at the scientist, and he flushed bright red.

"Damn," Matt muttered.

The scientist wrung his hands before throwing them in the air and shouting, "They are valuable. They must be preserved."

"And just what do you think I've been doing with them all these years if it wasn't keeping them safe? And my granny before me?"

"Everyone knows she was a mental case at the end. She might have destroyed these."

That did it.

She pointed to the doorway behind him. "Get out."

He glared at her, anger a bright glint in his eye, but he turned and walked away.

Genesis turned a cold eye to Matt. "Did you read this document?"

He nodded. "I do need to take several images back with me, and it needs to be verified. But I'm satisfied you and your sisters hold the deed. However, until the tests come back to prove that this is as old as it appears to be, I can't confirm your ownership. We might need to see it again."

She smiled thinly. "You won't need to. You'll never see it again. Or my cottage. Now get your small men and their little minds out of my house."

Matt backed up slowly. "I'll get the imaging equipment and take what I need for verification. You might need to bring that document into the lab for testing."

"This document goes where I go. It will not be released into any of these men's hands."

A second man stood in the doorway now. "I can understand how you feel. You are surrounded by artifacts of great value," he tried to explain. "We only wish to preserve it."

She turned her cold eyes on him. "And your colleague?"

He winced.

"Exactly." She turned back to Matt. "You have one hour."

CONNOR LEFT GENESIS alone in her room, giving her some time to calm down. He walked into the kitchen to the sound of men muttering angrily.

Matt said, "Enough. We have one hour. Now let's not waste it."

The men fell silent, but their short jerky actions spoke of barely leashed frustration.

Connor could understand. Empathize, even, but the property belonged to Genesis. The legacy of her family lines was her responsibility. She had to feel secure with what was happening, and it was painfully obvious she wasn't.

Matt walked over. "I'm sorry we upset her."

Connor nodded. "Especially now that she doesn't trust you."

"Me?" Matt asked in surprise. "Or them?"

Connor considered the issue. "You picked these men to come here. If she trusted you before, this would likely have made her doubt that." Connor nodded, indicating the men busily working. "She felt threatened by their actions, and I know she's scared now that they might do something to get their hands on these documents." He ran his fingers agitatedly through his hair. "For that I have to take some blame. This is her space. Her secret space. I'm now here, and I brought you here, and you brought them here."

"And that has shifted the energy." Matt winced. "I'll make sure these men can't find her place again."

"But if you can't get the idea out of their mind that these artifacts are here, they could hire other people to help find them."

"I'll do everything I can to prevent that. The biggest problem is they don't see her as the rightful owner," Matt said.

"True." Matt was correct there. "If we can prove to everyone that the three sisters are the heirs to this place, the granddaughters of the last stargazer and one herself, then it would change their minds." Connor thought for a moment. "She had DNA proof. Did she show you that?"

Matt nodded. "We need to take copies of that. And anything else that will help us to prove her lineage." Matt leaned forward. "I have yet to see her proof of ownership of the forest."

"There's been so much brought out, but I don't think I've seen that one either. Keep an eye on these guys, and I'll ask her."

With a backward glance at the men busily working, he walked into the bedroom. "Hey," he said quietly, watching her back stiffen and then relax again. At least she wasn't mad at him. "Did you find the deed to the forest?"

She sighed and turned to face him. "Not yet. It might be in one of these boxes. That's why I don't want them to leave until I've gone through them all."

"Would she have kept it in a random box like that? It's

pretty special. You'd think she'd have a second satchel for something that important."

Genesis turned to him, her lips twisting on a sudden thought. "And maybe she did."

CHAPTER 24

GENESIS FINISHED MARKING down the dates for the star charts on her bed and carefully laid them in an empty box to go into the vault. The rest of the documents needed to be gone through, but, so far, she hadn't found the other deeds. And she needed to. That proof was important.

In fact, according to Matt, it was everything.

She worked her way through the rest of the papers on the bed and sorted them into piles as ones to keep, ones to deal with, and ones that she could throw away. By the time she was done, the original stack had been decimated. She packaged the ones to keep. Then she reached for the first boxes Connor had brought down for her. They were all star charts. She marked the dates down and repacked the box, moving on to the next.

A cough behind her made her spin around. Matt stood in the doorway. "The agreed one hour is up." He motioned behind him. "We will leave, if that is your wish. However, the men could use another half hour to finish the imaging. We had trouble getting the light set up properly."

She nodded. "That's fine." She pointed to the four boxes she had packed up. "These can go to the vault. They are all star charts. I can go through them more thoroughly there."

His eyes lit up. "Thank you." He walked over and hefted a stack of two boxes. "I'll take them out myself."

With mixed feelings, she watched bits and pieces of her granny walk out of the cottage. Connor appeared in the doorway at that moment. He walked over and pulled her into a warm hug. "It's the right thing to do," he murmured.

"I know. It's just difficult letting go."

He smiled. "Caring hurts. But better to have loved and lost than …"

"Never to have loved at all," she finished for him. "I know. I just wish Granny hadn't had such a huge problem with the Center for Paranormal Activity."

"That would have been the idiots who headed the Center before me. Your granny and I got along fine." Matt walked over and picked up the second two boxes. "I promise, we will get these records properly preserved and available for the rest of the world. Our digital capabilities are so much more than what she would have known was available back then."

That helped. Granny hadn't had any technical knowledge, and knowing that Matt would preserve Granny's work made all the difference. And Genesis remembered that Granny had spoken well of Matt. Genesis turned to the remaining boxes.

With Connor's help, they zipped through all the ones he'd brought down. When they were done, he hefted several up, and, with Matt's help, moved the last of them to the hovercraft. She wandered behind them with the last load. The experts were still trying to take images of all the old vellum documents. The light glinted off one of the buckles on the leather satchel, and she suddenly realized that she'd seen the same kind of buckle before.

She went into her old bedroom and opened her old closet. Up top, in the very back, was an old engraved wooden box. She pulled it down and took it back to her new bedroom, shutting the door for privacy. Now the tears started to pour. This had been her treasure box when she was little. Somewhere along the way, this elegant box had fallen out of favor, and she'd started to use a brighter, more garish box. The stages of childhood.

With a deep breath, she opened the lid and spotted a teal satchel. Not as old as the one in the kitchen but pretty damn close. She unbuckled the front latch and pulled out documents. Ornate scroll patterns decorated the top, and official seals in wax decorated the bottom.

This was what they—she—had been looking for.

Several similar documents were in the satchel. She scanned them and realized they covered so much more land than she'd first assumed. Basically she and her sisters owned all the land around and in town. She shook her head in wonderment. The people had hated and feared Granny and had idolized Grandfather. And, all along, Granny had been the wealthy landowner and Grandfather the liar. He didn't own any of it. It was all theirs.

Jesus.

Had he known? He must have. Had he been behind the break-ins at her shop and apartment? Had he seen her chart in progress and wondered what else there might be? Had he been looking for these papers? The proof that he wasn't the owner? He could have had new ones forged, but only if the originals no longer existed.

She sat back and tried to figure out what to do next.

CONNOR WAITED IN the kitchen for the men to finish. Because they were rushed, things were going wrong and mistakes were being made. He kept one eye on Genesis's closed bedroom door. He wanted to knock and ask if she was okay, but she'd been the one to close it. If she needed a few moments, who could blame her?

He settled back to keep an eye on the men. The quiet *click* of the door latch caught his ear, and he turned to see Genesis walking toward them. She asked Matt, "How much longer?"

He inclined his head toward the men and said, "They are almost done."

"Good, ask them to step outside when that's finished. We need to image other documents."

She said it in such a low tone, Matt immediately straightened, and his face grew serious. He walked over to the two men and a few minutes later, they reluctantly left, shooting curious glances at her, as they went through the doorway.

Genesis looked at Connor. "Please stand by the door and keep them in sight."

Interesting. He did as she bid and watched as she returned with a blue satchel. And more old documents.

"Jesus." Matt shook his head as she held up the documents one at a time for him to read. "Well, as long as these are authentic—and, yes, they will need to be checked—that certainly answers the question of who owns the forest."

Then she held up the last document, and he choked. "Oh, shit."

Connor raced over to read the document. He raised his gaze to meet hers. "Really?"

She nodded. "All three sections of the forest, including the healing pools, as well as the quarter leading into town. The quarter Grandfather claims as his."

"And, … from the look on your face, you're thinking he's been responsible for the construction?"

She shrugged. "Think about it. Who else has as much to lose?"

Matt and Connor looked at each other, each listing off names. "Grandfather's heirs. His sister, brother, their kids. Peter, even."

Connor wanted to pick up Genesis and whisk her away from here. And, from the look in her eye, she wouldn't mind. She turned and walked away.

Matt had moved to the imaging machines and started documenting the papers. "As soon as I'm done, we'll head out." He made several adjustments, then started doing an electronic scan that would give them a digital and a 3-D reproduction of the document, something they could keep forever. The original would be kept as Genesis wanted, but the naysayers would have their proof. They could shut up after this.

At least, Connor hoped this would be the result. As a worst-case scenario, she'd have to bring the originals into a meeting for one time only. Then the documents could go back into safekeeping.

If this was stressful now, he couldn't imagine what a tribunal like that would do to her. He realized Matt was waiting for him to acknowledge his statement. "Good. She needs to get some rest. It's been an upsetting day."

"For all of us," Fenwick growled from behind him. Connor shifted so that the man couldn't see around him to understand what Matt was imaging. He turned around and glared the man back several paces. "You aren't welcome in here."

Fenwick sniffed but turned away. Connor stayed at the

door to make sure Fenwick didn't try to get back in. Connor wanted to believe Fenwick was simply concerned with the artifacts; he just wasn't sure what lengths he'd go to preserve them.

"Okay, I'm done," Matt said.

"Good. Let's get everything put away."

"That's done too." Matt stepped behind him. "Let the men come in and pack up the equipment."

Matt and Connor returned to Genesis's small bedroom to find her sitting on the side of the bed. Connor squatted down in front of her. "Hey, do you want to stay a little longer?"

She raised tear-drenched eyes to him. "There's so much to do here."

"And there."

"True." She rubbed her forehead, as if thinking hard. "Let's go with the star charts, so I can see them locked into the vault."

"And leave the cottage." He looked around. "Now that I know what's here, I'm worried."

That brought a real smile to her face. She said, "I can take care of that."

CHAPTER 25

GENESIS COULDN'T HELP the pang of loss she felt, as she watched her small cottage disappear into the mists below. At her insistence, they'd been the last hovercraft to leave, and they carried Granny's star charts. She'd refused to let any leave in the other hovercraft, as she no longer trusted the specialists.

Connor reached out a hand and said, "It will be fine, Genesis."

As cheerfully as she could muster, given the circumstances, she replied, "I know."

Matt twisted in the front seat to take a look at her. "Are you still worried about someone finding the cottage? I can clear the data from the hovercrafts, if that would make you feel better."

She shook her head. "No, that won't make a difference. Besides, no one will find my place again." She resolutely looked out the window. She'd already taken the necessary precautions. Granny had been very specific on how to hide the cottage and on making sure it was done every day.

Now that Genesis had seen for herself how other people believed they had the right to Granny's work, she understood why Granny had been so reclusive. To know all the land in town, around town, and the forests had belonged to her granny and now to Genesis and her sisters, well, that didn't bear thinking about. The townspeople had shunned her family, mocked them behind her back, and yet they were living on Granny's land. Free of charge.

It would get ugly.

Her sisters should be here.

Except it wasn't the right time for them to return. Genesis knew that. The charts had said that, but the charts could also be wrong, as she well knew. Still, it didn't feel like it was time for them to come home—but she wished it were.

The prime concern was seeing how the star charts would be looked after here at the Paranormal Center. If they cared for them properly, Genesis would consider bringing over more. There were hundreds, if not thousands, still in the cottage. It would be easier to leave everything untouched, hidden as Granny had. But Genesis wasn't sure that was the right thing to do either. Also she had to place her claim on the property to keep the forest safe. If Granny had done that decades ago, maybe they wouldn't be in this situation.

But she couldn't blame her beloved granny. Genesis and her sisters would have been lost without her. Especially as Genesis now knew about the adoption papers.

Or maybe she should call them *purchase papers*.

And life wouldn't be easy just because she wanted it to be.

They approached the Paranormal Center, and, from their height, she saw the other hovercraft had already arrived, and the equipment was being unloaded. Several other techs waited for Matt's hovercraft. They were also fully outfitted in special gear, presumably to handle the star charts.

With a pang, she realized she would have to let go of her charts and then trust these strangers. She was the first in her family to make such a decision, and it didn't sit easily on her shoulders.

As soon as they landed, the hovercraft was swarmed by staff. Like a mother hen, she hovered as each box was removed from the hold in the back of the hovercraft, hating to see the boxes leave her presence. When the last box was removed, she trailed behind the group to the vaults.

Seeing the awe on the men's faces, the reverence in the way they studied the contents of the boxes, she finally realized the star charts would be okay here.

"Are you still watching the men sort through the boxes? Matt needs to show you a few things."

She shook her head. "I won't leave until these are logged in."

"They've been logged in already," Connor said patiently. "You don't need to be here."

"The boxes have been logged in." She gave him a tight smile. "I won't be leaving until the star charts are individually logged in."

The nearest tech turned to look at her, his expression shocked.

She glared back. "Considering the behavior of one of your experts …"

The tech visibly winced, as he turned to see the experts, poring over the images in their hands at the back of the room. The tech nodded. "Makes sense. I'll log in everything first. Then we'll image each one and keep the originals in the special air-controlled vault."

And he proceeded to slowly remove each star chart, log it in, and set it to one side. He had the first box done in record time. A second tech brought over a second box for him.

Genesis felt her tension easing, as each chart was cared for. She didn't know how long she stood here, but she watched as each box was opened and as every chart went through the same process. When finished, each box was carefully repackaged and carried to a set of empty shelves in the climate-controlled vault, where they'd be joined by the others she still had in the cottage.

Hours passed.

"Granny, I sure hope this is okay with you." She chewed on her lower lip, as she worried through the problem. She wanted to do what was right. At least now Granny's legacy could be preserved and her name cleared of all the mockery that had risen to the surface, when her stargazing had been mentioned before.

Her stomach grumbled. She couldn't remember the last time she'd eaten. Her emotions had been too off the wall all morning, and now it had to be well into the afternoon. The muffins and sandwiches were a long time ago.

Hopefully the meeting with Matt would include food.

She walked into the large meeting hall to find Connor and Matt involved in heavy-looking discussions with several strangers. Then she caught sight of their faces. The men from her shop. The Portmans, father and son, and apparently an older Portman as well.

Instinctively she hesitated just inside the room, not liking the look of the men. But, at that moment, Connor saw her, his smile breaking out wide and happy. He stood and motioned for her to join them.

As she walked toward him, the conversation stopped abruptly, as the others turned to stare at her. Or maybe *glare* was a better word. They weren't hostile, but they obviously weren't happy at the interruption either. Well, she hadn't asked to be here. She'd come to protect her heritage.

She glared back.

Matt introduced her, his voice full of humor. "Gentlemen, this is Genesis, and it is because of her that we now have several boxes of star charts in our vaults."

"And she's the one who brought the rock back?" asked the oldest of the three men—the one she didn't know—his white hair and beard waving gently with the movement of his mouth and jaw. His tone sounded doubtful, as if he believed she were too young to have done that.

"Indeed, she is," Matt said, a smile playing at the corner of his mouth. "I was there with her, when she found it."

The youngest of the strangers narrowed his gaze at her. She gazed blandly back.

Genesis tried to study the men covertly, as Matt related the story of the stone. She was starving and was desperately in need of coffee, when someone in a waiter's uniform walked over and offered her a hot cup. She smiled and accepted. The local coffee was thick, like chocolate, and demanded cream or sugar to make it palatable. What it did have in common with the original stuff was its heady addictive properties.

There was a heavy silence, as she doctored her coffee, then took her first sip. She glanced from one to the other, keeping her gaze neutral. "Sorry, did I interrupt something?"

"No," Connor interjected quickly. "We've been waiting for you."

"Are you satisfied that the star charts will be safe here?" Matt asked, with a gentle smile.

Safe? She pondered that word, then decided honesty was the best option. "I'm satisfied that they've been logged in and will be respected here."

"You can also stay here to keep an eye on things," Matt suggested.

He opened his mouth to add something, when a man hurriedly approached from the doorway. He reached Matt and bent to whisper into his ear. Matt's face shuttered, and he motioned to Connor and said, as he stood, "If you will excuse the two of us for a few moments."

She nodded, her gaze following the two men.

"The experts are excited to see these artifacts," the old man said. "They are rare."

For the first time, one of the two younger men spoke up. "Stargazers have always been of the people, for the people. Your grandmother's work should be available for everyone."

His voice instantly set off her nerves. His words immediately set off her inner alarms.

"I'm sorry you feel that way," she said very, very softly. "I presume you are someone who treated my granny as if she were a leper. I suggest you don't go down that road again."

He leaned forward, his gaze harder than rock. "And if I do?"

She leaned forward, her hackles rising. "Then, as far as I am concerned, the star charts were better off back in my cottage."

The smile that stole across his face sent ice through her veins. "Now, isn't that too bad? Nothing that comes here ever leaves, and now that we know there are more available, you can be sure we'll go to the courts to force you to hand them over."

CONNOR STRODE QUICKLY behind Matt, trying to keep up with him. What the hell had happened this time? He hated to leave Genesis alone right now. She had no idea who those men were. Not that he knew much, but Matt and those men had been arguing steadily before her arrival.

The Portmans were men of power—and secrecy. They had little give in them. The oldest was just called Portman. His son was Portman Senior and the young upstart of a grandson was Portman Junior.

But Connor still didn't understand their role here.

And Genesis would have no idea of the power plays going on. She wouldn't like them if she did. She had no patience for politics. He remembered her granny had been the same. He'd never really known her. Now that Connor was back with Genesis, he wished he'd had the chance and had taken the time while Granny was still alive.

Now, as with so many things in his life, hindsight was wonderful. He forced his thoughts back to the present. He needed some answers. "Matt, what's going on?"

"It looks like Grandfather has heard that you are here."

Connor's footsteps faltered. Damn. How had that happened so fast? "I'll need to talk to him privately."

"This is Grandfather we're talking about. He doesn't do anything privately."

Sure enough, the sound of shouting and raised voices reached them from the end of the hallway. Damn it. Why could nothing be easy?

"You ready for this?" Matt asked quietly. "He won't take you quitting—or jumping ship, as he'll say—easily."

"No, he won't." And he had good reason. "He brought me out here to do a job."

"And have you done it?"

Connor gave Matt a hard look. "It's in progress."

Matt studied him carefully, then nodded. "How long do you need to wrap it up?"

"It's overlapping yours now, and a personal problem has

just stepped up into priority."

"Genesis?"

"Partially."

They reached the doorway to the meeting room and stood, waiting for the noise to die down.

Instead Grandfather caught sight of Matt and started toward them, but then his gaze landed on Connor, and he veered slightly off course in line with his new target. From the raging emotions creasing his features, Connor knew he was about to get blasted.

He braced himself. "Hello, Grandfather. What's the problem?"

He felt more than heard Matt's snicker.

Grandfather came to a complete stop. For all his size and his lion's mane of pure white hair, he appeared to be at a loss for words. Connor's question had taken the stuffing out of him.

"What are you doing here?" Grandfather asked abruptly.

"It's personal," Connor said quietly.

"Ha. You're on my payroll while you're here. There's no personal time on my watch."

"I have a lot of time coming. I took some."

Grandfather shook his head, as if gearing up for a shouting match, when Matt intervened.

"He was attacked. Twice. He's been recuperating. You might want to consider that you sent your man out on a dangerous mission alone. He had no backup and no way to get help, when he ran into trouble."

"What?" Grandfather roared. "What do you mean, you were attacked? By whom? When? Why didn't you tell me?"

"Because he's not back to normal yet," Matt said, his voice full of exasperation. "Now, can we tone down the damn yelling, please?" He strode into the conference-style room, all in dark mahogany and austere trimmings, and pointed to the set of chairs at the table. "And how about sitting down to discuss this like normal people instead?"

Connor immediately pretended to look like he had a roaring headache—which didn't take much acting, as one had started building the minute he had heard Grandfather was here. That man wasn't given to patience or understanding. He was all about power and taking what he wanted. Life was for the strong, according to him. The weak were the ones who were used—and used up—in the process. That was where they belonged—under his feet. Connor was ashamed to admit that it had been easy to ignore Grandfather's supposed underhanded practices while Connor worked out of town and remained involved in work he loved. Now however …

With the loss of his senses, he'd had a chance to reevaluate many things in life. If Grandfather had known, Connor would have been assigned a desk job.

Or fired.

Instantly.

"Connor, explain why you came here and didn't report in."

It didn't take long. Connor gave him a brief explanation of his two attacks at the caves, and Genesis finding him and bringing him to safety each time.

And he watched as the old man's face revealed just how little Grandfather liked that bit of news.

CHAPTER 26

NOT LONG AFTER that unpleasantness, Genesis sat motionless on the edge of the bed she'd shared last night with Connor in the Center, thinking over and over about her earlier conversation with the Portmans. Her mind flitted from option to option to option, as she tried to calm the panic firing inside her.

She had to leave the Center. Now. Before dark. The only question was how. Besides the fact that her nerves were shot, her stomach now knotted in fear, and her breathing so agitated it was hard to gulp enough air to function, she knew she wasn't safe here. What she didn't know was if the star charts were either. She wanted them to be. They were a huge burden on her and her sisters, and, since her two sisters weren't here, the star charts were a weight Genesis carried alone.

But she didn't have to. She could take them back home and keep them hidden.

She chewed on her bottom lip. But could she? Would she be allowed to remove them? Or was it a case of *they were here now, and here they would stay*, as the youngest Portman had said?

She held out her hand and looked at it, hating the fine tremor that slid through her fingers. There was another solution. Not only did she need to go to her shop tomorrow, having missed two days of being open, but she could pull another trick Granny had taught her. And, until she had the assurances she needed, she could make sure the star charts would be safe too. Maybe. It was the best she could do. The boxes were in a sealed chamber. Everyone would be working from the images now. So if Granny's trick worked, Genesis might pull this off. At least, long enough to make sure she'd made the right decision.

The three men downstairs? Now they'd been scary. And damn if she wasn't still afraid of them.

A gentle knock sounded on her door.

She got up and walked over.

A steward stood there. "Connor said to tell you that he would be a couple more hours yet. However, if you care to come down for dinner, he'll join you as soon as he can."

She smiled. "Thank you for delivering the message. Is there any way I could get a ride to my store? My vehicle is there," she said, forcing a sheepish-looking grin, "and I'd like to go there and take care of a few things."

"I can arrange for a ride. Do you wish to go now or after your dinner?"

She pretended to give it a moment's thought, but inside her mind was screaming, *Go now. Get out while you can.*

"Now would be better. Maybe Connor will be done by the time I get back."

"Good enough. Say five minutes at the front door?"

"Perfect."

She closed the bedroom door and quickly collected her belongings. With a final glance around the room, she walked down the hall to the elevator. She stopped and considered, then, following her gut, she bolted down the stairs. She couldn't help feeling that time was running out. She needed to make good on her escape, or, like her star charts, she might not manage to leave this place—ever.

The car was waiting, as promised. She didn't know the young driver, but, when she gave him the address of her shop, he nodded, as if he knew where it was.

Good thing. Still feeling very panicked, she knew she would have had a hard time giving him directions. She didn't like the games of men and power.

She was of energy and light ... and was so out of her element here. She no longer knew who was good or who was bad. All she knew was that she felt threatened at the most basic level. And, like any hurt or injured animal, she wanted to hide away in her home.

The drive took forever. She sat in the back seat, her fists clenched, her thoughts in turmoil, even as she kept her face schooled with detached interest.

For the millionth time, she wondered if she should try to find her sisters and to ask for their help.

Granny would say they all had trials to go through, and they would all be different from each other. The best course of action was to go through them alone and to learn from the experience, rather than sharing it and not reaping the full benefits. Depending on someone else to help and then not learning what was required to get through these times on their own wouldn't help a person grow.

How Genesis missed that old woman. Her gems of advice had been what had kept Genesis sane this last year. She wished her sisters had had the same comfort, but she doubted it. The four women had fiery temperaments, with Genesis being the softest and easiest to get along with.

However, being alone and gentle right now wasn't a good thing. She'd rather have some of Tori's backbone or

Celeste's courage.

Genesis felt very small and rather insignificant.

The driver pulled the car to a stop in front of her shop.

She thanked him and hopped out. She quickly unlocked the shop and stepped inside, immediately securing the door behind her. Peering through the window, she watched the Council's car disappear down the road.

Flicking the lights on, she turned and gave a strangled shriek.

Her shop was in shambles.

Again.

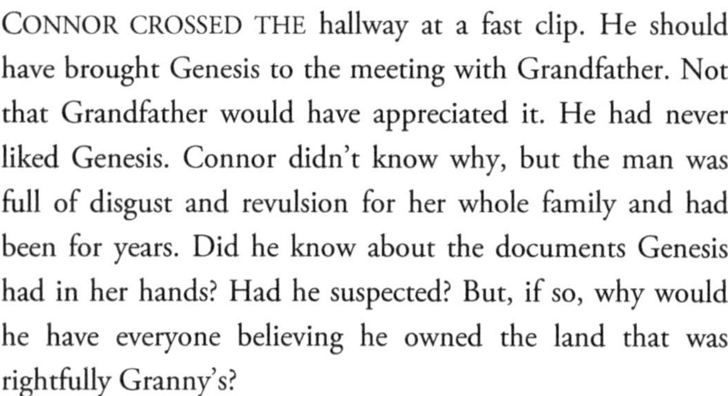

CONNOR CROSSED THE hallway at a fast clip. He should have brought Genesis to the meeting with Grandfather. Not that Grandfather would have appreciated it. He had never liked Genesis. Connor didn't know why, but the man was full of disgust and revulsion for her whole family and had been for years. Did he know about the documents Genesis had in her hands? Had he suspected? But, if so, why would he have everyone believing he owned the land that was rightfully Granny's?

Now they were all about to find out that Granny really was a stargazer, not to mention the largest landowner in the entire town. Connor couldn't help but wonder how their perception of her would change.

Would it darken? After all, they were guilty of some harsh judgments, and no one liked to have their behavior turned on them.

Connor's mind continued to whirl with all these thoughts when he walked into the dining room, looking for Genesis.

The room was empty.

What?

He spun, searching the small casual conversation corners around the massive room, hoping Genesis was tucked away in one of them, having coffee and waiting for him. He'd sent a message to her earlier, not expecting that he'd be so long. But Grandfather refused to be appeased.

He also wanted Connor back on the job. Now.

Connor winced at the memory. He'd managed to push Grandfather back for a few hours, got him to agree to a meeting later tonight.

He hadn't liked that either. Grandfather had already been gone for ten minutes, but it would take ten hours for the impact of his presence to diminish. It was one of the reasons why Connor had been happy when his job wasn't local. He was frequently out of town and didn't have to work closely with Grandfather or the family. Connor was related, but it was distant.

And how did he reconcile that with what he was learning about Genesis's heritage?

But first, he had to find her.

Damn, that woman could disappear in the blink of an eye.

CHAPTER 27

GENESIS STARED AT the wreckage of her shop. The last break-in had the look of some punk kids, showing how tough they were in front of their friends. Things had been broken but not many, and there was no serious damage.

This was different.

That mess had been disturbing and the invasion more so; this, however, was much uglier than that. Not one shelf still stood on the wall. A bowl of herbs lay shattered on the ground. The small packets she'd been busily creating before now lay on the floor, crushed under heavy boot treads through the small space.

The overwhelming scent of all the different crushed herbs assaulted her nostrils.

This was an act filled with anger. Violence. Hatred.

She shook her head, her fist pressed against her mouth, as she tried to hold back the sobs. Who could have done this?

What had she ever done to deserve such treatment?

From where she was, the cash register seemed still closed. Had the intruder even opened it? She didn't keep much in the way of money here.

Such ugliness filled this atmosphere. As if someone had been looking for something, and they hadn't found it. As a result, they'd taken their rage out on her shop.

The thought terrified her. To what lengths would these people go to in their search? Genesis decided that it was too late in the day to start cleaning up, and frankly she felt too violated right now to even consider it. She would just lock up and go to her apartment for the night and face the chaos in the morning.

And then the thought struck her. What if her apartment had been searched too? She kept the place for the days when she was in town, as it was convenient for work. If she'd been targeted, her shop singled out, then she had to assume the vandals knew about her home a block away too.

She picked her way through the shop to the back door, noting that the dried herbs hanging from the ceiling in the back were undisturbed. She should be grateful for that much. She could repackage herbs without too much effort, but finding them, picking them, and drying them took time. And it wasn't always possible to find the supplies she needed.

After trying to lock the back door and realizing it was broken, she made her way to her apartment. She stood hesitantly outside, looking up at the staircase and the entry door to her top-floor apartment, until she felt a warm hand slide into hers. "Remi, where have you been? I've been looking all over for you."

He chattered at her side. She picked him up and hugged him tight. He protested immediately, and she released him, with a laugh. "Sorry, I was worried about you."

She put one foot on the step leading to her apartment when Remi grabbed her hand and pulled her back. "Remi," she whispered. "What's the matter?"

He chattered at her angrily, tugging her farther back. She stared at her darkened home and wondered. Was something in there?

Or someone?

Remi chattered loudly again.

She sighed. "And what do you want me do then? I'm tired. I'd like to go home."

More insistent vocalizing came.

"Okay," she said, turning away. "You win."

Still a little daylight remained but not enough to make the street feel bright and normal. With the clouds moving in and the sun setting, a chill was in the air, even though the day had been hot and summery.

Remi's grip on her hand tightened, and he pushed her backward with an urgency that unnerved her. She moved from the open to the shadows beside a big truck and watched him.

That wasn't quite good enough for Remi. He chattered at her side and urged her to go around the side of the truck.

Hearing the panic in his voice, she slipped willingly around the vehicle. Now she couldn't be seen from her apartment or from the rest of the homes in the building. She peered through the driver's window to see if anything was going on.

The door to her apartment opened.

And damn if that young Portman from Matt's Council didn't walk out. She had no way to record his stealthy movements. Some people had imagers that they carried in a pocket, but she'd never had the money for such a thing.

What was he up to?

CONNOR STARED AT the steward. "She asked for a car?"

The steward nodded. "And our driver delivered her to her shop."

"But that's on the other side of town." He ran his fingers through his hair. "And you haven't heard from her since?"

The steward shook his head. "No. She said she hoped you'd be done by the time she got back."

Connor thanked him and turned.

Matt strode toward him. "We've got a problem."

"No," Connor snapped. "We have two problems."

Matt stopped. "You first."

"Genesis left. And she hasn't come back." He quickly relayed what the steward had told him.

Matt shook his head. "She's probably fine."

"*Probably* isn't good enough." Connor took a deep breath, willing his nerves to settle down. She'd just gone to her shop. Of course she had. He'd thrown her life into disarray these last few days. But inside, he couldn't calm the feeling that something was wrong.

"The star charts are gone."

Matt's tone, so deep, so dark, stunned Connor so much that he couldn't do anything but stare at him. Finally he found his voice. "That's not possible."

"It's not *supposed* to be possible," he corrected.

Connor spun, a dark stabbing sensation in his gut. "I'm going after Genesis. You find those damn star charts."

"Did you see the Portmans? They were with Genesis, and now I can't find any of them."

"I haven't seen them since we left the table either. Ask the steward," Connor called back, already rushing through the front door and heading for the rental car Matt had brought back from the caves for him.

The skies had turned dusky. Damn it. Why the hell had she left? She'd been safe here. But he and Matt had left her alone with the Portmans.

Would she have left because of them? Perhaps something they'd said or done?

As Connor reached the outskirts of town, another thought crossed his mind. Maybe she was feeling claustrophobic with all of them around her. Maybe she just wanted her independence back.

Something she was used to having.

He pulled up in front of the store and peered out the windshield. The lights were off, and the place looked deserted. Still … he got out and walked around the car to peer in the window. It took him a moment for his brain to process what he was seeing.

Her place had been trashed.

His blood froze. He reached for the front door and found it locked. If someone had broken in, then it should be unlocked. Unless she'd found it this way and had locked it again and had walked away. Several other small shops were in the same block. He walked past those storefronts, noting that they appeared to be undisturbed. He headed to the rear of the building, grateful his limited senses weren't picking up any traces of violence in the dark alleyway.

He tried the back door to her shop and found it unlocked. He pushed the door open. "Genesis?" The room was dark and silent. He flicked on the lights and grimly searched the premises for her. His instincts said she'd seen the damage and, despondent, had gone home.

He loped off in that direction, leaving his car behind.

She couldn't have gone far. That she might have gone to the cottage was something he didn't want to think about.

He would never find it, if that were the case. Worse, he would never find her.

CHAPTER 28

THE DUSKY NIGHT turned to jet-black, as clouds scudded across the sky to hide the moon. Now Genesis could see nothing. And that made the situation so much worse. She was hidden behind the truck, but she had no way of seeing her intruder or making sure he wasn't coming right at her. Running footsteps grew louder. She dropped to the ground and held her breath.

The footsteps raced past her. She popped up to look through the window. She couldn't see the intruder anymore, but now someone else was running up the stairs to her apartment. The man who'd just passed her. Was he meeting the other guy?

She waited. He knocked on the door. She bit her lip, not wanting to answer, not until she knew who this new person was.

After a long moment, the stranger pounded on the door again. Then he called out, "Genesis? Are you in there?"

Connor.

She breathed out a sigh of relief. Genesis stepped out in front of the truck and almost walked into another man. The darkness was so complete it was hard to see, but then the clouds parted and she saw him.

It was the intruder. Portman Junior.

She shrieked and bolted backward out of his reach.

"Connor, I'm down here."

"What?"

The sound of footsteps crashing down the stairs reached her as she kept backing up from Portman. "What were you doing in my apartment?" she demanded. "And did you break in and trash my store?"

"What are you talking about?" he snarled. "Stupid bitch." He stepped toward her, his hands still at his sides, a furious look in his eyes.

Connor barreled toward her. She took one look and threw herself into his arms. "It was him. He was in my apartment," she babbled, pointing to Portman. "I think he broke into my store too."

Connor stared at the man standing arrogantly in front of them both. "Were you in her apartment?" he asked incredulously.

"Don't be stupid. She's obviously mistaken me for someone else."

"Ha, the moon was out when I watched you climb down those stairs," she snapped, her own anger back now that she wasn't facing him alone. "What were you looking for?" Her voice rose. "And why did you trash my shop?"

He snorted. "I did nothing to your shop. I wondered who you'd pissed off this time and why they would do something so petty. If it were me, I would have burned the place to the ground." He gave them a mocking salute and walked to the other side of the truck. She watched as Portman climbed into an older-model Tortja. He was a wannabe rich person; he just hadn't quite made it there.

Then again, he was third in line for the family business.

With gravel spitting out from under his tires, he took off with the same arrogance he'd shown in their conversation.

As soon as he was out of sight, she turned to Connor. "Who are those people?" She cast a long look around and asked, "And why was he in my apartment?"

"I have no idea. They are from Big Glory. They run the Paranormal Center there, as Matt does here."

"Why would he break into my apartment?" she repeated. "I don't have anything."

"Well, in fact, you do," Connor said. "And it's quite possible that, even with our repeated warnings, word has gotten out already about the star charts and the other documents we imaged. If they were looking for the originals …"

"And, since they aren't at the shop or at my apartment, they will keep looking." Glumly she studied Connor's face, cast in shadows. "I should never have showed anyone."

"You had to, remember? With that construction going on in the pools."

She groaned. "Damn. You're right." But now what would she do? She wasn't safe anywhere.

"Come on. Let's get you back to the Center."

She shook her head. "No," she said sadly. "It's not safe there."

"Why not?" He looked at her, puzzled.

She snorted. "That's where the Portmans were." She quickly recounted the tense conversation she'd had with them. A thought struck her. "I'll bet they searched our room there as well."

Connor shook his head. "Not likely. The Center has good security." He paused and frowned in thought. "I doubt that extends to the many bedrooms though."

He led her toward her apartment. "Let's check to see if everything is still there."

"It should be. I've never kept anything important here, remember? And, besides, his hands were empty when he left the apartment."

"And you're sure it was him?"

"Yes. I watched him come out."

They reached the bottom of the stairs and started up. At the top, she turned the knob. The door opened easily. She flicked the light on and gasped.

The place had been destroyed. Even more thoroughly than her store.

She stood immobile, tears in her eyes. Connor wrapped his arms around her shoulders and tugged her against his chest. They stood, staring at the ripped cushions, overturned table and chairs, now-empty bookshelves, and dumped kitchen drawers. The carnage was everywhere.

Finally she whispered, "This is so much worse than before."

She felt him stiffen. "Before?" he repeated in a carefully contained voice. "What do you mean by before?"

"There have been several break-ins this last year," she admitted softly. "Both here and at the shop."

"Did you tell anyone?" he asked.

"Of course I did. The first time. Yet the cops didn't seem too bothered. I could never prove that anything was stolen. It was 'the weird herb store owned by that weird granddaughter of the crazy lady,'" she quoted. "No one ever really cared."

"Was anything ever taken?"

She shook her head. "Not that I could ever find." She motioned to the destroyed living room. "But it was nothing compared to this."

"This says fear to me," Connor said. "Someone is afraid

of you. Of what you might know. Of what you might own. And, if you didn't know about your ownership of the land, as most would assume, since you haven't come forward before this, the way would be free and clear for someone else to provide their own proof."

"Proof?" She snorted in disgust. "You mean, *fabrications. More lies.*"

"Exactly."

CONNOR PULLED GENESIS tighter into his arms. He couldn't shake the feeling that this had been a narrow escape. What if she'd already been in the apartment when the intruder arrived?

And was it Portman Junior who'd trashed the place? It made no sense if it was. Although he could have done a quick search and left. But why? Plus it would have taken time to create this much havoc.

"We can't stay here for the night." He led her back outside. "Let's go back to the Center."

She stopped. "Why is that any safer than here?"

He looked down at her. "Don't you trust Matt?"

She was quiet for a moment. Apparently that wasn't an easy answer to give. In a slow voice, she said, "I trust Matt, but I don't trust his specialists, and I absolutely don't trust the Portmans."

"After everything that's happened, that's understandable." He didn't know whether or not he should tell her about the star charts. He knew Matt was working to find out what had happened also, and she would never let any more out of her sight if she knew. Hoping Matt would solve the problem fast, Connor kept quiet.

Connor felt a tug on Genesis's shirt hem.

She glanced down. "It's been a long day, hasn't it, Remi?" She glanced toward the kitchen. "Remi wants his treats."

"How can you tell?" Connor asked curiously.

She froze.

And he knew he'd blown it. He cursed silently and said apologetically, "He's not visible all the time."

"He's not invisible to me anytime," she said, her temper starting to show on her face. "That you can't see him any longer is very concerning."

"I saw him once," he rushed to say.

She searched his gaze intently, then turned away from him.

Shit.

CHAPTER 29

GENESIS HATED TO walk into the Center again, but, with her apartment in shambles and her store in the same condition, she didn't want to make any move toward the cottage—in case she was being observed. She trusted Connor, but the fact that he could no longer see Remi, and Remi refused to show himself to Connor, said volumes about the relationship between them.

She also didn't like the things going on at the Center. But the cold, hard truth of the matter was that her choices were limited. Tired and dispirited, she followed Connor inside the building.

And found a highly agitated Matt waiting for them. The two men greeted each other, while she sidled past, heading for the same room they'd stayed in last time, when she realized she didn't want to be in the same room. She wanted some space.

"Genesis, a meal will be served in five minutes."

So much for sneaking past unnoticed. She paused. Damn, she really needed food. Without saying a word, she changed directions and headed for the dining room. She heard muted voices continue behind her, but she was too tired to care.

Until she heard the words *missing* and *star charts* in the same sentence. Her footsteps slowed, and she closed her eyes.

Shit.

She opened her mouth, ready to turn to the men and say something about what she'd done, but the hot sting of tears threatened, and she didn't dare trust her emotions after the day she'd had. So she took her seat and stayed quiet, not wanting to explain. For now. As soon as she sat down, a hot bowl of fettle soup was placed in front of her.

Her stomach growled. She dug in, without waiting for the men to be seated. This was no time for proper manners.

And then Remi's paw landed on her thigh.

She dropped her spoon and sat back, feeling even worse somehow. "I'm sorry, Remi."

"Don't be," Matt said. "I'll have something brought for him."

The power of money and position had Remi soon served greens and treats. She watched as Darbo slid to the table and was served a small plate himself.

In spite of herself, she smiled.

"Now I think that's the first smile I've seen on your face all day," Matt said gently.

"It's been a crappy day."

"Tell me about it."

She shook her head. "Connor can. I'm too busy eating."

With only half her attention on the food, she listened to Connor fill Matt in on the vandalism and damage to both her apartment and the shop.

"I'll have it taken care of," Matt said, anger in his voice. "I will also speak to Portman Junior."

"That won't do any good," she said, with a small sneer. "He'll deny everything."

"Yet you are positive that he came out of your apartment?"

She nodded. "He did, didn't he, Remi?"

Remi chattered, his words directed at Darbo. Darbo replied by making odd singsong sounds. Matt frowned, his attention on Darbo. It was the way of the animals and their human partners. There was an understanding between them that circumvented language.

"Good enough," Matt said.

She hid a smile. How amusing to think the director of the Paranormal Center would believe her statement because her plumer had backed up her story.

Instantly she felt better. She slid her gaze sideways to see what Connor was thinking and watched his jaw working. He kept his gaze on the table setting in front of him. Disbelief and … sadness were written all over his face, and she could do nothing to help him. It was hard to watch. He said he'd seen Remi, but now he couldn't. Was it the energy of the pools that had helped? His abilities had certainly strengthened again with the healing energy.

She didn't know.

The thought of the pools sent pangs of homesickness invading her soul.

She needed her pools tonight, more so than she had in a long time. She was hurting something awful inside. And that was something that most healing pools did a better job in fixing than doctors.

But it was too far to travel tonight. And she couldn't risk being watched or followed.

AFTER DINNER, CONNOR excused himself. It was time to go see Grandfather. "I need to talk to him."

"Unfinished business?" Genesis asked.

He nodded. "This is something I have to do alone." He glanced over at Matt.

Matt shrugged. "It needs to be done."

"I'll be back in an hour or so." He looked at Genesis, wondering at her particular silence, at her absent gaze, at the spacing of her chair from his. She seemed distant. He wanted her to be with him, but this wasn't the time. This wasn't the moment. He had to leave. There'd be time for explanations and discussions later.

He nodded goodbye to Matt and headed to the front door. Surely she'd be waiting here for him when he came back. At the door, he paused and turned around to look at her. She sat motionless at the table, her head bent. Defeated.

He strode back quickly, tugged her chair backward, and hauled her up and into his arms.

And proceeded to kiss her. Hard.

After her initial shock, she responded. Not with the passion he'd hoped for, but with a gentleness that scared him more than anything he'd felt yet.

"I'll be back as soon as I can. … Whatever is bothering you, we can discuss then." He released her, turned around, and walked out.

Outside, night had settled with a vengeance. Deep, dark, and black. With the cover of darkness came a mess of high winds and a light misting of rain.

Once in the car, he turned the vehicle in the direction of Grandfather's huge estate. As he reached the edge of the property lines, he had to wonder. Did Genesis really own this? It was massive. Little Glory wasn't as big or as prestigious as some of the cities that had popped up around the planet. But, due to Grandfather's position, Big Glory had taken off, and he was the biggest landowner in the community. With that position came power. And more wealth.

Connor had to wonder—how had he made that wealth? He ran many companies by now. Were they legitimate? Or had he pushed the envelope that way as well? Did he know that his claim to the properties was false? What if he had inherited the land from his father? From his grandfather? Maybe he had no idea that it didn't belong to them.

Then Connor considered the old man and the way he wielded power. The ruthlessness. He brooked no resistance. If he did know about Genesis, … what then? Just how ruthless was he? Connor had heard a lot about Grandfather but hadn't seen nasty behavior firsthand. And nothing concrete against Granny or Genesis.

That brought his thoughts back full circle to her.

Had Grandfather had something to do with the vandalism of her store and apartment? Connor frowned. He didn't think so. What would be the point?

But, if Grandfather thought Genesis had proof of what she owned, no way he would stand by and let someone else take away what he considered his—even if it wasn't.

Connor pulled into the long curving driveway and parked at the front steps. The building rose in front of him, austere and pompous but elegant. As an afterthought he added *cold*. That was the one noticeable thing about the place. It oozed money, but there was no warmth to it.

He reached for the knocker only to have the door open under his hand.

Mason, Grandfather's right-hand man, stood there, waiting for him. "He's expecting you."

Connor nodded. "I'm a little late." He followed behind, as Mason led him to Grandfather's office.

Grandfather looked up, piercing blue eyes staring at him

from under heavy brows. "About time you got here."

Determined to not be cowed by a man who crushed others so easily, Connor took a seat across from him. "It was a late kind of day."

"Now tell me again, what the hell is going on?"

Considering that Grandfather was paying his salary and mindful of Connor's position and upcoming change, Connor launched into a repeat of his earlier report.

"And you have no idea who hit you the first time or who downed you the second time?"

As much as he hated to say so, Connor said, "No. I don't."

"Did the pools mess up your senses or something? How is it someone got the drop on you two times?"

Grandfather's question was probing. Typical.

Connor shrugged, as if unconcerned. The last thing he wanted was for Grandfather to know how unstable his abilities were. And, if Connor didn't fully understand the situation himself, how could he explain it to someone else?

"I'm hearing rumors. Slight noises that you are having some difficulties with your abilities."

Connor's eyebrows shot up. "Really? From whom?" he demanded.

"It doesn't matter. The question is, are you?"

"Not as much now as I was," Connor said honestly. "They were bothering me before but appear to be improving slightly."

"What caused the problem?"

"No idea."

Grandfather glared at him. "I can't use an investigator if his senses aren't up to par."

That was a perfect opening.

Connor nodded. "Understood. So this is as good a time as any to tell you that I'm giving you my notice." He smiled at the shock on Grandfather's face. No one quit the family business. Grandfather might fire someone, but they didn't quit.

It was a power thing.

"And, no, I don't know what I'll do at this point," he added, smoothly forestalling Grandfather's ire that was threatening to blow. "I am, however, going to spend some time with Genesis and figure out just what I do want to do." He stood. "To that end, I'll say good night."

While Grandfather was still frozen in shock, Connor walked out of the room.

And right out of the house.

As soon as he stood out in the open air, he realized how much freer he felt. He hadn't realized it before now, but being with Grandfather had felt like his only choice. It wasn't that there weren't plenty of jobs available, there just weren't many in his field.

"I wouldn't go back to her, if I were you." Mason's voice came out of the darkness behind him.

The hairs on the back of his neck stirred. Connor turned slowly. "Why not?"

"She's the one responsible for your diminished senses. I'm surprised you never put it together. They've been on the decline since you left her a year ago. Now that you're back in her clutches, they are strong again—at least as strong as she wants you to be—but not so strong that you're back to being normal."

Mason tapped his pipe on the railing, knocking out the used tobacco inside, and then turned and disappeared back into the house.

Connor stood in shocked silence, his mind racing.

Mason was many things. But, in this instance, the timing of everything was exactly as he'd said.

Had Genesis really been responsible for Connor's so-very-personal loss?

His heart broke slightly, as he contemplated such a betrayal. His heart said it wasn't possible. But logic demanded he consider the possibility.

He didn't want to think that she would do that. But she had been upset back then. Angry even. Women who'd been scorned were often wild cards.

Could she have done this unintentionally? Unknowingly? Done something on a subconscious level? By the same reasoning, could someone else have done this to her?

There was no doubt that he started having trouble after their breakup, although it had been slow to manifest. Or had he just been so disbelieving of a problem even existing that he'd refused to acknowledge it until it became too big to ignore?

The same way he couldn't ignore the puzzle pieces now as they snapped into place—thanks to Mason.

CHAPTER 30

GENESIS WALKED UP to her room. Matt had excused himself earlier, once he'd made sure she was fine. She'd smiled and insisted she was. As soon as he'd left the dining area, she finished her cup of coffee, refilled it, and carried it up to her room, Remi at her side. Only she didn't want it to be her room.

She entered and stood just inside the door. It felt wrong now. She had no logical reason for it to be that way, just that things had changed, and it no longer felt *right*.

Was it possible the room had been searched? It felt different.

She returned to the hallway and glanced in both directions. Many rooms were here. She had yet to see anyone else come or go. She walked to the closest room and knocked. There was no answer. She turned the knob and realized it was locked. After a quick look both ways down the hallway, she zapped a little energy and smiled when the lock clicked open in her hand.

She opened the door and found it to be an identical room to hers. She contemplated the ramifications for a long moment and then put her coffee on the night table. As she didn't have any belongings with her other than her bag, the move was simple. In the new room, she showered and crawled into bed. She didn't have a ready explanation for

Connor, but maybe, given the lateness of the hour, he wouldn't ask for one.

She turned out the light and, within moments, dropped into a deep sleep.

Hours later, she woke in a panic. Something was wrong. She leaned up on her elbow. There was an unsettling disquiet to her room.

"Remi?" Her voice sounded fragile and small in the darkness.

No answer. She bolted upright and searched the room. She couldn't see anything, but a painful unease rippled through her. She didn't know why his absence was so upsetting. Remi took off on a regular basis, sometimes for hours. He wasn't physically attached to her, and he often left her alone.

But this? … This didn't feel normal.

She ran to the window. The curtain blew toward her as she approached. Her heart thudded in her chest. She hadn't left the window open, had she?

She tugged the sheers out of the way and peered out into the night. The moon was nonexistent, and only shadows moved.

Then she heard the sound of murmured voices. "We can't leave her here."

"Why not?" demanded a second voice. "How else are we going to get the rest of those damn documents? At least if she's here, she won't know we're looking for them."

"Who would have thought she could produce those at this late time?"

"Grandfather must be ready to commit murder right now."

"Well, we are, so he'll be as well."

"We have to find the documents before he does."

"Why don't we just make new ones, forcing her to 'sell' the land to us?"

Genesis couldn't identify the voices, although the gist of what they intended to do was enough to make her blood run cold.

"She won't willingly. And, if she disappears or turns up dead on the heels of allowing the documents to be imaged today, it'll be obvious what's happened."

"That won't matter if she's not here to do or to say anything about it."

"No, but all the suspicion will shine on us. We want to make sure it shines on Grandfather."

After a loud snort, the voices started to drift away. She strained to hear the last bit.

"What you're forgetting is that Grandfather will make his own plans."

"And who do you think he'll blame, given what has happened these last few days? I'd say Connor is the one with the target on his back."

Genesis choked back a gasp. Her stomach knotted. Why Connor? He was part of Grandfather's family.

What had she missed? She squeezed her hands together against her chest and bowed her head. She knew she should never have come forward. The argument carried on in her head.

But how could you not?

Granny should have done this.

She wasn't strong enough. Besides, she was protecting you.

Now what was Genesis to do? She wanted her sisters here to help. But, if they were here, what difference would it make?

She slumped on the side of her bed and realized it wouldn't make any difference at all. She was here. It was her job to protect the forest and their heritage.

She didn't know what was going on with Connor, but it felt like shades of last time. He was involved in the relationship, but not on the same level she was. She knew that was the likely scenario going into this, but the reality she faced wasn't one she had hoped for.

And she didn't like it.

Those men, whoever they were, were hunting for her documents. That meant she had to double her efforts to make sure they didn't find them.

But knowing of their plans gave her a slight advantage. It meant she could actually catch them in the act.

But the big question now was, who could be counted on to help her? And who would not be safe to mention this to? It would be impossible to stay here and to keep her actions from Connor. Regardless of where their relationship was heading, he would know something was wrong.

How could he not?

And Matt? She wanted to trust him, but did she? She wanted to trust Darbo, but did she?

The answer to those questions came from deep inside. Yes. That much she did. By extension, then, she trusted Matt. Maybe not to take her side but at least to do what was right.

And Connor. No. Not the same. She trusted him not to hurt her, but there was no doubt something wasn't quite right here. His abilities coming and going. His supposed ability to see Remi, then not again. He'd gone to Grandfather tonight. She could hope Connor was quitting his job and going to work for Matt. Then doubts assailed her if that would be better or worse.

Staying at the Center was no longer an option if every-thing she owned was in danger. She'd done what she could to protect her cottage, but other people were out there with abilities. What if someone could find her secret sanctuary?

Then what would she do? She glanced out the window and realized that the sky was a shade lighter than it had been. Her uneasiness grew. She glanced around the room. "Remi?"

Closing her eyes, she reached out for him mentally and realized she couldn't sense him. There was a dullness to their link. One that scared the crap out of her.

She had her own wheels now, after driving here ahead of Connor. So she could leave at any time.

And she couldn't get rid of the feeling that anytime meant *now*.

CONNOR STOOD IN the shadows behind his bedroom window. His, not theirs. She'd moved out. He'd almost panicked, until he met the steward, who'd informed him that Genesis had moved into the room beside him. He understood she'd considered that the room had been searched earlier, but that didn't explain what changing rooms would do. If the intruder had searched one room, they could just as easily search a second room.

And she'd moved out, but she hadn't moved his belong-ings with hers.

As a message, it was pretty clear.

That he had mixed feelings about her actions said much for his state of mind. The stuff Mason had said? ... Was it even possible? He'd been searching his mind for another explanation and so far hadn't come up with one.

But he was good at puzzles. He'd get to the bottom of this one too.

Movement outside his window caught his eye, and he watched several men move through the parking lot.

An awful lot of activity was going on for the middle of the night. He wasn't close enough to hear the conversation, but several men got into a vehicle and drove off, while Connor watched.

Faint rustling noises from the other room told him that Genesis was moving around. He listened carefully, hearing her door open and close. Then her footsteps receded down the hallway. Now where the hell was she going?

He ran back to the window and looked out. Sure enough, a few moments later, she left the building, her bag under her arm. She walked to her car and got in.

Making no attempt to hide his actions, he leaned out the window to watch which direction she turned when she left the parking lot.

She turned left. He would bet anything she was going home. The question was, which one?

And why hadn't she said goodbye?

CHAPTER 31

GENESIS DROVE CAREFULLY in the dark. Her night vision wasn't great, and she didn't want to use her abilities to make it easier. She wasn't recharging well. That could be because of the damaged connection to Remi.

The early morning sun was just rising over the hills by the time she reached the park. No other vehicles around.

Good.

Even now, she couldn't understand her need to run from the Paranormal Center. She should have told someone at the Center that she was leaving. But it had been dark, and the others were sleeping. She would have felt bad if she'd woken them up.

So she'd snuck off. Although it had felt more like she was running away. She didn't like that. But there was nothing saying she couldn't go back. She would check on the cottage, make sure all was well, and then return to catch a few more hours of sleep. She sighed, her hand trembling as she brushed the stray hairs from her forehead. To say she was exhausted would be an understatement. A deep-seated weariness had built over the last year. Now, underneath it all, fear went through her. Where was Remi? She tried to stomp down the panic. It would incapacitate her.

The birds were noticeably silent, as she trudged through the bushes. She missed Remi. She called out to him. She could sense him, a reassurance she badly needed, but not feel him. She whistled a long, low animal-like whistle that she often used.

He didn't come running. But still she had that same sense that he was around but maybe not as close as she'd like him to be. He was alive, but … something was definitely off. At least being able to sense him eased the constriction around her heart.

She reached the caves quickly and slipped inside Granny's entrance. She carefully made her way down the stairs to where she'd found the heavy equipment and where she'd found Connor. The equipment was still here, but the cavern was silent and deserted. Good. Just the way it should be. Better yet, get the equipment the hell away from here.

Except she realized that, while the machinery might be silent now, it had been working all day. The cavern wall had been dug out more on the left, and shards of rock lay on the cavern floor. Anger rushed through her at the ruts in the cavern floor.

This had to stop.

On the spot where she'd found Connor, she realized it would have been hard to creep up on him like that. She knew he'd been handicapped with his senses not functioning properly, but it was the first time she realized just how much danger he'd been in this last year. He was blind in a way that most people wouldn't understand.

She studied the energy around the room, sensing the strongest waves coming from the left. If Connor had been here, had the man just jumped him without saying anything? No doubt Connor had been badly hurt. But had he seen his attacker? Known who it was? Did he remember? Or was it all a dark hole in his brain?

The healing energy of the pools pulled at her. She could collapse in here quite nicely, but she'd also likely sleep and could wake to any number of unpleasant scenarios.

Better she make it to her cottage, where she would be safe. She carried on to the back exit and moved through the brush. The woods were even quieter—if such a thing were possible. It made no sense, but the closer she got to her cottage, the more unsettled she became.

Was someone else out here? Had they found her cottage? Granny said no one could ever find it, but maybe she'd been wrong. More and more abilities had been showing up in each new generation. Who knew what anyone could do nowadays? Genesis had done everything she knew to keep it safe.

But was it enough?

She barely noticed that she'd gone from a fast walk to a jog and was now barreling through the woods at top speed. Instincts drove her. She didn't have Remi with her to find the best way through, so she just beelined in the direction she needed to go.

She broke through the last line of greenery into the clearing where her cottage belonged. Only it wasn't there.

She'd cloaked it, after all.

And neither was she alone.

Portman Junior stood in front of her. He had a grin on his young face that made her blood turn to ice. But it was the look of joy in his eyes that made her feel physically sick.

In his arm, he carried her spirit pet.

An unconscious Remi.

CONNOR DRESSED QUICKLY, ready to leave the Center and chase after Genesis. At the heavy knock on his door, he raced over to find Matt standing in the hallway, anger and a hint of fear on his face.

"Darbo is gone," he said, without prelude.

Connor shook his head. "Does he not go off on his own?"

"Not really. He's connected to my energy. He won't survive on his own for long," Matt said baldly. "The loss will affect my energy and abilities soon afterward."

Connor stared at him. "Really? How soon?"

"I don't know." Matt shrugged. "It's never happened before." He rubbed his temple. "I have to adjust to being slightly off. Disconnected."

"Genesis left."

Matt stared at him, his gaze widening in shock. "Why?"

"I don't know," Connor admitted. "I got back, and she'd moved into a different bedroom." He could feel the muscles in his jaw locking. "I couldn't sleep and was standing by the window an hour ago. I heard noises out-side—a group of people leaving the Center—and then, while I was studying the parking lot, I heard Genesis leave from next door. I watched her get into her car and head toward town." He motioned to his own fully clothed form. "I'm going after her."

Matt's gaze narrowed. "I hate to ask this, as I know it's a sore point, but did you see Remi with her?"

"No," Connor said shortly. "I didn't. Then again, I ha-ven't since that time in the pools."

Matt nodded. "I was afraid of that."

"Why could I see him there and not since?"

"The pool would have amplified your senses."

"Do you think something happened to Remi, like to Darbo, and that's why she bolted?"

"At the very least, I think she's been alone a very long time and has never had anyone to go to when she was in trouble. Her instincts are telling her something is off."

"Her store and apartment have both been trashed. There's nowhere she can go except to the cottage."

"And what if that's exactly what someone is hoping she'll do? She'll lead them right to it."

Shit. Connor closed his eyes briefly. "Damn it. I shouldn't have let her go. Hell, I shouldn't have left her alone last night. I could sense something was wrong but didn't understand it. By the time I got back, she'd already distanced herself."

"With Darbo, Remi, and Genesis gone," Matt said, "I'm very much afraid it's all related to her land ownership documents. Genesis holds the key to it all, so we need to go to the cottage."

"Let's go. We can get there faster in the hovercraft."

Connor was already out the door and halfway down the hallway when he turned back to Matt striding behind him. "Except for one thing. How will we find the cottage?"

CHAPTER 32

GENESIS STARED, AND a scream choked back in her throat. Her mind had stalled, then kicked into overdrive. She didn't know why or what this was about, but given the documents she'd finally brought out, it couldn't be anything else. Then she remembered the break-ins earlier.

"What do you want?" She was proud her voice came out normal.

"Don't play games."

She raised her eyebrows. "Games? This coming from someone who's holding my unconscious pet in a threatening manner?"

"He's not all I have." He gave a hard laugh, reached into his pocket, and pulled out an equally unconscious Darbo.

Oh no! Matt had to be going ballistic. He'd be able to track Darbo, but would he know this was a trap?

"So I repeat. Besides kidnapping pets, what do you want? Are you trying to ransom them?" she asked, stalling for time.

"Like hell." He glared at her. "I'm not a petty criminal."

She shook her head. "Really? So you have nothing to do with the security guard or construction going on here?"

He snorted. "No way."

"Then what do you want?" Waving an arm behind her, she said, "I didn't come without bringing help."

"You're alone," he scoffed. "What do you think I am?"

A fool, but she kept that thought to herself. "How did you find this place?"

The grin that spread across his face was terrifying. "My abilities. It can't find places like your cottage, but it allows me to recognize energy trails, like the paths you and these critters took to get here. So I know it's here, I just can't see it."

"And the animals?" she asked cautiously. "Why bring them?"

"Leverage." And that smile deepened.

She hadn't understood the look in his eyes before, but now she did. It was delight. He was enjoying this. The process. The unconscious animals. Her fear. He had plans, and she expected that inflicting as much pain on her and them was a highlight for him. That he was doing this as a means to the end was one thing, but this guy would enjoy the job. "Who is paying you?"

His eyebrows lifted. "Why would you expect anyone to pay me to do something I'm happy to do?"

Her stomach sank. "Because there's no reason for you to do this unless you are getting something, more than a few hours entertainment from it." She kept her voice smooth, adding, "So—Portman or Grandfather?"

A look of surprise glinted in his eyes, before being quickly masked.

"Or better yet, Portman Senior wants you to make it look like Grandfather did it."

When he snorted, she realized something else. "No, of course not," she said slowly. "He'd love it if you would, and, for all intents and purposes, it probably looks as if you are following orders, but you like games too much and the payout isn't big enough."

"What the hell are you talking about?" he demanded, but his gaze shifted to the left.

"No." She studied him. "You're doing this for Grandfather. He'll help you take over your family's company."

He laughed, but anger twisted his features.

"I'm right, aren't I?" She caught sight of Remi's eyes opening slightly and choked back a cry. *Easy, Remi. Don't move.*

"You don't know anything," he said in disgust. "You're just fishing."

"No. See? That's the thing about my abilities"—her untapped abilities—"energy doesn't lie. And when I asked you about doing this for your family, you were disgusted at the concept. Your energy showed it. You're a young powerful male, and you don't want to wait for them to step down, so you can take your proper place at the top of the line. Your father was never ambitious like you. He was content to work for his father."

"He's weak. He has no drive. He will never run the company."

"Of course not. He doesn't have the right stuff for it, does he?"

"He's nothing." He waved his hand, the one holding Darbo. She held her breath, afraid Darbo would go flying. When he swung his arm back again, Remi reached out his long arms, snagged Darbo, and bolted.

It happened so fast that Genesis barely saw the sequence of events. And she knew Portman Junior hadn't.

"What the hell?" he blustered, turning around to look at where the animals had gone. She knew he could track Remi's trail, but she doubted he could once they went down to the pools.

But she couldn't take the chance.

Genesis watched as Junior glanced in her direction and froze.

She wanted to laugh, but she didn't dare. She had no idea what he could see.

She'd gone invisible, but, if he saw tracks, maybe he saw her.

The look on his face said he saw something but what?

"Bloody hell. You can go invisible."

And he grinned, a nasty malicious grin that had her moving in the opposite direction—and fast.

She had to get to the safety of the pools.

Before he could catch her.

She tore through the bushes, hearing him behind her.

At least she knew the area. If she could do a few circles and confuse him about her tracks, she'd gain a little time to slip away.

At least, that was the plan.

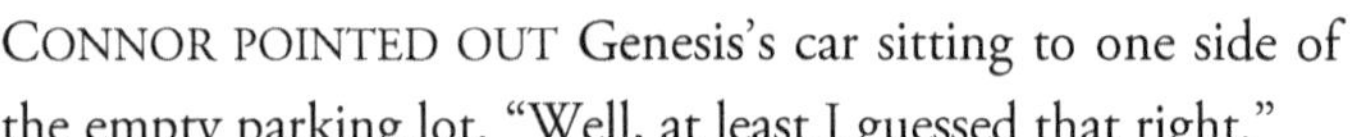

CONNOR POINTED OUT Genesis's car sitting to one side of the empty parking lot. "Well, at least I guessed that right."

"Darbo is here too." Matt stepped out of the Razor and looked around.

Connor strode forward. He could sense Genesis was ahead. He had no idea whether that was because he was close to the pools or his damaged senses were getting stronger. And, if that were the case, why had they become weak overnight? Unless it was the distance from the pools.

"Uh, Connor, why are you going that way?"

Connor looked behind to see Matt racing after him,

dodging the bushes and trees.

Matt shook his head, calling out, "You know there's a path on the other side?"

"I know, but it meanders through the woods. This one is a straight line."

"Except it's not a path."

Connor stepped into a clearing and stopped. "Darbo was here." Connor turned to stare at Matt and the hard look on his face. "So was Genesis."

There was an awkward silence.

"Are you saying she has Darbo?" Matt asked, shock in his voice.

"No." At least he didn't think so. "At least she didn't bring him here. Whether she has him now or not, I don't know."

The longer he stayed here and studied the air around him, the stronger he could sense something else. The energy signatures wove in front of him. He was delighted to see them. But he wished they'd stabilize so he could memorize them. "Someone else was here too."

"Can you tell who?" Matt demanded.

"No." But Connor didn't move. He studied the energy, looking for similarities to other people, locking the signature down in his memory. "But I'll recognize it again."

"So your abilities are stronger here and less capable the farther away you go?" Matt asked in a slow considered way. "Interesting."

"And reassuring. It means that, if I spend some time here, I should be able to fully recover."

"It would explain why you had your abilities when you were here earlier too."

"Exactly." Connor chose the path with the strongest energy and raced ahead.

"Are we following Genesis or the newcomer?" Matt asked from behind him.

"Both. Genesis is ahead of the other."

"I'll take that as *not* a good sign."

"No, but she's on the move, so that is positive."

"Not if he's following behind."

Connor came to a stop at one of the entrances to the healing pools. "Damn it. They've gone in."

"Maybe that's a good thing," Matt said beside him, studying the small entrance in the cliff. "Darbo is down there too."

Connor nodded. "I can see two vague animal energies." He groaned. "Why couldn't I see them earlier? I knew Genesis was upset that I couldn't see Remi. I think she thought I made up my earlier sighting."

"I can't blame her. The ability to see the animals connected to our partners is key in a relationship. Like having a secret life you can't share with someone you love. It doesn't work."

A note of something was off in Matt's tone. Just about to step inside the cave entrance, Connor looked back at him. "Is that what happened to you and Celeste? Could you not see her animal?"

Matt winced. "It was a little more severe than that."

As it related to Genesis and affected everything she saw in relationships, Connor needed to understand. Connor waited, his gaze steady.

Matt sighed. "Darbo used to be hers."

CHAPTER 33

GENESIS COULD ONLY hope the energy of the pools would confuse Portman Junior. So far, she hadn't had any luck in throwing him off her track. But she was smaller, lighter, and faster. And she knew the area. She'd laid several crisscross trails to confuse him but needed to lay a few more. She could go down to the lowest pool, but she really didn't want to lead the asshole down there as well. She didn't know what his final agenda was but knew it would be bad for him to take Remi and Darbo. He'd crossed a line with that action.

She slipped around a corner and hid, waiting to see if he was still following her. Hating that her breath was raspy enough to be heard, she held her breath and closed her eyes. He could track her energy, but the caves were full of it. It was more an issue as to whether the energy pooling where she stood would show stronger than the other trails. She took another step deeper into the shadows and felt a small hand slide into hers.

Oh God. It was Remi! She reached down and pulled him into her arms. She didn't dare cry out in joy or make any motion that would attract attention. He chattered briefly and quietly, but it was mostly a sigh and a heavy breath. Then she felt something so soft and so gentle it brought tears to her eyes. Darbo. Tiny paws patting her cheeks, as he slowly moved to sit on her shoulder, one arm hooking around her ear.

She smiled, loving the little body cuddling close. The good thing here was that Darbo's presence made her feel closer to her sister right now. And, in her moment of homesickness, that connection was so special that she rejoiced in the sensation.

She cuddled the animals, so grateful to have them in her arms.

But that also meant that they weren't safe. She'd so hoped they would be long gone. Away from here. But, of course, Remi had come for her.

How could she use this new scenario to make her escape?

Remi whispered against her ear. She couldn't make out the details, but the message was clear. Use them to save her.

She sat here in silence, as she contemplated mixing Remi's and Darbo's energies with hers. Would that create a strong band of pooling energy to make them more visible, or was there a way to spread it so thin that her kidnapper couldn't see any of them?

How could she do it?

As she pondered the question, Remi slipped from her grasp and disappeared. She listened to his soft scuttling sounds as he ran down one corridor and back up another, then did it all over again. She smiled. She didn't have to spread the energy; he was doing it for her.

When he was done, he pulled her out of the shadows and led her down a different corridor. They didn't see Portman Junior anywhere.

Good.

With Remi leading the way, she moved through the caves to the other side, where she could gain access to her cottage. Once there, she'd be safe. She knew that. She just had to make sure she didn't give away her position.

With one ear listening hard for sounds indicating Portman Junior was following them, she moved through the blackness, loving the dark. Loving being one with nature. Having Darbo on her shoulder just added to the comforting feeling. She wished she could contact Celeste. See her sister's face just for a moment. Hold her sister in her arms for a hug. The triplets had always been close.

Genesis would love to sit down with Tori too, but she knew her sister had left angry. Not at Genesis but at Devon. Her fiancé and soul mate, and yet another victim of Grandfather's machinations. Given what Genesis knew had transpired, she knew her sister wouldn't come back anytime soon.

But, damn, she missed them. Feeling the tears in her eyes, she sniffled back the sobs threatening to break free.

As she reached out mentally for her sisters' love, she felt them reaching back. She rested for a moment, letting the memories fill her with joy and love, then feeling stronger and more in control than ever, she closed the last bit of distance to her cottage.

The brushes rustled around her but in a calm, serene way. There were no unexpected noises or disjointed silence. Birds sang. The wind blew gently.

She searched for any signs of Portman Junior, any dark or disturbed energy, but there was none.

Not sure it was safe but needing to take the next step anyway, she called to Remi. He came immediately. "Remi, take us inside without showing the house."

She repeated the same request inside her head.

A gentle answer rumbled through her mind. She smiled

and finally understood one of the lessons Granny had tried to teach her about invisibility. She had been trying too hard. It wasn't an outer action; it was an inner relaxation.

Still using the invisible energy from Remi, she shed her soul-bound existence and, using the lessons of her granny, Genesis spread her energy outward, connecting with Granny's energy through the past and the present and stepped inside the camouflage, becoming one with it, becoming it.

Inside the barrier, she stopped for a long moment, feeling the energy of Darbo, Remi, everyone she'd loved and had lost, flowing through her. The only way energy became invisible was by joining with it—all of it.

She could barely breathe, as her cells filled and released, over and over.

Then she stepped through to the other side. She opened her eyes and smiled.

She was home.

CONNOR KEPT MOVING forward, his mind busy on Matt's words about Darbo having been Celeste's. What could Connor say? There was a whole story in itself over that issue but it did explain, at least a little bit, about why they had broken up. Matt was private. He wouldn't tell tales out of turn, and Celeste was not here to ask.

Genesis hadn't mentioned the breakup either. Neither had she mentioned Tori's disappearance. Then again, as they'd all left at the same time, himself included, better to not ask Genesis yet. She and Connor needed to resolve a few problems first.

They would have time, after they sorted themselves out,

to explain about the others. He understood that Matt was hoping Celeste would return, but who knew if that were even possible?

The tunnel had widened to the point that the two men could walk side by side. They'd long passed the heavy construction equipment and the pools at the top layer. Connor was looking for Genesis's private exit that led to the cottage. He only had a vague memory of the trip, as he'd been injured at the time.

"You can't see it?" Matt asked, his voice low, deep, his fatigue evident.

"It's through here," Connor pointed, worried at his friend's state. "But I can't remember much. The trip got fuzzier as we traveled. Honestly, by the time we got to her place, I was barely on my feet."

"I'm surprised she managed to get you there."

Connor nodded. "I think I remember her talking to Remi at the time, but I didn't know what I heard, and I certainly couldn't see anyone. Figured it was my imagination."

"It's difficult to see spirit animals. They're not just pets but creatures we are connected with on a most intimate level."

"You're speaking from experience, I presume?" Connor took a few steps into the closest tunnel, realized it didn't look right, and backed out.

"Absolutely. I had no one in the family with spirit animals. None with abilities or power of any kind. I was as unlike the rest of my family as could be imagined."

Connor glanced over at him. "That would have been difficult but not unusual. My situation wasn't much different."

"It was what it was." Matt shrugged. "But it cemented the relationship with Darbo in a way that I couldn't have imagined."

"Why, when I had abilities, didn't I ever have a spirit pet? It would have made my relationship with Genesis much easier."

"Would it?"

When Connor sent him a narrow-eyed gaze, Matt just grinned and said, "Maybe it would have."

Ignoring the smirk on his friend's face, Connor finally recognized the next tunnel. "It's this way."

The tunnel was short, the exit taking them to the bushes again. He stood at the edge of the massive green space and said, "This is the edge. Look at how big, how vibrant everything is."

Matt gave a low whistle. "Something is definitely going on here." He reached out a hand and stroked a palm leaf the size of a huge chair. "How is this possible?"

"I think it's from Genesis herself."

"But she has an affinity with water, not plants. I think that's Tori's affinity."

"Right. Maybe they all have some abilities in common," Connor said, with a nod. "Are they all stargazers though? I wonder."

"Likely. Different stages, different levels maybe. They are all so similar yet very different personalities. Different abilities overlapping among them makes sense."

"What about that damn parentage issue?" Connor brushed back a large bush slightly so he could walk beside it. No path was here. The bush appeared to be so dense as to be impassable. Genesis's work, no doubt. "Who the hell were their parents?"

"That's the question, isn't it?"

"And just how did they end up with Grandfather's sister?" Connor asked.

"No idea. Just more mystery with those three," Matt muttered. He stopped suddenly. "Jesus, we can't get through this, can we?"

Connor stopped as well, feeling the sweat on his brow. "I'm thinking this will be impossible."

They both stopped and stared, as the wall of foliage fell back into place in front of them, thicker than ever.

Connor had a thought. "Can you still sense Darbo?"

Matt stopped and tilted his head. "Actually, … yes. He is here."

"Really?" Connor turned to look at him.

Matt's grin widened. "And he's answering. Not sure why he wasn't before, but he is now."

"Can you call him? Could he help lead us in?"

Matt frowned. "I don't know. I haven't ever asked much of him. He's so tiny, and he's been more of a friend than a coworker."

"Sure, that makes sense. However …" Connor turned his gaze from Matt to the foliage and back again. "Darbo is friends with Remi, right?" He lifted a hand to the bushes. "And Remi lives in this environment. Maybe you could tell Darbo, and then Darbo could tell Remi that we are here."

"And tell Genesis?" Matt asked, curiosity in his voice. "Yeah. I say we ask permission to enter and hope she lets us in." Matt closed his eyes.

Connor observed his friend carefully. Connor had been honest when he'd admitted that he'd never had a spirit pet before. He'd had a dog, but he'd lost him a long time ago. His beloved lab, Kona. He'd deliberately buried those memories. At least he thought he must have. Everything was obscure. Foggy. Searching his past was even more frustrating now with his limited abilities. He had just turned away, rather than dig deeper. Still, it would be much better if he could at least see these spirit animals.

Maybe he'd have a better understanding of Genesis. She'd missed out on so much. And he was only just realizing what he'd asked of her a year ago. It still hurt that she'd chosen to stay, rather than leave with him, but, as he was just seeing for himself, it had hurt her that he'd taken off. He hadn't told her about his job and traveling lifestyle when they'd gotten together a year ago. She'd been so young and innocent. Fresh to his jaded emotions.

He'd fallen hard, and, with all the arrogance of a young male, he'd left with the tattered remains holding him upright, never thinking what it had cost her to stay behind.

CHAPTER 34

GENESIS CLOSED HER eyes with relief, as she slumped into her kitchen chair. Was there anything quite like being home? While Darbo and Remi raced through the place, chittering delightedly to be back, Genesis reached for a granola bar. She was tired. Hungry. Thirsty. And heartsick. Her body ached, and her heart trembled. Something ugly was happening, and she didn't know how to stop it. She understood she was in the middle of several power plays and couldn't, for the life of her, figure out how to get out.

She put on the teakettle and waited for it to boil. She was so tired; she planned to take her tea to the pool and climb in. Maybe after a long, long session there, she would come out clearheaded and able to cope with the sudden changes in her world.

That Connor was back was tough already. That they'd returned to the same state as when he'd left in mere days one year earlier said much about what their relationship was not. Yet she wasn't quite sure what—if anything other than her chaos—was the problem. She hoped they could work it out, but, from now on, they would have to work on it out of bed.

She didn't want the distractions of their unbelievably hot sex life taking precedence over working out the bigger issues.

Although one of those issues appeared to be solved—if he, indeed, went to work for Matt, that is. She would love for that to happen, for him to break away from Grandfather. Connor was a good man, and he deserved a break—even if she wasn't at his side.

In her position, she really didn't have much choice.

The sound of the teakettle blowing off steam interrupted her musings. She made a cup of chamomile tea and carried it to her pool. The room looked open and fresh, the water inviting.

For some reason, she only stripped to her underwear today. Normally she couldn't wait to shuck her clothing. Maybe it was seeing Portman Junior so close, or the fact that both Matt and Connor could be on their way, arriving at any moment, that stopped her from going in nude. She didn't know if any of them could find her, but she didn't want to get caught without her clothes on, if that were the case.

She slipped into the water, moaning with pleasure. The water rose up her thighs and cradled her, as she stretched and sank into the welcoming waves.

She so needed this. At the splash at her side, she opened her eyes to see Remi diving and swimming around her.

"Darbo? Do you want to come in?" She turned to see Darbo stretch out a super-long leg and dip a toe in the water. The healing waters stretched up his leg to his knee. Darbo scrambled backward. Still, he was intrigued. He couldn't take his eyes off Remi, as the plumer dove and swam, then floated in the water, obviously safe and equally at home in the water.

Remi, noticing Darbo sitting on the edge, floated over and chittered at him encouragingly. Darbo wasn't having anything to do with it. When Remi held out his arms, Darbo stared at him, undecided. Then in a move that made Genesis laugh, he jumped off the ledge to land on Remi's tummy.

And that's how the two of them stayed. Remi floating on his back, Darbo riding his tummy, his long arms trailing in the water. They looked so peaceful that Genesis couldn't help feeling the same sense of security slipping through her. The healing waters were doing their job. She felt better now. More rested. The aches and pains easing, the confusion clearing.

She was home, and that was the one place she wanted to be.

Even if she was alone.

For the first time, she could understand Granny's reasons for avoiding the townsfolk and living out her life in seclusion. There was acceptance, peace, and tranquility to be had here. For Granny, who'd spent so much of her day, every day, on the star charts, it would have been a perfect existence.

Maybe that was what Genesis should do too.

Just as she closed her eyes, prepared to sleep for a few moments, Remi bolted upright and chittered loudly.

Genesis sat up and stared at him. "What's wrong?"

He didn't give her an answer. Instead he slung Darbo on his back and bolted to the other room. She heard the door open and close as he left the cottage. Why? Where could he be going? There could be any number of reasons. But, as he hadn't been distressed or angry, it couldn't be related to Portman Junior.

Anyone else she could deal with easily enough. She stood up and dried off, dressing carefully, as she was still slightly damp. Taking her tea out to the kitchen, she looked out the window just in time to see Remi leading Matt by the hand, with Darbo on Matt's shoulder. With his other hand, Matt led Connor forward.

Well. Wasn't that great? Now she had the whole lot of them to deal with. She opened the door and grinned. "What took you so long?"

Matt laughed. "Without Remi, we would still be struggling to find a way through, as you very well know."

"I suspect it was more a case of you calling for Darbo, Darbo asking for Remi's help, and then you bringing Connor through." She shrugged. "Still, you're here now. You might as well have a cup of tea."

"Sounds good." Matt entered the small cottage, instinctively ducking under the low doorway. He sat down across from her chair.

She turned to study Connor. He watched her every move but had yet to say anything. He also hadn't entered. He stood in the doorway and stared, a hard look on his face.

"Before we get too cozy, tell me why you left."

She raised an eyebrow. "Meaning, if we get cozy, I won't tell you? How does that work?"

"I want answers, and I want them now," he said in an aggrieved tone.

"You might get them. But only when I'm damn good and ready to give them." She narrowed her gaze at him. "You don't have to come in and have a cup of tea if you don't want to, but you do have to drop the anger and the attitude. It's not welcome in my house."

And she turned her back on him and walked over to the teakettle. She filled it and put it back on the stove. There wasn't a sound behind her. She bowed her head and groaned softly. Damn that man.

She turned around to find he hadn't taken a step forward or back.

He glared at her.

She glared back.

"I came back last night to find that you'd moved out of our room, and then, in the early hours of the morning, you pack up and sneak out of the building and drive away?"

The way he said it made it sound so much worse. Ignoring Matt, who was watching the exchange with interest, she snapped back, "I'm certain the old room had been searched. It didn't feel right anymore, so I moved next door. And I didn't pack up in the middle of the night. I had nothing to pack, if you remember. Also, the damn men outside woke me up, and, after I heard about their plans, I decided I wanted to be back home, where I could look after the place and its very valuable contents. At the same time, I realized Remi was in danger."

At his look of astonishment, she added, "And I was planning on coming back. At least until I realized Portman Junior had kidnapped both Remi and Darbo here and had plans for me. He's still out there, you know? I don't know why you didn't see him, but that man is dangerous."

On a roll now, she walked over to stand in front of him.

"And besides, if you knew I'd moved to a different room, why didn't you come to my room then?" she demanded. "Or was it Grandfather's warnings that kept you the hell away from me?"

Silence fell in the small room after her outburst. Remi swung up her body to sit on her shoulder. He chittered once at Connor.

She said, "Don't bother, Remi. He's not listening to either of us."

CONNOR DIDN'T KNOW what to say. He should have

knocked on the door last night and actually talked to her. Not brushed off her concerns about their room being searched. So, of course, she'd taken matters into her own hands. Wasn't that what Matt had said? She'd been alone a long time and wasn't used to depending on anyone? Or having anyone there to help her. Connor had expected her to come to him, but she likely hadn't even considered the possibility.

Instead, he had done something about it but hadn't told her.

"I spoke with Matt's head of security," Connor said. "He was going to check the video feed from the security cameras to see if there'd been any intruders in our room."

"And?" she asked curiously. "Were there?"

He flushed. "I didn't get a chance to ask him."

She nodded. "There hasn't been that much time."

Of course she would let him off the hook. She may bluster and tell him what was wrong, but then it all blew over. That was the thing about Genesis. She was a peacemaker and so easy to get along with. Too easy. It had allowed him to forget about something that had bothered her. "I'm sorry."

"You had a lot on your mind."

She turned away to make the tea, once again forgiving him and letting him be in the wrong without the guilt. He felt guilty enough for a number of reasons. "Maybe, but I should have checked up on it." He stepped forward, grabbed a kitchen chair, and turned it around before sitting down on it. "I told Grandfather that I wouldn't work for him any longer." He watched for her reaction.

She froze. Not turning around to face him, she asked, "And how did he take that?"

"Much better after he realized I had lost my abilities.

Then he couldn't get rid of me fast enough." That was the truth as far as it went. He didn't want to talk about what Mason had told him on the way out.

At least, not with Matt sitting here and watching.

"You didn't tell him that your abilities were coming back?"

He shook his head.

"Why?"

"I wanted him to be happy I was leaving." He gave her a small, crooked grin. "He would have held the door for me, if he could have."

She gasped. "But you're family."

"Very distant. I'm not one of his sons, and, if I don't have my abilities and if I can't do my job, then I'm no good to him."

"So you're unemployed." She frowned.

"Hardly," he protested. "Matt has offered me a job, and I've decided I'd like to give it a try."

"Damn glad to hear that." Matt spoke up for the first time.

Connor glanced over at him to see Darbo curling up against his neck. As the sight was such a surprise for him, he stopped and stared. The little thing was literally curled up on his shoulder, Darbo's long arms wrapped around his ear, and it appeared that Darbo was sleeping after his ordeal. "Why can I see Darbo here? The only other time I've seen him was at the pools," Connor complained.

Genesis laughed, and even Matt grinned. "Probably be-cause you brought his human back to him," she said.

Connor slid her a sideways look. "Really?"

At her nod, he continued to study her but couldn't see Remi. Finally he asked, "And Remi, your spirit pet, why can't I see him?"

She shrugged but answered in a low voice, "Maybe he doesn't trust you."

"Or," he said just as quietly, "maybe he's making a decision based on your emotions, and you're the one who doesn't trust me."

And, damn, if she didn't turn away.

CHAPTER 35

G ENESIS HATED TO think that Connor was right, but, with the truth staring at her, it was hard not to see it.

Remi *would* pick up on her feelings and take them into account. But, if Connor had his abilities and was working on gaining the rest back, he should see Remi all the time, especially after having seen him once. The same for Darbo.

For some reason, it wasn't happening. She frowned, staring into her tea. Why not?

"Where did you lose Portman?" Matt asked gently, thankfully changing the topic.

She waved her hand outside. "Out there. He can see and track energy signatures, so he could still find us." She started, staring out the window, suddenly realizing she hadn't hidden the men's tracks. Shit.

At that moment, a cacophony of sound filled the air as Remi and Darbo screamed in alarm.

Genesis bolted out of her chair as Portman's dark form filled the doorway. He scowled, then yelled, "Shut them up."

Instead of subduing the animals, the sound of his raised voice had the opposite effect. The animals went into overdrive, screeching and chittering loudly. Outside, the birds joined in, raising a raucous racket. Genesis tried to calm Remi down, and, when that didn't work, she sent him to the pool. As he passed Matt, who had his hands full with screams of terror right at his ear, Remi reached out and snagged Darbo; then the two of them raced from the room.

Matt stood, his back straight and his face dark. "So you're the one who stole Darbo."

"Darbo?" Portman said. "Wait until the Council hears about your spirit pet. Hell, couldn't you have at least found one that had balls?"

"I don't need you to tell me who and what my pet should be," he said, with a murderous glare and no hint of embarrassment over Darbo. "That's none of your business. Kidnapping—people or spirit pets—is a crime you will pay for."

"Oh, really?" Portman Junior sniggered. "And what will that be? Will I do community service with the local animal doctor?" He was obviously having too much fun laughing at the lot of them.

Then Genesis realized something else. As Portman was a man of power, he could have a spirit pet of his own. Given his comments, she knew that chances were it wouldn't be a small sweet one, like Remi or Darbo.

"What is your spirit animal?" she asked warily. She'd never seen the bigger, more dangerous ones, but she'd heard stories about them.

"I don't have one," he said dismissively.

Only it wasn't that easy. And then she knew. "You killed it, didn't you?"

He turned that cold gaze on her. She swallowed bravely but refused to back down.

"Why would you say that?" Connor asked. "I don't have one, so obviously not all of us do."

"The reason you don't is quite different from the reason he doesn't," Matt said. "He wouldn't like the connection.

The dependency. He would consider a spirit pet a weakness—not a strength."

"They are a weakness. God, Matt here looks ridiculous with Darbo on his shoulder during the meetings." Portman sneered. "Quite silly, really."

"Not at all," Matt said smoothly. "Darbo may look like a useless decoration, but he's anything but."

Portman stared at him, but Matt didn't elaborate.

"A miscalculation on your part," Genesis noted. "How did you find my cottage?"

He laughed. "I told you that I can read energy signatures. This place is lit up with all of you here. You cloaked the cottage but not the inhabitants."

Damn. She'd never thought to do that.

"I'm not leaving without the proof of ownership documents."

"And what makes you think they are here?"

He laughed, the sound humorless and cold. "Of course they're here. Your granny is related to Grandfather. There's no other place they'd be safe. Grandfather can't cross this threshold. Granny made sure of that a long time ago." That laugh of his darkened. "But now that you removed the star charts, the barrier she set up has been weakened, and now he can. Or, in this instance, I can."

Could she really be related to Grandfather? Her insides knotted in panic. Her mind screamed in denial.

Surely not. He despised her. His sister had sold her back to Granny. No, it didn't make any sense. Unless no blood was involved here. Maybe Grandfather belonged to Granny's husband, but not Granny. Although Genesis hadn't heard anything of Granny having been married, it didn't mean such a thing hadn't been possible. She'd had a child at some point, although she refused to talk about it. The girls never did get an explanation of what happened.

Yet, if they were related to Grandfather by marriage, … it might explain how Grandfather came to think the land was his. Maybe he thought he would inherit it. Maybe he'd assumed he owned it—or worse yet, maybe he did own it.

No. If he owned the land in town, then he also owned the land around the forests, and that he hadn't claimed. The deed was clear. It was all the same parcels and ownership. There'd been no subdividing of the quarters. It was all Granny's and had been given to Genesis and her sisters. But Granny had been gone for a year now. Maybe Grandfather was prepared to stake a claim after all this time, thinking no paperwork was available.

Did he have a bigger claim over granddaughters?

Surely not, when the documents stated the property belonged to the three of them. She reached a hand to her throbbing head and closed her eyes.

"Genesis?" Connor asked briefly, his hand landing on her shoulder to massage gently. "Are you okay?"

She shook her head. "I'm *not* related to Grandfather." She wasn't. She didn't know how or why, but she knew she wasn't his kin.

"Damn right, you're not. Why do you think he's so pissed off over you now trying to stake a claim on his land?"

She glanced over at Matt, seeing the same puzzled look on his face that she felt. "That's because I am *Granny's* kin—not Grandfather's. I don't know what line of bull he fed you, but that crap can stop here."

"Ha." Portman Junior pulled a small object out from his pocket and held it up.

Crap. She stumbled backward.

A black rock.

"See? Besides seeing energy, I have an affinity for the Glory rocks. They are great little indestructible things. And when I combine my senses with it, I can see energy in a way other people can't."

Genesis stared at the rock in his hand. He wielded the black rocks?

"What ability do they have on their own?" Matt asked. He stood up and took a step toward Genesis.

"I wouldn't come any closer if I were you," Portman Junior said, a big manic grin on his face. "These rocks are all about negative energy. They aren't your typical nice, positive-vibe kind of rock. Like everything in life, this is the polar opposite. Just like my abilities. I work dark energy, like these rocks."

Genesis was repelled but intrigued. She worked energy more than many people. She understood the difference between positive and negative energy in a big way, but she didn't understand this. "But this isn't like the rest of the rocks on Glory."

He laughed coldly. "No, of course not. I made this one. It does take a bit of time and effort for bigger rocks, but I've found it to be very helpful to keep one around."

Of course. She stared at him and the rock, her mind connecting the dots. That was why the pools had been so agitated. The negative energy of the rock skewed the healing balance. At one point, in its own effort to return to normal, the rock would be trying to reverse the process and to become positive again. But the requirement to do so was energy. And that meant positive energy. Either by stealing a little bit from everything around it, which, in turn, caused all those rocks, plants, waters, to turn and to seek out more positive energy to reassert their own balance, or by taking a lot of positive energy from one thing.

Like a man.

Like Bernie.

"You tried to kill Bernie with that?" she whispered.

"Not at all. The rock from the pools couldn't take the energy from the water, as it's too highly charged in positive ions, so it was looking for the closest source of energy it could access. As I'm the one who removed the energy, it knew human energy would be a viable source. Besides, Bernie was supposed to throw the rock in the pool and run, but, like an idiot, he forgot the last part of his instructions."

Connor coughed softly. Not enough to catch Portman's attention and interrupt his egotistical monologue, but enough for Genesis to look his way and catch Matt studying Connor's face at the same time. She readied herself for action. She just had no idea what form it would take.

She did know the rock would decimate them if they didn't act now.

She shifted her weight to the balls of her feet and leaned forward slightly. And felt Remi slip his hand into hers. Right. Then she remembered what she'd done last time. Using Remi's energy, she carefully sent out probes of energy to wrap up the black rock and defuse the weapon.

Portman stared down at the rock. "What the hell? What's wrong?" he cried out. "It's getting hot."

"Hot? Why would it get hot?" Matt asked. "Why would it have any temperature for that matter?"

"It's supposed to be cool. Absence of light. Absence of anything."

Portman lifted his gaze to Matt and studied him intently.

Shit. He was searching for the energy flow, but hopefully, with all of them in the small cottage, Junior couldn't see who was working the energy. Turning away slightly, Genesis shut off the flow of energy in her hand, hoping he couldn't see. In order to distract him, she said, "You have to leave. Now. Or else that rock will destroy us all."

"Oh, I don't think so," he snapped. "You're going to give me the damn documents I need, or I'll use this rock on both Connor and Matt."

She turned back to face him, her actions slow, studied. "Oh no you're not."

He laughed and tossed the rock at Matt. "Here. ... Catch."

Instinctively Matt held out his hands and the rock landed in his right hand.

"Good thing you caught it, Matt. It's a small bomb if dropped." The smile on Junior's lips never reached his eyes.

Genesis shivered. She could easily imagine the damage if that rock had been dropped. That meant Junior didn't care who or what survived.

She had to get him out of here before Granny's life's work exploded in the blast.

For the first time, she fully realized that maybe the star charts and documents *should* be in the Paranormal Center. They'd be safe there. Providing all this mess could be handled first.

Her mind twisted on the possibilities, searching for a solution.

And came up blank.

CONNOR STARED AT a man he'd known for years and yet

hadn't ever known. How could anyone have foreseen this? There had been a sour displeasure at the world around Junior, but Connor hadn't seen this darkness inside.

He had to wonder if it wasn't a result of creating these black rocks. As if the very act of causing so much damage in other things caused the very same damage in himself.

"These rocks are killing you, Portman," Connor said quietly, his gaze studying the gray cast to the man's skin, the early graying of the man's hair—a man within several years of Connor's own age. Then there was the odd shine to Portman's gaze. A fanatical, obsessed look.

"Like hell, but go ahead and try to convince me to give it up," he snickered.

Connor shook his head. "No point. You don't want to hear anything I have to say. As far as you're concerned, I'm not even here."

"You're a broken old model that should have been discarded last year, when you lost your abilities. It was foolish of you to let her do that to you."

Connor felt rather than saw Genesis's start of surprise. "Stooping to eavesdropping now, are you?"

"I was sitting on the deck a little farther down. Could hardly miss that conversation. Not to mention it was pretty damn obvious she'd kinked your abilities the same as she'd put you in a kink." And he laughed raucously at his own joke. The door behind Portman Junior slammed shut. His laughter cut off, and he swiveled to look behind him.

"Genesis," Matt called out.

From the corner of his eye, Connor watched as Matt tossed the black rock to Genesis, before slumping weakly against the wall.

Time to act. Arm back, Connor launched forward and

drove his fist into Portman's face.

Portman Junior slammed backward against the closed door. Connor was on him in an instant. Bigger and stronger, Connor had him down in seconds, but Portman was meaner.

He pulled out a second black rock and held it against Connor's hand.

"Christ!" He pulled his hand away, but where there'd been pink and warm flesh before, there was a white circle the size of the rock. With his good hand, he kept Portman Junior pinned to the ground at the neck, his thumb pushing into a chokehold spot in the man's throat.

A paw covered his injured hand, and something hot jetted into his skin. Burning. Cooling. Healing. An animal shape wavered at eye level. He couldn't make out anything clearer.

"Who the hell is that?" Portman snapped. "Jesus, what's wrong with you people? Dirty animals freakin' everywhe—"

Connor dug his thumb in deeper. "I wouldn't finish that sentence if I were you."

Portman Junior choked back the next words, but his gaze spoke volumes.

"I have men coming," Matt said, now standing in front of them. "Can you hold him until then? Sorry, I'm still recovering."

"No problem," Connor said, through gritted teeth. "I'm more than happy to."

"Won't matter," Portman Junior snapped. "Grandfather will get me out of here."

"Yeah," Genesis said in a dry tone. "Which grandfather?"

Silence. Then Portman started laughing, the sound maddened by the energy abuse.

Connor stared down at him in disgust. "That's what comes from playing with things you don't understand."

Portman Junior snickered. "You haven't a clue. Look to your side piece. She's the one you don't understand."

Asshole. Still, enough things had been said recently to make things a little fuzzy. He trusted Genesis. But what did he trust her to do? Protect Granny's life work? Save Remi? Save herself?

Slowly he looked over at Matt to see him busy on his phone, then he studied Genesis. She stood on guard, waiting. Watching, as if to see where she could help, or waiting for something else to happen.

As he watched, some of the animal energy slipped from her side toward him. He frowned, confused, as the energy glow became brighter, stronger. A golden Lab appeared in the mists in front of him. A dog that looked very familiar.

He shook his head, glancing back down at Portman, who was still giggling madly.

"You don't even know. You poor, lovesick idiot."

"What don't I know?" Connor shook the man. "What?"

"It's your own spirit animal. Your disbelief leaves it disconnected. Unloved. Unattached. So it came to the one who was open to it. Willing to heal it. Willing to give it a life."

Connor glared down at Portman Junior. "Not possible. He died a long time ago."

"And sometimes, when the bond is so strong, they become a spirit animal. But you didn't want that. You didn't care."

"That's not true. I cared too much." And, for that moment, he was a kid again, lost in the joy of having the best dog in the world. A dog just for him. An animal who loved him. Someone for him to love.

He'd cared so much back then.

Could it really be Kona? God, he'd loved that dog. He'd been completely devastated when he'd died in a car accident. He cast his mind back to those dark days. Days when he'd been inconsolable and determined to not be hurt like that again.

As truth after truth slammed into him, he felt his foundation shift. Memories rippled through his mind, replaying the effect of that decision. He'd never seen Kona again— afraid Kona wasn't real—and afraid Connor would be hurt again if he did acknowledge Kona's presence. For the same reason, Connor had walked away from Genesis. It was better to be the one who walked and not the one who'd been walked out on.

He stared at Genesis. Was it the same thing? Had he lost all he'd cared about simply because he didn't want to believe? Even his beloved pet dog of so long ago? A tremor rippled down his spine at the ghostly image in front of him. Had he lost Genesis because once again he hadn't trusted? Not in Kona. Not in Remi. Not in Genesis. Not in what they'd had.

Even now, he'd wavered because of Mason's words. Portman's accusations. His own insecurities.

Christ. He bowed his head.

What the hell had he done?

CHAPTER 36

STANDING WITH HER back to Connor and Portman, Genesis pondered the conversation going on behind her. Interesting that everyone appeared to be blaming her for Connor's loss of abilities. It was her fault, but not for the reason they all believed. She had had no choice in the matter. She'd also thought it could be the natural order of things. But apparently that order had changed. And he wouldn't appreciate the way it was now. Not if he didn't love her.

She also had no idea how to handle it.

High above the cottage, she heard the sound of a hovercraft approaching. She walked around the men on the floor, so still and so accusing she could barely hold back the tears, and opened the door. She opened up the cloaking energy to allow them to land. She had no wish to have anyone here anymore. They could all leave. And the sooner, the better.

She'd learned several major lessons this last year, and they'd all brought her closer to understanding Granny. There was much to find in this cottage, and, for the first time, she realized this was a journey she needed to take.

For herself.

For her sisters. She'd send them a message now. Give them an update. Let them decide whether they would stay away or come home.

They had much pain to face here. Now she understood.

She would face hers and would walk forward alone. As she always had. She didn't know whether that would be alone or not. She had no idea where she stood with Connor. Or where he wanted her to be in his life. There'd been so many revelations and accusations, she had to wonder if he knew either.

As she waited for the hovercraft to land, she worked on closing up the gap in the energy behind them. She didn't want anyone else here than those who needed to be here. At the moment, she was thinking that closing down her shop and apartment might be the best too. She would become a hermit, like Granny. At least until things died down a little.

She tilted her face up to the sunlight, feeling the burning tears threatening to fall. They weren't going to. She wouldn't let them.

"Planning to hide away after this?" Matt murmured behind her.

"How did you know?" she said quietly.

"I suspect it's what your granny did. She saw a little too much of the dark side of society and decided to dedicate her life to her star charts."

The tears burned hotter. Genesis shook her head. "No. She dedicated her life to me and my sisters. She had nothing to be ashamed of in that."

"He'll learn the truth eventually, you know?"

"Will he?" She couldn't stop the snort of disbelief. "I wonder when. I went through this a year ago. Now again. I'm good. I don't need to go through this a third time."

"Did you know it was his spirit dog?"

"No," she said softly. "Granny collected lost spirit animals the way she collected us orphans. Many were here over the years. She found homes for some, and some disappeared when she passed. They had become hers and left when she did."

The hovercraft sounded louder and louder. They watched it crest over the trees.

"That's very special."

"She was."

"Connor just needs to learn the truth."

"He needs to find out the truth himself."

And, with her words, the hovercraft settled in the front of the cottage. Portman, Portman Senior, and Grandfather all exited the front cab.

Outraged, she turned to face Matt. "You were supposed to take away the enemy. Not bring them here."

He shook his head, confusion and anger blistering his face. "They weren't supposed to come here at all."

"Shit," she said softly. "It's the wrong hovercraft."

She closed her eyes and chanted silently for her grandmother's charms to work their magic and protect her cottage and her precious heritage inside. Only it wasn't working. Portman Junior inside had busted the seal wide open. He was a negative energy she couldn't oust—at least not in time. "Hurry," she cried. "We need to get him out of the cottage."

Opening the door, she motioned to Connor. "Get him out here now," she screamed.

He stood, hauling Portman Junior upward. Thrusting him in front, he shoved the other man outside. As soon as the door closed behind them, she started again. Calling to Remi and Darbo and her sisters, her grandmother long dead, she closed the energy barrier, just as the men reached her …

The cottage disappeared from sight.

AS THE COTTAGE disappeared in front of his eyes, Connor turned to look at the three grim-faced men walking toward them.

"Grandfather." He tilted his head in acknowledgment at the other two men. "I'm surprised to see you here."

"I'm not surprised to see you though," Grandfather growled. "Keeping company with that bitch."

Connor straightened. "There won't be any of that here."

"Haven't you bedded her enough yet? Gotten her out of your system?" He snorted. "She must be good—"

"You don't want to go there," Connor snapped, clenching his fists. "This topic will never be broached again."

"Ha. She's got you, hasn't she?" Grandfather pulled his bushy brows together, his eyes bright, scornful. "Just like the rest of that damn family."

"What do you know about the rest of her family?" Matt interjected smoothly. "She's a little short on personal history."

"Granny was a freak of nature. That's what I know," he blustered. "And her grandkids were made from the same damn mold."

Connor had never hit someone older than him, but, damn, if there was ever a time and a place, it would be right now.

"Meaning?" Matt kept his voice even-tempered.

Connor admired that. Especially considering that one of Granny's freak granddaughters was the love of his life too.

But they needed to find out the truth. And with both Grandfather and Genesis here at the same time, maybe they'd get it out in the open.

"Granny was married to my grandfather for a few short months. A union in hell if you listened to my father. Granny divorced him, after finding out he'd had a few affairs. The damn woman was disgusting. Of course he had affairs." The look on his face showed such revulsion at Granny's lack of understanding that Connor wanted to laugh.

Matt once again returned the discussion back to his line of questioning. "So Granny never bore any children?"

"Hell no. Never. Those kids she adopted aren't her own kin, no matter what the bitch says."

Connor took a step forward, gaining some satisfaction as Grandfather scrambled backward several steps. The Portmans stood rigid at his side, identical glares on their faces.

Regaining his ground quickly, Grandfather continued, spite coloring his voice. "My father gained the lands through the marriage, and, although she tried to reclaim them after the divorce, it wasn't possible."

A loud gasp could be heard from behind him. Connor understood that Genesis was listening in, cloaked in her own invisibility energy.

"How did Granny get the land in the first place?" Matt asked. "It must have been in her family line."

"Sure. The whole family damn near owns half the planet. Little Glory wasn't named after the planet Glory but after Granny's great-grandmother, who was named Gloria. Back then, hardly anyone lived here. They had all the land."

"And now?" Connor asked in a hard voice. "What did Granny own when she died?"

"Nothing," Grandfather spat. "She owned nothing. It was all my grandfather's, and now they're mine. Damn ingrate, trying to say the place was hers."

"And the stargazer part?"

"Crap, that's all. They were all charlatans." He pointed a finger at Connor. "They can't be trusted. Not any of them."

"Why is that?"

"They lie, cheat, and steal." He threw his arms out wide. "You've seen them. They attract men, steal what they want, and toss them aside."

Connor held his hand up behind his back in warning. He was afraid Genesis would completely lose it. Something was so chaotic about her energy.

It occurred to him that, once again, he could see energy. Feel her energy. His abilities were stronger here in this environment where there was a healing pool. And where Genesis was.

That also meant he could see Grandfather's energy for the first time. And the deception in his aura. Why hadn't Connor seen that years ago, when his abilities were fully functioning? Connor wanted to beat the truth out of him. He glanced over at the Portman clan, silent since their arrival. Their energy swelled and wafted with distaste and anger, but the anger was directed at Portman Junior.

"What do you intend to do with him?" he asked them, not sure he wanted to release this man into their care. "He's a danger to us all."

Portman Senior nodded. "We will look after him."

"You're misunderstanding," Matt said coolly. "It's not an option for him to be free."

Portman Senior glared at him. "We take care of our own."

"Really? You do realize he was planning to take over your company by joining up with Grandfather here?" Connor smiled glacially at them. "Maybe you should be a little more careful about your power-hungry son."

"He has power beyond anything we've seen in this family," Portman Senior admitted sadly. "And he is the only one to want to use it for all the wrong things."

"He attacked Genesis, kidnapped and injured several spirit animals"—at that, the other two men winced, but Matt carried on—"broke into Genesis's cottage and attacked us all. He's used his black rocks to damage the pools in the forest and as weapons against us."

Startled murmurs began, as Genesis stepped out from behind Connor. She carried one of the black rocks in her hands and held it out to them. "Of course you'll want to take this with you," she said quietly.

They held up their hands and stepped back. "No. We've seen what those things can do."

"And yet you brought them here."

"Business meetings with Grandfather, that is all. We wanted to commercialize the pools. Grandfather owns the land." They both smiled genially. "Just a business meeting."

"Are you responsible for the guard who attacked Connor?" Matt asked, frowning.

The two men shook their heads. "He was hired by Grandfather's security company. Just overzealous in doing his job."

"The pools can never be commercialized," Genesis said, giving Grandfather a glare. "And, since they aren't his to sell, I suggest you go back to where you came from and keep him"—she pointed to Portman Junior, now standing at his father's side, with a huge manic grin on his face—"locked up so he can't hurt anyone again."

"Or else?" Portman Senior asked gravely.

"Or else," Genesis responded just as seriously, "I'll make sure he loses his abilities forever."

Connor stared at her in shock. "So you did do that."

She gave him a scornful look. "No, I didn't," she said

shortly, "but I could." She switched her glare to Portman Junior and added, "And I will, if I ever see him again." She pointed to the hovercraft. "Get him out of my sight."

The two men grabbed Junior and hustled him to the waiting craft. Then she turned her wrath on Grandfather. "You dare stand before me, being the liar, cheater, thief that you are, and accuse my granny of those things?"

"As you were playing invisible, you were proving my words, so your accusations hardly count."

"This land is mine. The land you claim as yours is also mine," she added quickly. "It's mine and my sisters'. All of it. The woods. The pools. The meadows. The whole damn town. We own it all."

"Rubbish," he snapped. "You are nothing and always will be nothing."

"Granny was a stargazer. The land here is stargazer land. It stays in stargazer hands. It can never be handed over by marriage. It can't be. It can never be sold or given away. Maybe your grandfather should have looked at the deeds more closely before you started making accusations you couldn't back up."

His face turned so red that Connor wondered if he would collapse. He watched warily, waiting.

"You little upstart. You don't own anything. I don't know what fake documents you showed Matt here to turn him against me, but I know they aren't real."

"And how do you know that?" Matt asked.

"Because I have the real ones at home," he snapped. "And I'd be happy to show you."

Connor turned to look at Genesis, but she was smiling. A cold, clear smile that demanded retribution for today's events. From the look on her face, she appeared to believe she held the missing ace.

He hoped so, for her sake.

Not that he cared. He didn't understand the energy stuff, hadn't made any attempt to really learn it over all these years, and hadn't realized what a mistake that was, until he'd lost it all. But he would make up for it. He had much to learn. Much to gain. Much to be.

Now he knew that, regardless of what she'd done, if anything, Genesis was part of his heart. And he'd do whatever he had to do keep her there.

He turned his attention back to Grandfather—and swore.

Grandfather stood tall in front of them.

A high-energy impact gun in his hand.

CHAPTER 37

"UNCLOAK THE COTTAGE, you little bitch."

Undecided, but not liking the look in his eyes, Genesis complied.

"Now inside …" At the wave of the gun, they all followed his orders. Genesis stood at the edge of the pool room, glaring at the man who'd made her family's life hell.

"Move the rock back to the pool." Grandfather motioned in the direction of the healing pool. Genesis opened her mouth, but the wave of the weapon in his hand persuaded her against arguing. She had no idea why the healing pool, but she'd take anything at the moment to staring down the gun.

Then she noticed the gray cast to both Connor and Matt. As she watched, a startled cry escaping, both men staggered, then fell slowly to the ground. She wanted to go to Connor's side, when the gun lifted in her direction. She stopped. Glaring at him, she snapped, "What did you do to them?"

"Knocked them out. My ability isn't as refined as some of the ones I've seen lately," he snapped, "but I make up for it in power."

She nodded. "And is that what your grandfather did? Knocked Granny out, so she woke up married, and he figured he owned her lands?"

"Think you're so smart, don't you?" His eyes darkened menacingly. "What makes you think we had to do anything?"

"Granny loved someone a long time ago. She would never have remarried willingly, and, even if she didn't want to be alone for the rest of her life, she understood people, and she would have seen the truth of your grandfather's energy. She would never have married him," she said in a flat voice. "Therefore, she was tricked into marriage."

An odd silence followed, as Grandfather contemplated her with a serious look. "You're right, you know. He drugged her and married her while she was unconscious."

"So it wasn't even legal," she said in disgust. "Typical. You want something, and you don't care what you have to do to get it."

"According to my grandfather, when she woke up, besides being livid, she was laughing her head off, saying it wouldn't work." He waved her in the direction of the room again. "Only it did work. We had already been living on her lands as it was, so we just stayed there, but now as the rightful owners."

"But you're not the rightful owners, and Matt knows this now. The whole Council will know this soon."

"You're lying," he scoffed. "They don't know anything."

"The documents I have are centuries old," Genesis said, "and they are very clear. The land can't be sold. It's handed down from generation to generation of stargazers." She waited a beat then added, "They carry the stargazer's seals." His look of astonishment made her laugh. "You've gone along with your family's machinations for years and for what? Nothing?" She loved the look of shock on his face. "Now everyone will understand what you've lied and cheated to get."

"That can't be true."

"It is. Your grandfather and your father can't own the land. You can't own the land, and neither can any of your family."

As his face worked, she brought up the one bit of the story that had been bugging her. "How did your sister end up with me and my sisters?"

His shock turned to anger. "Granny's daughter ran away as a young woman and had an affair. She argued with her mother and felt she couldn't come back here. She lived on my sister's kindness, until she was killed in an accident. My sister ended up caring for you girls as long as she could."

"No." She shook her head. "That's not true." It couldn't be.

"You don't want to think of your grandmother as anything but perfect. Well, she wasn't. My sister, once she realized who the children belonged to, contacted Granny and arranged for her to have you all back."

"And not for the first time," Genesis said, remembering something that had been brought up earlier. "Doesn't your sister look after orphan children and find families for a price?"

He snorted. "So what? That's called an adoption fee."

It wasn't. Still, it had been a godsend to Genesis and her sisters that the triplets had been returned to their blood grandmother. Somewhere were letters Granny had written to the three of them. Genesis had found hers and had learned much. Maybe her sisters' letters would offer more bits and pieces to help fill in the missing blanks.

"And the pools, are you involved in trying to commercialize them, as the Portmans said?"

He shook his head. "Hell no. I don't want tourists through here. Damn place is crawling with enough strangers as it is."

She didn't know whether she believed him or not. His energy had a darkness to it that she didn't recognize or understand, but she respected the destructive power within it. She turned to her healing pool, reaching down a hand to trail her fingers through the water. Immediately the water surged upward to coat the palm of her hand, her wrist, and forearm.

"Why anyone would want anything to do with that water, I don't know," he said, stepping up beside the pool. "That's just creepy."

"You've never been in?"

"No way."

"That's why it's so active then. Your body is in great need." Although Genesis figured it was his mind the waters really were drawn to help. She should just let the water have him. Who knew what he'd be like when he came out? "Why don't you step in?" she invited him. "The waters will help you."

"Not happening." He motioned with the gun. "Walk past the pool and go up into the attic. I want all the documents down here, where I can see them."

She stared from him to the attic, then back to him. "You can't have them, you know," she said in a calm voice. "Hundreds and hundreds of star charts are up there."

"I only want the ones she drew about my family."

She narrowed her eyes and gazed at him. "Why?"

"They say things about the family. I want those. No one in the Paranormal Center needs to know anything about my family's past, present, or future," he said in a hard voice. "If

I'd realized she had these still, I'd have done something about it earlier."

"Wow, I really opened up a nightmare by taking home the one star chart I'd been working on, didn't I?"

He laughed coldly. "And that was a fluke. A junkie broke in to your place and saw it and tried to sell the information to Mason." With another wave of the gun, he added, "You wanted recognition for your granny and a place in society for yourself. It's to be expected. No one wants to live as the crone in the haunted house. Only I now know that the charts my father spoke about actually do exist. They speak about my family's destiny. Our individual powers. We can't have that. Too much knowledge isn't good. In fact, in this case, … it's downright dangerous."

And she understood. "Because madness is in your genetics, isn't there? A sickness brought on by using your powers with such negative force." She motioned toward where Matt and Connor were passed out. "I can see the deterioration in your own energy. The darkness in your soul."

He shrugged. "Power is addictive, and, once you use it to get your own way, it's hard to stop using it."

"And can you make people do things that they don't want to do?"

"Not really, but we can use our abilities to get them into a state where they can't fight us. We can then force them to do things—things they wouldn't normally do."

"Nasty."

"Nothing like what your granny and those damn star charts could do to my family, if that mess ever came out. That old woman was a vindictive bitch. She would have stopped at nothing to get you back after all these years."

Here it was. The truth. Everything he'd said earlier—a

fabrication. She asked softy, "After your family arranged for us to disappear?"

"Your mother. We made her disappear." He smiled. "To get back at Granny. She had one of the original star charts with her."

"And she was pregnant." It had to be. That was the only thing that made sense. Pregnant with triplets.

He nodded. "My father killed her lover only weeks after they were married. When he came back to check on her and saw she was heavy with child and working star charts of her husband's death at an incredible speed, he knew it would only be a matter of time before she understood. But when he went to kill her, she went into labor. He couldn't kill the babies. Instead, he gave them to a young family on the edge of town. It took years, but Granny finally found out. She came after you all with a vengeance. To get you back, she had to pay—and in a big way. She had to agree to destroy the star charts."

He glared at her. "We thought it was over. Until that junkie broke into your apartment looking for easy money."

Genesis reeled with horror at what had happened to her family. This man and his father and his grandfather had killed her parents. Made her life hell and that of her sisters and made sure Granny lived the life of a pariah. Shunned by all. "She didn't deserve that," Genesis said. "She was a good woman."

"She owned too much, knew too much, and did too much," he snapped. "She deserved everything coming to her."

Her heart sinking, Genesis asked in a small voice, "Did you kill her?"

"No." His headshake was immediate. "We didn't need

to. She passed on her own."

Tears of relief came to her eyes. "Oh, thank God."

"Of course she'd rather we'd killed her than take you out, as I will soon."

"And then I'll take you out." Portman Junior's voice from the doorway was a welcome distraction. Until she saw the look in his eyes.

She shuddered.

Grandfather swiveled, shock on his face. "What are you doing here? You're supposed to be back at the hovercraft."

"Nah, change of plans." Without warning, he fired his weapon at Grandfather. A bolt of light zapped across the small room, hitting Grandfather square in the chest. He clutched at his heart, stumbling backward with the force of the shot, and tumbled into the water.

"Good. That should take care of him."

And that was a sure sign Portman Junior had lost his marbles. Grandfather had fallen into a healing pool—and one of the strongest available.

She studied the youngest Portman. "Now what?"

"I want the star charts and the land documents."

"And again, not being a blood member of the family, you can't hold the title to the land."

He shrugged. "But that's only as long as the documents exist."

Uh-oh. She watched him pull a dozen small black rocks out from his pockets. "Where did those come from?" She was afraid to hear the answer.

"I made them."

"You can do that to those rocks so quickly?"

"Sure can." He threw one into the healing pool. Instantly the water hissed and boiled in agitation. Grandfather's body tossed about in the choppy waves. She raced over to the edge of the pool.

"Oh, I don't think so."

A zap of blue energy sparked. She dove behind the raised edge of the pool as the blue streak crackled overhead, just missing her.

She pulled energy around herself, becoming invisible once again, soft chitters at her ear. She crawled forward and made it to the far wall behind the chairs and table.

A kerfuffle just out of her line of vision had her peering warily across the room.

She watched as Connor tackled Portman Junior to the ground—again.

A few hard swinging fists, a few more grunts, and then Connor leaned over Portman's prone body, his chest heaving and his head hanging low, as he caught his breath, struggling against the forces zapping his energy. "It's okay, Genesis. He's out cold."

She threw off the cloaking energy and raced to her healing pool, only to find that Remi already had the rock out of the water and carefully wrapped up in his energy. "Thanks, Remi." She stood for a moment, studying Grandfather, but he was alive and appeared to be in a healing stupor.

She turned back to Connor. He had turned Portman over on his belly and held his hands behind his back. "Those black rocks are deadly," he said, "but they did do something good."

She walked closer, studying changes in Connor's energy that she could see but couldn't understand.

"As they pulled on my energy to reassert their own balance, they removed something I hadn't known was there."

"Oh? And what was that?"

He motioned to Grandfather floating in the pool. "A layer of suppression energy he'd used to keep me in his network."

Crouching beside him, she looked to see his energy from a different perspective. "You have your abilities back for real this time, don't you?"

He grinned. "Sure do. I don't know why he was allowed to infiltrate my system like he did though."

"*Um,*" she said, "I might be able to explain that part. After you left a year ago, your energy weakened the farther apart we got." She shrugged. "No, I didn't do it, but, as we'd already aligned perfectly, our energies were happy that way. After you left, we both became weaker for a time, until we healed. In your case, that gave Grandfather the opening he was looking for."

She pondered the issue, then added, "Chances are he'd been doing that in a light way for a long time, so you couldn't see him for what he was."

"How could he keep that up though? Especially with so many people around him."

She shrugged. "The difficulty is more in the initial setup. After that, as long as he had that pathway in place, he could feed it whenever he needed to." He was very strong and in a very sneaky way.

"And that would explain why my abilities were always stronger when close to the healing pools. They could heal the damage his energy caused and heal the grief and loss from losing you."

"Exactly."

CONNOR STARED AT the woman so many people had

accused of hurting him in wonder. "I've been a fool."

"No." She shook her head. "You were operating without your normal level of intuition. You couldn't tell the truth from the lies."

"And now I can again." He smiled gently. "And I can see that there never was any artifice. It's all open honesty with you."

She grinned. "It's the only way a healer can be."

"My spirit dog …" he said hesitantly in a low voice. "When he died, I was heartbroken."

"He found Granny. So did dozens of others. She tried to find other people for him, but he'd become attached to her." She looked down at the floor. "When she passed, he stayed here."

"Is there a way for me to have him back?" He didn't know what to say to make such a thing happen. If it were even possible.

"If you want him." She gazed into his eyes. "I think it's why he's been hanging around. He knew you were here one year ago. Then you left, and we were both brokenhearted. He's rarely been around since."

Connor reached out and snagged her close. "God, I'm so sorry."

"So am I," she whispered, "but maybe it's the way things needed to happen."

"Maybe," he admitted. "I'm certainly a lot wiser now." He tilted up her chin. "But I wouldn't hurt you for anything."

"Then promise to not do it again, and I'll forgive you." She laughed. "Actually I forgive you anyway."

He bent his head, and, just before his lips took hers in a searing kiss, he said, "I promise."

"*Uh*, I hate to disturb you two lovebirds," Matt interrupted, "but the hovercraft from the Center is looking to land, and they can't find the place." He faced Genesis. "Did you cloak it again?"

Genesis laughed. "It was only partially uncloaked." She rose to her feet. "No problem. I can fix that." And she smiled. "Actually now I feel like I could fix anything."

"Speaking of fixing anything, did you by any chance have something to do with the missing star charts at the Center?"

She gazed at him. "Are they missing?"

He studied the look on her face, then groaned. "You cloaked them, didn't you?"

A chuckle escaped. "Let's just say that you shouldn't have any trouble finding them when you go looking again."

Connor looked down at the still-unconscious man, whipped off his belt, and tied up his hands. "Just in case." And then he realized something else. "Remi is moving all the rocks so they surround him," he said in surprise. "Why?"

"The rocks want to return to balance," she said gently. "He stole energy from them, and they are getting their own energy back."

He shuddered, watching as Portman Junior's skin took on a deep-gray cast.

"Will it kill him?"

"I don't know, but he created this. As long as they aren't reaching for my energy, then I don't really care." She brushed past Matt to go outside.

Matt walked over to Connor. "You can see Remi now?"

He nodded and quickly explained about Grandfather's energy used to suppress Connor's abilities.

Matt sighed. "What a damn mess."

"Yes, but it's a good one now." Connor stood. "We'll get to the bottom of everything eventually. Genesis will be safe, and the documents and star charts will be preserved forever."

"We'll need to bring her sisters back," Matt said, his tone deepening.

Connor laughed. "Will they come? That's a whole different story."

"They'll come," Genesis said from the doorway, a beaming smile on her face. "When they are ready."

Matt nodded, staring at his shoes, reminding Connor of his friend's own unfinished business.

"Let's hope it's soon."

Connor glanced over at Genesis, who had a faraway look in her eyes. She laughed softly and pointed at Grandfather. "He has started something, … set something in motion. I can't see the details, but I know that Tori will be back soon."

Matt brightened. "And Celeste?"

Genesis studied him carefully. "When the time is right, she'll be here too."

That deep gaze of his locked on her face. "Promise?"

"I promise," she said seriously. "There are different pathways for different people. I'm just so grateful that I have come to the end of mine."

In two strides, Connor was at her side, swinging her up into his arms. "Not the end, just the beginning."

And he kissed her.

This concludes Book 1 of Glory: *Genesis*.
Read the first chapter of Glory: *Tori*, Book 2

Glory: Tori (Book #2)
Chapter 1

TORI CHANDLER CHECKED her watch. Damn. She had just two minutes to make a decision. Her break was only fifteen minutes, and she didn't dare be late. Not with a new job and a strict boss. Should she risk a trip to the bank? She could always walk out if the line wasn't moving fast enough.

She needed the little cash she had for her rent. She had to pay daily until she had a month's worth saved up, and she was already behind. Her landlord had caught her in the hallway this morning and had given her an ultimatum. Moving again wasn't an option. She needed that hideaway. It was walking distance to her new job and saved her bus fare. That meant keeping her landlord happy until next week when she'd get her first paycheck from the health food store. She'd already given him the last of her cash, and there was no way she was using plastic. It was too traceable. She didn't know if she was still on anyone's radar, but she just knew she couldn't take the chance. She'd left in secret and had planned to stay gone. Except for her sisters, there was nothing left for her back home.

In the past year, she still hadn't found another place to call home. Pain and anger had sent her on this journey, and now she was afraid she didn't know how to stop.

Moving a lot meant no accumulation of stuff. She had so little to her name that if her landlord dumped her belongings outside when he kicked her out, it would take no more than a single tote bag to pack them up.

This was her first chance to settle down in a long time. Now if she could just make it work.

"Tori, go for your break now," Mary, her supervisor, said. "See you back in fifteen."

"Thanks." Tori smiled. "I'm just going to hop over to the bank."

Mary frowned. "Bad day for that. It's the last day of the month."

"And that's why I have to go." Tori gave her a bright smile. "Not to worry, if the line is too long, I'll just come back."

That brought a smile to Mary's face. "Good idea. You've been a model employee so far. You know how the owner feels about tardiness. Best not to push it."

Tori rolled her eyes at Mary's back as the woman walked away, then she bolted for the front door. Did no one in this world understand that sometimes shit happened and had to be dealt with?

The bank was only a few stores over, in the big strip mall. Thankfully, it was a small branch and served mostly locals. Regardless, it was still almost noon, and that meant there'd be a rush. As the building came into view, she saw that there was no one else hurrying to get inside. That, at least, was a good sign. Tori pulled open one of the two glass doors and rushed inside.

Blissfully cool, an air-conditioned gust hit her, but she barely noticed. Her senses went on full alert.

All around here, there was an eerie silence. She stopped in her tracks and looked at the service counter. The tellers were all staring at her, a mixture of fear and anger on their faces … and horror.

She straightened and realized that something was very, very wrong. Instinct screamed at her to run. *Get the hell out of there.*

Then she heard it. *Click.* And something round and hard was shoved into her back.

"What a nice day for you to come to the bank." A gravelly voice spoke in her ear, accompanied by the smell of beer and stale pizza, mixed with the remnants of a sour belch that almost dropped her to her knees. "Welcome to the party."

Tori closed her eyes. Shit happened, all right.

But why did it always happen to her?

Book 2 is available now!

To find out more visit Dale Mayer's website.

https://geni.us/DMtori

Author's Note

Thank you for reading Genesis! If you enjoyed my book, I'd appreciate it if you'd leave a review.

Dear reader,

I love to hear from readers, and you can contact me at my website: www.dalemayer.com or at my Facebook author page. To be informed of new releases and special offers, sign up for my newsletter or follow me on BookBub. And if you are interested in joining Dale Mayer's Reader Group, here is the Facebook sign up page.
http://geni.us/DaleMayerFBGroup

Cheers,
Dale Mayer

About the Author

Dale Mayer is a *USA Today* best-selling author, best known for her SEALs military romances, her Psychic Visions series, and her Lovely Lethal Garden cozy series. Her contemporary romances are raw and full of passion and emotion (Broken But … Mending, Hathaway House series). Her thrillers will keep you guessing (Kate Morgan, By Death series), and her romantic comedies will keep you giggling (*It's a Dog's Life*, a stand-alone novella; and the Broken Protocols series, starring Charming Marvin, the cat).

Dale honors the stories that come to her—and some of them are crazy, break all the rules and cross multiple genres!

To go with her fiction, she also writes nonfiction in many different fields, with books available on résumé writing, companion gardening, and the US mortgage system. All her books are available in print and ebook format.

Connect with Dale Mayer Online

Dale's Website – www.dalemayer.com
Twitter – @DaleMayer
Facebook Page – geni.us/DaleMayerFBFanPage
Facebook Group – geni.us/DaleMayerFBGroup
BookBub – geni.us/DaleMayerBookbub
Instagram – geni.us/DaleMayerInstagram
Goodreads – geni.us/DaleMayerGoodreads
Newsletter – geni.us/DaleNews

Also by Dale Mayer

Published Adult Books:

Shadow Recon

Magnus, Book 1

Bullard's Battle

Ryland's Reach, Book 1

Cain's Cross, Book 2

Eton's Escape, Book 3

Garret's Gambit, Book 4

Kano's Keep, Book 5

Fallon's Flaw, Book 6

Quinn's Quest, Book 7

Bullard's Beauty, Book 8

Bullard's Best, Book 9

Bullard's Battle, Books 1–2

Bullard's Battle, Books 3–4

Bullard's Battle, Books 5–6

Bullard's Battle, Books 7–8

Terkel's Team

Damon's Deal, Book 1

Wade's War, Book 2

Gage's Goal, Book 3

Calum's Contact, Book 4

Rick's Road, Book 5

Scott's Summit, Book 6

Brody's Beast, Book 7

Terkel's Twist, Book 8

Terkel's Triumph, Book 9

Terkel's Guardian

Radar, Book 1

Kate Morgan

Simon Says… Hide, Book 1

Simon Says… Jump, Book 2

Simon Says… Ride, Book 3

Simon Says… Scream, Book 4

Simon Says… Run, Book 5

Simon Says… Walk, Book 6

Hathaway House

Aaron, Book 1

Brock, Book 2

Cole, Book 3

Denton, Book 4

Elliot, Book 5

Finn, Book 6

Gregory, Book 7

Heath, Book 8

Iain, Book 9

Jaden, Book 10

Keith, Book 11

Lance, Book 12

Melissa, Book 13

Nash, Book 14

Owen, Book 15

Percy, Book 16

Quinton, Book 17

Ryatt, Book 18

Spencer, Book 19

Hathaway House, Books 1–3

Hathaway House, Books 4–6

Hathaway House, Books 7–9

The K9 Files

Ethan, Book 1

Pierce, Book 2

Zane, Book 3

Blaze, Book 4

Lucas, Book 5

Parker, Book 6

Carter, Book 7

Weston, Book 8

Greyson, Book 9

Rowan, Book 10

Caleb, Book 11

Kurt, Book 12

Tucker, Book 13

Harley, Book 14

Kyron, Book 15

Jenner, Book 16

Rhys, Book 17

Landon, Book 18

Harper, Book 19

Kascius, Book 20

The K9 Files, Books 1–2

The K9 Files, Books 3–4

The K9 Files, Books 5–6

The K9 Files, Books 7–8

The K9 Files, Books 9–10

The K9 Files, Books 11–12

Lovely Lethal Gardens

Arsenic in the Azaleas, Book 1

Bones in the Begonias, Book 2

Corpse in the Carnations, Book 3

Daggers in the Dahlias, Book 4

Evidence in the Echinacea, Book 5

Footprints in the Ferns, Book 6

Gun in the Gardenias, Book 7

Handcuffs in the Heather, Book 8

Ice Pick in the Ivy, Book 9

Jewels in the Juniper, Book 10

Killer in the Kiwis, Book 11

Lifeless in the Lilies, Book 12

Murder in the Marigolds, Book 13

Nabbed in the Nasturtiums, Book 14

Offed in the Orchids, Book 15

Poison in the Pansies, Book 16

Quarry in the Quince, Book 17

Revenge in the Roses, Book 18

Silenced in the Sunflowers, Book 19

Toes up in the Tulips, Book 20

Uzi in the Urn, Book 21

Lovely Lethal Gardens, Books 1–2

Lovely Lethal Gardens, Books 3–4

Lovely Lethal Gardens, Books 5–6

Lovely Lethal Gardens, Books 7–8

Lovely Lethal Gardens, Books 9–10

Psychic Vision Series

Tuesday's Child

Hide 'n Go Seek

Maddy's Floor

Garden of Sorrow

Knock Knock…

Rare Find

Eyes to the Soul

Now You See Her

Shattered

Into the Abyss

Seeds of Malice

Eye of the Falcon

Itsy-Bitsy Spider

Unmasked

Deep Beneath

From the Ashes

Stroke of Death

Ice Maiden

Snap, Crackle…

What If…

Talking Bones

String of Tears

Inked Forever

Psychic Visions Books 1–3

Psychic Visions Books 4–6

Psychic Visions Books 7–9

By Death Series

Touched by Death

Haunted by Death

Chilled by Death

By Death Books 1–3

Broken Protocols – Romantic Comedy Series

Cat's Meow

Cat's Pajamas

Cat's Cradle

Cat's Claus

Broken Protocols 1-4

Broken and… Mending

Skin

Scars

Scales (of Justice)

Broken but… Mending 1-3

Glory

Genesis

Tori

Celeste

Glory Trilogy

Biker Blues

Morgan: Biker Blues, Volume 1

Cash: Biker Blues, Volume 2

SEALs of Honor

Mason: SEALs of Honor, Book 1

Hawk: SEALs of Honor, Book 2

Dane: SEALs of Honor, Book 3

Swede: SEALs of Honor, Book 4

Shadow: SEALs of Honor, Book 5

Cooper: SEALs of Honor, Book 6

Markus: SEALs of Honor, Book 7

Evan: SEALs of Honor, Book 8

Mason's Wish: SEALs of Honor, Book 9

Chase: SEALs of Honor, Book 10

Brett: SEALs of Honor, Book 11

Devlin: SEALs of Honor, Book 12

Easton: SEALs of Honor, Book 13

Ryder: SEALs of Honor, Book 14

Macklin: SEALs of Honor, Book 15

Corey: SEALs of Honor, Book 16

Warrick: SEALs of Honor, Book 17

Tanner: SEALs of Honor, Book 18

Jackson: SEALs of Honor, Book 19

Kanen: SEALs of Honor, Book 20

Nelson: SEALs of Honor, Book 21

Taylor: SEALs of Honor, Book 22

Colton: SEALs of Honor, Book 23

Troy: SEALs of Honor, Book 24

Axel: SEALs of Honor, Book 25

Baylor: SEALs of Honor, Book 26

Hudson: SEALs of Honor, Book 27

Lachlan: SEALs of Honor, Book 28

Paxton: SEALs of Honor, Book 29

Bronson: SEALs of Honor, Book 30

Hale: SEALs of Honor, Book 31

SEALs of Honor, Books 1–3

SEALs of Honor, Books 4–6

SEALs of Honor, Books 7–10

SEALs of Honor, Books 11–13

SEALs of Honor, Books 14–16

SEALs of Honor, Books 17–19

SEALs of Honor, Books 20–22

SEALs of Honor, Books 23–25

Heroes for Hire

Levi's Legend: Heroes for Hire, Book 1

Stone's Surrender: Heroes for Hire, Book 2

Merk's Mistake: Heroes for Hire, Book 3

Rhodes's Reward: Heroes for Hire, Book 4

Flynn's Firecracker: Heroes for Hire, Book 5

Logan's Light: Heroes for Hire, Book 6

Harrison's Heart: Heroes for Hire, Book 7

Saul's Sweetheart: Heroes for Hire, Book 8

Dakota's Delight: Heroes for Hire, Book 9

Tyson's Treasure: Heroes for Hire, Book 10

Jace's Jewel: Heroes for Hire, Book 11

Rory's Rose: Heroes for Hire, Book 12

Brandon's Bliss: Heroes for Hire, Book 13

Liam's Lily: Heroes for Hire, Book 14

North's Nikki: Heroes for Hire, Book 15

Anders's Angel: Heroes for Hire, Book 16

Reyes's Raina: Heroes for Hire, Book 17

Dezi's Diamond: Heroes for Hire, Book 18

Vince's Vixen: Heroes for Hire, Book 19

Ice's Icing: Heroes for Hire, Book 20

Johan's Joy: Heroes for Hire, Book 21

Galen's Gemma: Heroes for Hire, Book 22

Zack's Zest: Heroes for Hire, Book 23

Bonaparte's Belle: Heroes for Hire, Book 24

Noah's Nemesis: Heroes for Hire, Book 25

Tomas's Trials: Heroes for Hire, Book 26

Carson's Choice: Heroes for Hire, Book 27

Dante's Decision: Heroes for Hire, Book 28

Steve's Solace: Heroes for Hire, Book 29

Heroes for Hire, Books 1–3

Heroes for Hire, Books 4–6

Heroes for Hire, Books 7–9

Heroes for Hire, Books 10–12

Heroes for Hire, Books 13–15

Heroes for Hire, Books 16–18

Heroes for Hire, Books 19–21

Heroes for Hire, Books 22–24

SEALs of Steel

Badger: SEALs of Steel, Book 1

Erick: SEALs of Steel, Book 2

Cade: SEALs of Steel, Book 3

Talon: SEALs of Steel, Book 4

Laszlo: SEALs of Steel, Book 5

Geir: SEALs of Steel, Book 6

Jager: SEALs of Steel, Book 7

The Final Reveal: SEALs of Steel, Book 8

SEALs of Steel, Books 1–4

SEALs of Steel, Books 5–8

SEALs of Steel, Books 1–8

The Mavericks

Kerrick, Book 1

Griffin, Book 2

Jax, Book 3

Beau, Book 4

Asher, Book 5

Ryker, Book 6

Miles, Book 7

Nico, Book 8

Keane, Book 9

Lennox, Book 10

Gavin, Book 11

Shane, Book 12

Diesel, Book 13

Jerricho, Book 14

Killian, Book 15

Hatch, Book 16

Corbin, Book 17

Aiden, Book 18

The Mavericks, Books 1–2

The Mavericks, Books 3–4

The Mavericks, Books 5–6

The Mavericks, Books 7–8

The Mavericks, Books 9–10

The Mavericks, Books 11–12

Standalone Novellas

It's a Dog's Life

Riana's Revenge

Second Chances

Published Young Adult Books:

Family Blood Ties Series

Vampire in Denial

Vampire in Distress

Vampire in Design

Vampire in Deceit

Vampire in Defiance

Vampire in Conflict

Vampire in Chaos

Vampire in Crisis

Vampire in Control

Vampire in Charge

Family Blood Ties Set 1–3

Family Blood Ties Set 1–5

Family Blood Ties Set 4–6

Family Blood Ties Set 7–9

Sian's Solution, A Family Blood Ties Series Prequel
Novelette

Design series

Dangerous Designs

Deadly Designs

Darkest Designs

Design Series Trilogy

Standalone

In Cassie's Corner

Gem Stone (a Gemma Stone Mystery)

Time Thieves

Published Non-Fiction Books:

Career Essentials

Career Essentials: The Résumé

Career Essentials: The Cover Letter

Career Essentials: The Interview

Career Essentials: 3 in 1

www.ingramcontent.com/pod-product-compliance
Lightning Source LLC
Chambersburg PA
CBHW071212210726
48293CB00002B/403